DUE RED
MANTICORE REBORN

The helot reached for her wrist with its one remaining hand, but it wasn't strong enough. Red ripped back, coming away with a handful of flesh and metal hoses. The worker sank to its knees, spitting blood and breath from the wound, and twisted away onto the deck.

Red dropped the handful next to the convulsing worker, then turned to see the bald woman trying to get the hatch open. "Oh, for sneck's sake!"

She walked quickly over to the hatch, grabbed the woman's shaven head and bounced it off the metal. The Iconoclast sagged like a loose sack, crumpling among her own robes.

Durham Red created by **John Wagner**,
Alan Grant and **Carlos Ezquerra**

Special thanks to **Dan Abnett** and **Mark Harrison**
for character and continuity of the Accord

DURHAM RED

MANTICORE REBORN

PETER J EVANS

BLACK FLAME

To Dave, Lee and Tracey,
The Addington Crew:
One day you'll read one.

A Black Flame Publication
www.blackflame.com

First published in 2006 by BL Publishing, Games Workshop Ltd.,
Willow Road, Nottingham NG7 2WS, UK.

Distributed in the US by Simon & Schuster, 1230 Avenue of the
Americas, New York, NY 10020, USA.

10 9 8 7 6 5 4 3 2 1

Cover illustration by Mark Harrison.

ISBN 13: 978 1 84416 323 6
ISBN 10: 1 84416 323 7

A CIP record for this book is available from the British Library.

Printed in the UK by Bookmarque, Surrey, UK.

The Legend of Durham Red

It is written that in that year of 2150, the skies rained down nuclear death, and every family and clan lost father and brothers and sons. The Strontium choked our beloved homeworld and brought forth mutants, squealing and twisted things.

Yet such mutants were not weak things to be crushed underfoot, for the same radiation that had created them warped their bodies, making them stronger than any normal human. They became hated and feared by all, and were herded into ghettos and imprisoned in vast camps. There they plotted rebellion and dreamed of freedom amongst their own kind.

Some, it is told, were able to escape from the shadows of ruined Earth, to join the feared Search/Destroy Agency. They tracked wanted criminals on worlds too dangerous for regular enforcement officers. They became known as the Strontium Dogs.

The one they call Durham Red became an S/D Agent to escape the teeming ghettos of her devastated homeland. Shunned even by her own kind because of a foul mutant blood-thirst, she soon found that her unsurpassed combat skills served her well as a Strontium Dog. The years of continuous slaughter took their toll, however, and the tales relate that in the end Red willingly entered the deep sleep of cryogenic suspension, determined to let a few years go by without her.

All know of the unexpected twist that the legend took. Her cryo-tube malfunctioned. Durham Red woke up twelve hundred years late.

While she slept, the enmity between humans and mutants had exploded into centuries of total war, leaving the galaxy a shattered shell, home only to superstition and barbarism. Billions of oppressed mutants now worship Saint Scarlet of Durham – the mythologised image of Red herself! The bounty hunter from Milton Keynes has now become almost a messiah figure for mutantkind – and a terrifying blasphemy in the eyes of humans.

Half the galaxy is looking to her for bloody salvation. The other half is determined to destroy her at any cost. The future is a nightmare, and Durham Red is trapped right in the middle of it...

PROLOGUE. 627YA

The bridge was on fire. Lucius Verax could smell the stench of burning plastic, the raw, acrid stink of melting insulation and deck plating. Whatever had struck the heavy cruiser *Redeemer* had done so with enough force to rip a hole clear through the command tower, and secondary explosions had hammered into the bridge from all sides. By the smell of ozone and roasted human meat, Verax knew that one of the core power feeds must have been sheared.

He sat up, shakily, trying to ignore the hot sparks of pain dancing through his chest. For a moment he wondered if he was blind, his eyes destroyed by a flash fire or light from the power feed's discharge, but then he put his hand to his face and realised that his eyelids were glued shut with blood.

There was a dreadful noise all around him, a thunderous gonging that made it difficult to even think.

From what he could hear past the gongs, the bridge was in chaos. There were screams on all sides, shouts of pain and fear, and the thick, choking moans of the dying. People were running past him, boots heavy on the deck, and someone to his right was shouting over and over for a damage report. Verax heard the hiss of fire extinguishers, the crack and spark of shattered electronics, and below that, the deep, vibrating groan of a starship deck being stressed by forces it was never built to withstand.

One of Verax's sleeves was hanging off at the shoulder. He tore it free and used the cuff to wipe the worst of the blood from his eyes, finally getting them open, and blinking furiously to clear the blur in his vision. He felt a warm trickle of fluid above his right eyebrow and dabbed at it with the torn sleeve, noting with some surprise that the fabric came away glistening red. There must have been a sizeable gash in his scalp somewhere, to have bled so profusely.

Light and shadow played in his vision, little more than watery blocks of colour. He blinked again, cursing under his breath as he wiped his eyes, and gradually the scene around him began to resolve.

A patch of wavering yellow light to his left shrank into fire and vapour: two of his officers were wielding canisters of flame suppressant, trying to douse the flames with clouds of freezing extinguisher. At least three of the workstations along the port wall were destroyed, burned and split from the explosion. There was a twisted, smouldering object in one that might once have been a human being.

Verax stood, pulling himself upright on the arm of his control throne. "Sanicus? Where are you?"

A young woman darted over to stand before him. He didn't recognise her, couldn't have named her if he'd tried, but the rank pips on her jacket told him that she was a junior officer, a midshipman.

The woman stood stiffly to attention. "Commander Sanicus is dead, sir."

Verax nodded dully. His vision was still only partly clear, and his head was pounding. The impact of the mutant weapon must have knocked him senseless. "Dead?"

"Aye, sir."

"What's that noise?"

"Damage alerts, sir."

Verax took a deep breath and shook himself. There wasn't time to stand here like a fool, no matter how hard he had hit the deck. He had to regain his wits, and fast. "What's your name, girl?"

"Midshipman Seela Tertius," she replied. There was fear in her voice, but she was hiding it well.

"Very well, Seela Tertius, here are your orders. Get me a trauma kit, find the most senior officer still on his or her feet and bring them to me, and then shut that bloody racket off."

"Thy will be done." The girl raced away.

Verax manoeuvred himself around into the command throne and dropped back into it, wincing as a ripple of pain shot through the sides of his chest. He'd broken ribs in the attack, that was certain.

The gonging died away, taking with it several lesser rackets that Verax hadn't even noticed until they were gone. The shouts and screams remained, although the fires had been brought under control. Verax knew his duty was to get back to his feet, bring the bridge back to order and continue the fight, but his head wouldn't stop spinning. He'd be no use at all until it did.

Tertius scrambled back to his side, bearing a trauma kit. Verax used some antiseptic wipes to clean his face and eyes, while the girl filled a pressure syringe with war-balm, injecting him in the side of the neck.

The balm raced through Verax like a clear mountain stream, freezing the pains in his chest, wiping the grogginess from his mind. He closed his eyes for a second, just to let the last dregs of the impact wash away. "Midshipman, I asked you to find me a senior officer."

"I'm sorry, captain. No bridge crew above my rank survived. Until we can regain access to the rest of the tower, I'm your most senior officer."

He looked across at her and gave her a grim smile. "Consider yourself promoted."

It took some time to get even narrow band communications back on line. Verax's primary concern was making sure the injured were treated, if for no other reason than to stop their cries distracting the rest of his crew. The damage *Redeemer* had taken to its command tower had effectively trapped everyone on the bridge, but the repair helots were already clearing the shattered compartments below. It would only be a few hours, they had assured him, until the way was open.

For the moment, Verax ordered the command tower's devotional chapel to be used as a temporary infirmary, and had the worst of the injured moved there. Some insisted on staying at their posts, and Verax didn't deny them. He needed everyone.

He also needed information, and orders. The surviving sense-engine operator was tasked with giving him the former, but the latter could only come from one place.

Some of the newest Iconoclast vessels were fitted with holographic communication chambers, although Verax had never seen one. Rumour had it that the new dreadnought class killships would have completely holographic instrumentation, but those awesome machines were still years, if not decades, away from service. *Redeemer* still relied on flat screens to display information to the crew, just as they had since humankind had regained the stars. Verax's comms chamber was ringed with video panels of the most traditional kind.

Several of the screens weren't working. The blast that had wrecked *Redeemer*'s bridge had taken down part of the ceiling in the comms chamber, and Verax had to step over several pieces of shattered gantry and dislodged plating before he could get to the controls.

The screens showed static for a few seconds, until the quantum link established and an image of Fleet Admiral Deodatus fizzled into view. Deodatus was a skeleton of a man, immensely tall and thin, a total contrast to the stocky Verax. "Hail, captain," he said, as the static cleared. "It's good to see you in one piece."

"I'm in better shape than my ship, fleet admiral. Whatever the mutants threw at us, it struck like the wrath of God."

"What's your status?"

"As far as I can tell, not good." Verax had been given a partial damage report by Midshipman Tertius just before going into the comms chamber, but it was fragmentary at best. Too many parts of the ship were still cut off. "We've lost primary power, which means the lasers are down and the main drives are at reduced efficiency. There's no contact from the torpedo rooms on the port bow, nor from the port hangar pod. As it stands, we've got no way to dock any of our fighters. As soon as the general comms are back up, I'll instruct them to berth with other ships if they haven't already."

Deodatus frowned and his gaze dropped. "That may not be so easy, captain. We've been unable to make contact with most of the ships in your battlegroup."

A cold knot of horror began to grow in Verax's belly. "How many?"

"We've heard from *Gideon*, the *Magnificat*, and the *Benedictus*. *Vespasian* reported in with serious reactor damage, but then their comms went offline ten seconds before we picked up a neutrino flare. That's all."

Verax reached out to the comms control panel to steady himself. Four ships out of a battlegroup of twenty-eight, and if Deodatus had picked up a neutrino flare it could only mean that *Vespasian* had gone nova. Fleet headquarters was on Bacchylus, ten light-seconds from the battle site.

Four ships left. Thousands of Iconoclasts dead. "I had no idea. I thought *Redeemer* must have taken an unlucky hit."

"From what I hear, Verax, you were the lucky ones." Deodatus looked to one side, nodded to someone outside the video pickup's field of view, and then returned his attention to Verax. "Give me your report, captain. What hit you?"

"I'm not sure, fleet admiral." Verax shook his head in exasperation. "We don't even know where it came from – the first we heard of it was a proximity warning, but we saw no jump flares. It turned up out of nowhere."

"A Tenebrae vessel?"

"It has to be. They attacked us without provocation."
Deodatus nodded to himself. "Go on."

"The battlegroup had dropped out of superlight in the
Kentyris system. A regular patrol, that was all. We'd
heard reports of pirates operating out of Kentyris Secundus. I had my sense-operators on full alert, looking for
any unauthorised traffic. If there had been a jump-
point, fleet admiral, we would have seen it."

"Your conclusion?"

"They were waiting for us."

The fleet admiral nodded his agreement. "I'll petition
his holiness for a series of punitive strikes. Let's see
how strong the Tenebrae stomach is once we start razing mutant cities. In the meantime–" He stopped
abruptly.

Verax realised that Deodatus was looking past him.
He turned to see Tertius standing in the hatchway
behind him, a slender silhouette in the light from outside. "Forgive me, captain," she stammered.

"I'm assuming it's important."

"Sir, the primary power core is online. We have
comms, and access to tactical sense-engines."

"Good work, Commander!" Then she stepped forward, into the chamber, and Verax saw the expression
on her face. "What's wrong?"

"The enemy, sir. It's attacking the planet."

The bodies had been cleared from the bridge by the
time Verax got back, but their stink was still in the air.
In a way, he welcomed that. It would be a continual
reminder of what he was up against. He went straight to
the command throne and sat down.

Tertius took up position at his side. "Sense-operator,"
she called. "Full tactical display!"

"Your will." The operator worked at his board, and a
moment later the viewscreens around the bridge walls
sequenced into life, surrounding Verax with stars.

He turned his head left and right, gauging the situation instantly. Kentyris Secundus, a human colony of some thirty million people, filled the screens to port. To starboard, splinters of bright metal, surrounded by identification graphics and vector markers – the last remnants of the battlegroup. And dead ahead, drifting a thousand kilometres above the planet's surface, was the dark mass he had spotted in the few seconds between the proximity alert and the blast that had holed *Redeemer*'s tower.

"Enhance view, centre screen," growled Verax. "I want to see that bastard's face."

A grid appeared around the attacker. Verax found himself leaning forward, half out of the throne, hands clenching in anticipation. "Come on," he breathed. "Show yourself…"

The grid expanded, dragging the attacker's image forward in a rush. Verax flinched as it billowed to fill the screen – a rounded, nearly spherical mass of glossy black metal. It was hard to see in any detail. The shell of it was so dark, so gleaming, that the ship appeared to be nothing more than a vague series of reflections. There was a hint of panelling, of complexities beyond what Verax could actually see, but they were only suggestions. The machine was as unknowable and as distant as a thunderhead.

"In the name of God," gasped Tertius, beside him. "What is that thing? Captain, have you ever seen the like?"

"I've not," Verax replied. "Sense-op, is that thing as big as it looks?"

"At least fifty kilometres across, captain. Mass is off the scale."

It has to be a trick, Verax told himself. No one in the Accord had the facilities to build a vessel of such size, least of all the mutants. It was as big as a temple station, bigger than most, and yet it was drifting between the stars like a warship. "Impossible. The sense-engines must have lost calibration. Sense-op, full comparison check. Get me a real reading on that thing."

"Thy will be done." The man began to tap at the keys of his control board, but a moment later he drew up short. "Captain! Energy surge from the attacker!"

The magnified view shrank away, allowing Verax to see threads of blinding white light flicker between the enemy's bulk and the surface of Kentyris Secundus. The threads lasted only for a fraction of a second, just long enough for their brilliance to burn a track across Verax's vision, but wherever they touched the planet great domes of white light erupted in their wake.

Each one of those domes, Verax realised, was the size of a city. Millions were dying under those fireballs. "Drives to maximum thrust, prime all weapons! Charge lasers and activate any torpedo room we can contact. Tertius?"

"Sir."

"Hail the rest of the group. Tell them to follow my lead. If we don't stop that thing it'll boil the planet and everyone on it."

The deck shuddered as the drives fired, hundred-kilometre cones of plasma erupting out from behind *Redeemer* as the ship surged forward. To starboard, the metal splinters grew their own streams of hazy light and began to move ahead.

"Torpedo rooms, fire when ready. Laser crews stand ready. We'll be in range in…" He checked a status display set into the throne arm. "Ninety seconds."

The attacker was growing in the viewscreens, but as Verax glared at it, the machine started to rotate. It span slowly around its axis, bringing the side it had been aiming at the planet around towards the approaching ships.

On that side, a huge crater flared with orange light. It must have taken up half of the rounded vessel's diameter, a gaping maw that glowed like a minor sun. "Open fire," snarled Verax. "Pour cleansing fire right down its throat."

"Energy surge," cried the sense-op again. "It's firing."

For a split second, light connected the centre of the glowing crater to the carrier *Benedictus*. Verax saw the Iconoclast ship touched, the thread of light fade out, and a sphere of white light suddenly spring from the ship's core.

Benedictus began to keel over. The ball of light at its centre was growing by the second, swamping the carrier. Sparks flickered around it as the fighters it was launching detonated in mid-flight.

"All ships, evasive action!" roared Verax. He was on his feet now. "Pilot, bring us over, hard to port and zed-minus thirty. Drives to emergency thrust. Get us out of here!"

Tertius gave a moan of terror. "Too late..."

Verax saw a thread lance out from the attacker, as fleeting as that which had struck the *Benedictus*. The impact of it came up through the deck. He felt it through the soles of his boots. "All hands, evacuate. Anyone who can get to an escape pod, do so – we are lost."

White light, a perfect sphere of roiling energy, was expanding to fill the viewscreens.

Captain Verax stayed at his post, Tertius at his side. The sphere was too big to evade, too fast growing to outrun. In moments it was fading up through the bridge floor, flooding the chamber with light. In a heartbeat more it had reached him.

The last thing he saw was his newly appointed commander's hand, reaching down to grip his own.

1. HOSTILE ACQUISITION

Aura Lydexia heard the Salecah artefact before she saw it. When the comms operator reported that he had picked up a transmission, she ordered it diverted to the chant sounders. It was a decision she regretted almost instantly.

As soon as the key was pressed, howls filled the bridge. The artefact was emitting a hellish racket, a stuttering, multi-layered cacophony that bellowed from the sounders like the lament of lost souls, drowning out the shipboard chant and hammering Lydexia's ears.

"God's blood, Alexus!" she cried. "What in damnation is that supposed to be?"

"Apologies, doctor-captain. I had no idea it would be so…" Alexus trailed off, working at his board, so Lydexia finished the sentence for him.

"Insanely loud?"

"Strong signal. Hold on." A moment later, the din throttled back to a gentler level. "There."

"Well, I can hear myself think again. That's a bonus." Lydexia got up from the command throne and crossed the bridge to Alexus's workstation. "Any idea what it might be?"

"I believe so, doctor-captain." Alexus looked up at her, his thin, pale face half-hidden by the heavy sensory prosthesis he wore. "But I need to filter it. If I may?"

"Be my guest."

Alexus turned his multi-lensed head back to the board and worked the controls once more. As he did, Lydexia heard the transmission begin to alter.

Slowly, its wails and squawks fell away. The sound attenuated, smoothed out, reducing layer by layer, until after a minute or so, it had shrunk back to a soft, plaintive warbling. It was as though the instruments in an orchestra had been removed one by one, leaving only a single flute to play on alone.

Lydexia listened to the sound for a few seconds, trying to determine its meaning, but it told her nothing. If anything, it was more uncomfortable to hear than the previous commotion had been. Although it was nothing more than a single cadence repeated over and over, it gave Lydexia an unavoidable impression of awful, aching loneliness, like a lost child crying in the dark.

She shivered. "What is it? What did you do?"

"There was more than one signal, doctor-captain." Alexus kept his attention firmly on the comms board. "Several hundred, in fact, each sending the same information in a different format. This is the closest to our frequencies."

Lydexia glanced around the bridge. *Vigilant* was a fairly small vessel, with a command crew of only twenty, herself included. Nineteen Archaeotechs hunched in their pod like workstations, attention fixed on their instrument boards, visibly trying to shut the noise out. "What's it sending?"

"Its own co-ordinates, doctor-captain."

It wants to be found, Lydexia thought hollowly. "Record it and shut it off, Alexus. This sector is worrying enough without that ghost clamouring in our ears."

"Doctor-captain?" That was Nivello, *Vigilant*'s pilot. "I have the artefact in visual range."

Lydexia found herself hesitating. What would the artefact look like, after singing such a painful song?

She steadied herself, bringing a calming catechism to the front of her mind. Its complexities stilled her worry within moments. "Let's see it. Full magnification."

At her command, the holoscreen at the forward end of the bridge sprang to brilliant life and blue light flooded over the deck. At first Lydexia was unable to make sense of what she saw there: it looked as though an open, summer sky had been twisted into some kind of whirlpool, roiling around in a hazy spiral and shot through with bars and discs of pure black. Then a shadow passed across that sky, and the scene's perspective turned inside out.

Lydexia wasn't looking up at a blue sky, but down into the swarming cloud layer of a minor gas giant. The clouds were tainted a pale azure by the chemicals within, and wrenched into a tight whorl by some powerful confluence of rotational forces. From what Lydexia could see on her secondary scans, the planet Salecah was covered with storm systems of similar dimensions, but she wasn't paying much attention to those. She was looking at the artefact.

It hung just above the atmosphere, its lowest point brushing the haze, drawing a continuous storm of electrical arcs that lit the clouds from within. From above, it was clear that the object had been built around a trilateral symmetry, with three long spines emerging from its body to join smaller discs, and three more raised at a sharper angle, each terminating in a spear point as big as one of *Vigilant*'s landers.

A board next to Lydexia's throne chimed, and she looked back to see a holographic image of the artefact building itself in the air behind her. In three dimensions it was even more baffling – a slender spindle projecting up from a massive central dish, capped with smaller domes at either end. The dish was upturned and filled with great pods and cylinders. It looked like a spear thrust through a fruit bowl, if the spear had been a kilometre long.

Tiny motes flocked and circled around the object. Some kind of flying creatures, Lydexia guessed. She'd have to factor those into her bioscans.

"Very well, Archaeotechs. Our task begins. *Per cognitio, ad salus*."

The rest of the bridge crew murmured a response. Lydexia began tapping at the control boards set into the arms of her throne, uploading area designations to *Vigilant's* tactical array. Quick, colourful descriptions that could be easily remembered: the arena, the outriggers, the punchbowl.

"Run preliminary sense sweeps, full bio and power emanation series. Nivello, bring us to within a thousand kilometres and then keep position. Tell the *Lamarion* to circle at ten thousand. Ruida, I'm picking up a breathable gas trace around the artefact. Can that be right?"

Ruida was *Vigilant's* sensor tech. She was very young, her shaved head barely marked by the division's ritual circuit tattoos. Lydexia saw her studying her board holos, checking her facts one last time. "It is, doctor-captain. The main atmosphere is nitrogen, methane, a little water-ice. Nothing you'd want to breathe. But there's a thin layer of breathable gas just above that, maybe ten kilometres thick. Probably a gravity capture."

The artefact had been stationed right in that layer, hung there on its grav-lifters and left to sing its haunting, lonely songs into the night. "That answers one question," Lydexia announced. "The artefact isn't here by accident. Someone knew just where to put it."

She stood up. "Nivello, you have command. I'll be down at the lander racks until acquisition."

"Thy will be done," nodded the pilot.

Lydexia saluted the back of his head, and then made her way off the bridge. As she left, she noticed that Alexus still hadn't shut the artefact's transmission off.

Its lament was in her ears all the way down to the racks.

Vigilant was a standard design of Archaeotech procurement clipper: five hundred metres of drives and pressure cylinders hung beneath a diamond shaped wing, and studded with sense-engine pickups. The vessel had little in the way of weapons. Most of its bulk was taken up by the lander racks, a double row of fast cargo shuttles held in powered launch clamps. It was an unlovely vessel, built for one purpose only: to transport an Archaeotech acquisition team to their target site, provide them with huge amounts of scan data and then let them scour the site for artefacts in as short a time as possible. If it came to a fight, and such things were always possible, it would be up to *Lamarion* to protect the clipper.

Then again, *Lamarion* was a fully armed killship, a dreadnought class war vessel. It was quite capable of protecting *Vigilant* from most things.

All except time, thought Lydexia as she headed down to the racks. Time was always an Archaeotech's worst enemy. From the moment a site was discovered, the clock was ticking. Harvesters, nomadic communities of space-going scavengers, listened in on many of the comms channels that the Archaeotechs used to locate their quarry. They would descend on any target they considered ripe for picking, be it a lost starship, a forgotten battlefield, even an alien construction like the Salecah object. Once they were done making their profits, there would be precious little left for the Archaeotechs to pore over.

There were the Tenebrae to consider too – wandering bands of mutant extremists, eager to claim any place or object they considered to be of religious significance. And most dangerous of all, in many ways, were the Iconoclasts themselves. Although nominally all part of the same military force, few other divisions shared the Archaeotechs' passion for lost technologies. Most considered such things heretical, forbidden, dangers to be wiped from the face of the universe. Lydexia couldn't allow herself to consider how many priceless artefacts might have been lost to the hunger guns of superstitious admirals. The thought was too upsetting.

If all the factors were taken into consideration – Harvesters, Tenebrae patrols, unsympathetic Iconoclast commanders petitioning the Patriarch to have their protection edicts overturned – an Archaeotech acquisition team could consider itself lucky to get ten days at any newly discovered site. In some cases, the actual time was less than ten hours.

Lydexia, who had been on acquisition missions before, had a countdown display fitted into the wrist of her uniform armour. She tuned it to ten hours as she entered the lander rack airlock, and set it ticking.

There was a small staging chapel between the lock and the racks, where the mission leaders would equip themselves and make final devotions before embarking on their tasks. Lydexia had been supplied with a full complement of four researcher-lieutenants for the Salecah acquisition and, in accordance with Archaeotech custom, all were in the chapel before her.

As the airlock opened, they turned to Lydexia and bowed.

That froze her, just for a second. Salecah was her first acquisition as mission leader, her first selection since she had been promoted. She thought she had gotten used to the idea, but the salute from five men and women who had been, until not very long ago, her fellow Researchers almost stopped her in her tracks.

"At ease," she said, trying to keep her voice level. Reflexively she put a hand up to her head, ran it back over her scalp. The newest set of tattoos there still itched. "We'll go over the primary scans now, agreed? There's no telling how badly these transmissions are going to affect lander comms once we're in flight." There were a couple of nods when she said that, and Lydexia relaxed a little. One correct decision today, at least.

"Quartus," she continued. "What are the conditions like down there?"

The Researcher took a pace forwards. "Cold, doctor-captain. Salecah itself is throwing out some heat, but don't expect the ambient to rise past minus thirty."

"But the air's breathable?"

"For a while. If we're down there for any more than thirty hours I'd recommend breathe-masks."

Lydexia raised an eyebrow. "We should have such luck." Salecah was outside the coreward edge of the Accord, several light-years into the lawless, sparsely populated sector known as the Vermin Stars. That, coupled with the volume of the artefact's siren calls, made her wonder if this mission wouldn't set a new record for brevity. "I'll personally buy everyone double rations if we're here for more than ten. And don't look like that, Dema. I consider my stipend safe."

"I've no doubt, doctor-captain," replied Dema. She was the youngest of the four researchers, just a year or two older than Lydexia. Like Alexus, she'd had a sensory prosthesis fitted across her eyes to augment her vision. One large lens gleamed on the left, balanced by a cluster of smaller sensors on the right. "I've analysed the gravity field surrounding the object. It appears stable on the main body, averaging about point-nine standard gees. That only fluctuates at the three outriggers."

"Gravity anchors?"

"It seems likely."

"Very well." Lydexia crossed the chapel, halting at the armoured locker that contained her field equipment. She held her crypt-disc to the door panel, and the magnetic latches thumped back into their housings. "Dema, your team will investigate the outriggers. I'll let you choose which one." She saw Dema smile wryly: all three outriggers were identical. "Get whatever hardware pertaining to the gravity anchors you can, but don't do anything that might unbalance the artefact until the last minute. If needs be I'll have *Lamarion* blast one free for you and we can tow it home."

"Your will, doctor-captain."

Lydexia was already shrugging into her cowl, a long hooded cloak of rubberised impact armour, jet black like the rest of her uniform. She sealed it around her waist, making sure it hung loose and free around her legs. "Quartus, you'll take the arena. Try not to get too close to the edge: there's no rail that we can see, and a sheer drop of eight hundred metres into the punchbowl."

"I'll make sure my helots are well tethered."

Lydexia had a small cache of specialised detection equipment in the locker. Her technicians would carry the usual sensing gear – quantum tracers, maser rangefinders, and so on – but there were some devices that were unique to her speciality, and therefore under her purview alone. She touched another crypt-disc to a secondary locker inside the first, and this too slid open, its lid hinging up. "Ortina?"

"Yes, my lady?"

"Set your team down into the punchbowl." This was the main body of the artefact, an upturned dome of rusting metal plate three hundred metres across. "Find what you can there, and then begin working your way up into the habitation cylinders. Lotonus will begin at the upper pods and work down, so once you meet in the middle, join forces and spread out into the pressure spheres."

"Doctor-captain?" Lotonus was plainly surprised. "Forgive me, but I thought you'd take that honour. Surely the richest pickings will be in the habitation cylinders."

She turned to him and smiled. "That all depends on what you consider valuable, my friend."

He bowed and stepped back. It was Lydexia's privilege to pick her own target areas, after all. "Thy will be done, doctor-captain. And your guard?"

"Commander Hirundo will take that task." She glanced at the countdown display. "We'll be using all ten landers, and five full squads of Custodes. Remember that we are very far from home here. The reputation of the Vermin Stars isn't an idle one. We've lost people closer to the core systems than this."

"You anticipate danger?" asked Dema. The woman's eye-lenses whined as they rotated in nervous counter-focus. "There are rumours…"

"Of what?" Lydexia had heard nothing.

Dema glanced briefly at her fellows and leaned closer. "Some of the helots have been heard talking. They say that the artefact has something to do with Durham Red!"

A blunt fist of panic appeared momentarily under Lydexia's ribs, squeezing her gut. She forced it away. "Dema, you must know that's folly. If High Command thought there was even a chance the Blasphemy had been here, we would never have been granted a protection edict."

"But what if High Command doesn't know?"

"Are you saying our helot-workers know more about the Blasphemy's whereabouts than High Command?"

Dema dipped her head. "Of course not. Forgive me, doctor-captain."

"Don't fret, Dema. This isn't the Inquisition – no one's going to indict you for heresy. Besides, we all know full well that the average helot worker has more sense than the whole of High Command combined." She put her hand on the researcher's shoulder and gave it a firm squeeze. "I need you focused on the task at hand, not so frightened by rumours of the bitch saint that you can't do your job, yes?"

Dema just nodded. Lydexia gave her shoulder a light slap and stepped away to address them all. "The clock is ticking, Archaeotechs. If any of you have heard this rumour, or any like it, put it from your mind. Say extra prayers if you have to, but say them from your landers on the way down."

With that, and a few extra words of encouragement and respect, she finally got them out of the chapel. It was only when she was alone that she could turn back to the locker, grip its sides hard and let out a long, shuddering breath.

This task would be hard enough without thoughts of Durham Red.

Even the Scarlet Saint's name sent a crawling itch down her spine. The vampire was a nightmare Lydexia had grown up fearing from earliest childhood, the ultimate enemy of humankind, the hidden darkness at the heart of every mutant.

But Durham Red was no longer just a story. She was a very real force, potent and terrifying, roaming the galaxy in search of blood and victims. Tales of her murderous exploits were already becoming legend, despite High Command's best attempts to suppress them.

In the year and a half since the fall of Wodan, Durham Red had caused untold woe to humanity across the

Accord. She had unleashed some kind of demon in the Lavannos system, something so terrible that the starship crews charged with scouring the system refused to even speak of it. She had been linked with the razing of Pyre, the attack on the Irutrean Conclave. And, in an indignity that Lydexia felt all too personally, she had boarded and robbed an Archaeotech clipper in mid-flight.

If that wasn't enough, it seemed she could bend even the strongest Iconoclast to her will. Her power over the unfortunate heretic Matteus Godolkin was well known, but more recently the once respected Admiral Huldah Antonia had become the vampire's slave. Even a special agent, Major Nira Ketta, had gone renegade under her awful influence.

It was horrifying, unthinkable, but impossible to deny. Ketta was a rogue now, pursuing some unspeakable business in the Balrog Cusp. Huldah Antonia had died along with her treacherous fleet in the Broteus system, unless one believed the persistent rumours of her survival. And the Scarlet Saint flew free among the stars, hunting for more Iconoclast blood to slake her sickening thirst.

Could she have something to do with the artefact?

Lydexia took several deep breaths, forcing her heartbeat to slow, her lungs to take in less air. She called forth the seventh cognitive catechism, letting it fill her mind for a few seconds, letting it calm her as it always did: *Beati expiscari, quoniam ipsi Deum videbunt...*

Once her heartbeat had slowed to a normal level, Lydexia opened her eyes and calmly began taking her detection gear from its layers of protective foam. There was something on this artefact that was more important than fear, something that had called her across four hundred billion kilometres. She alone on this mission had the means to locate it, and she would do so if she had to rip the object open with her bare hands.

· · ·

Within half an hour the landers were down and the artefact was swarming with Archaeotechs.

Lydexia could see dozens of them from her target point
on the lower dome. Her team was spreading out across
the artefact's rust brown surfaces, black-clad technicians
scanning and recording data, directing helot workers to
the most likely pieces of hardware. Students, with their
slate grey hoods and masks, watched from the sidelines,
and the hulking, brooding forms of the Custodes
Arcanum, the Archaeotech division's trained warriors
were everywhere.

The artefact was seething with activity. Light drills
and power cutters sparked and flared everywhere that
Lydexia looked, as the helots sliced their way through
its armour and into the systems beneath. It was a brutal process, violent and destructive, more like the work
of rampaging barbarians than that of scientists and
seekers of knowledge. The plain fact of the matter was
that there simply wasn't time to study the artefact as a
whole. As much data as possible had to be gathered
before the cutting began, of course, simply to provide
more clues about how the various pieces of hardware
worked in concert. The real work was done, by neces-
sity, back at the Archaeotech labs. Once in the safety of
their temple-factories, the division could study their
newfound treasures at length, poring over each frag-
ment, picking each system apart bolt by bolt, scanning
and recording until every secret was revealed. A few
hours butchery here could provide the division with
years of research, and the Accord with untold techno-
logical riches.

Per cognitio, *ad salus*, Lydexia reminded herself.
Through knowledge, to salvation. It was the principle
every Archaeotech lived by, their motto and their most
fervent belief. It had only been through projects like
this that humanity had regained the stars, after centuries of war had reduced them to little more than
savages.

Still, she thought ruefully, it would have been nice to spend a few weeks teasing secrets out of the artefact, rather than ripping them free in a matter of hours.

Her lander, and that containing her Custodes squad, had set down on one of three petal shaped platforms inside the upturned lower dome. Like most of the artefact's gross structure, the three petals were identical. Or rather, they should have been. The pilot had spotted anomalies on one of the platforms, which had made Lydexia's decision about which one to land on very easy indeed.

As soon as she left the lander, she could see what the anomalies were. This platform had suffered catastrophic damage.

Lydexia strode between hills of buckled plating, a small forest of broken and ruptured pipe work. Hirundo, the Custodes commander, kept close by, his bolter held at high port. "Take care, doctor-captain. This area could be unstable."

"If it starts to give way, you'll just have to grab me." She turned and gave him a grin. Hirundo's expression was unreadable, his dark eyes narrow above his breathe-mask, but she wouldn't be surprised if he was smiling too. Although Scholars and Custodes rarely mixed in normal circumstances, she and Hirundo had become something close to friends over her years in the division.

"I'll do my best," he replied. His hair, swept back in a long tail, whipped in the freezing wind. "All joking aside, my lady, I'm certain that this damage was caused by a crash. Something landed here, and did it badly."

Lydexia had to agree. She had found several long streaks of pigmentation among the plating, colours that had no place amidst the artefact's almost uniform rust brown. Her chemical tests had dated them as only a few days old. "Someone beat us here, then."

"They would have had time. The chronoplast wave was detected fifteen light-days away."

This meant that the artefact had appeared around Salecah fifteen days before that. Chronoplasts travelled at light speed once they were released – Lydexia herself had proved that in a series of experiments five years earlier. According to an Iconoclast survey vessel that had passed through the system a month ago, there had been nothing previously in orbit around Salecah. It was safe to assume that the artefact had simply appeared above the gas giant, springing into existence in a burst of chronoplasts.

How, Lydexia could only guess. But chronoplasts were a very rare kind of particle, generated only by objects travelling through time. That fact alone made solving the Salecah object's mysteries a maximum priority.

"It couldn't have been Harvesters," she muttered, her words emerging as steaming clouds in the frozen air. "There'd be nothing left if those scum had been here."

She looked upward. Her sky was a great curve of red brown metal, the base of the punchbowl. She could see detail above it through the myriad gaps in the plating. Whoever or whatever had built the artefact seemed to have done so out of random scraps of ferrous metal, and every section of it was half-finished, filigreed by missing segments. Even the landing platforms beneath Lydexia's feet showed the blue haze of Salecah in a hundred patches.

There was no beauty to this machine, she decided, despite its song. It was an industrial thing, and purely functional. Although what that function might have been, she couldn't begin to guess.

Flocks of flying creatures swooped and dived around the punchbowl, startled by the activity. Alexus had identified them as filter feeders – pale, birdlike things native to the gas giant's upper layers. They never rested, Lydexia saw, never set down on the structure or stopped moving. Which made sense, of course – where would they ever have rested before the artefact's arrival?

There was a chime from her belt. Lydexia tore her attention away from the fliers' hypnotic wheeling; her chronoplast wave detector was sounding an alert.

She unclipped the device and checked its gauges. The detector was an unlovely thing, hand-built by Lydexia herself, little more than a flat box set onto a pistol grip, with a narrow funnel at one end. Lydexia aimed the funnel downwards and saw the signal decrease. An upward tilt had it at full strength again.

A second later, the chiming stopped. The waves of chronoplasts, pitifully small compared to the burst which signalled the artefact's arrival, were growing steadily weaker and less frequent. Any one of those she had picked up might be the last, and each gave her only the haziest indication of where they were coming from.

That had been from *Vigilant*, however. This signal, taken from the artefact itself, was far more precise. "I have you," she whispered. "By God, I have you…"

"My lady?" Hirundo was looking at her quizzically, his forehead creased.

In explanation, she lifted the wave detector. "A time machine," she said simply. "And it's close."

Given the range and strength of the wave signal, there was only one feasible location for the chronoplast source. The device sending out pulses of time bending particles had to be in the short, thick stem that joined the lower dome to the punchbowl.

Lydexia had known that the source was somewhere in the lower part of the artefact, but couldn't be any more certain than that. Luckily, a pulse had occurred while she was standing practically on top of the thing. For all her dozens of technicians and hundreds of helots, she might still never have found it otherwise, not in time.

Getting into the stem wasn't easy. There were hatches, but they were locked with some kind of crypt-pattern that defeated her best data-picks. Eventually Hirundo had opened one with a shaped demolition charge, and even that only cracked a locking panel, enabling him to force the hatch aside. This part of the artefact was massively strong.

The interior of the artefact was even stranger, if that was possible, than the outside. It was a bizarre mix of narrow, cramped chambers and cavernous vaults, connected by a maze of tunnels. Stairs and ramps seemed to lead off into empty space, while access ducts narrowed after every turn, until not even her smallest helot could squeeze through. Some of the rooms were booby-trapped, too. Lydexia lost a helot worker to a monofilament web that diced him where he stood, another to a pair of iron rams that pistoned from the walls of a corridor at head height, leaving the unfortunate worker dangling with her skull pulped between them.

Things progressed more slowly after that, but the stem was a finite size. It was only a matter of time until the most sensitive of Lydexia's chrono-locators sounded its reedy chimes, telling her that she had found what she had crossed half a sector for.

"So this," she breathed, "is what a time machine looks like."

Hirundo was still with her. He'd not left her side during the hazardous trip into the stem's heart. "Are you sure, my lady?"

"Sure?" She didn't look at him. She couldn't take her eyes off the machine. "No, I'm not sure. I won't be sure until I've taken it back to Chorazin and made it work, and maybe not even then. But this is the closest I've ever been, Hirundo. The closest anyone's been."

The Custodes drew closer to her. "In which case, my lady, I'd advise it be stripped out of this place now, and taken aboard the Vigilant. Anything else on the artefact is secondary to this find."

He was right, of course. Lydexia allowed herself a few more seconds to watch the machine move, before calling over her technicians and attendant helots. Getting the device off its column would be difficult enough, and as for removing it from the stem... Lydexia started seriously considering whether one of Lamarion's fusion lances would be enough to cut a hole in the artefact's shell.

The machine itself wasn't overly big, perhaps the size of a small groundcar. The chamber it occupied must have taken up an entire level of the stem: it was a broad, flat cylinder, the circular floor a great spread of pipes and ducts that fed in through the walls to meet at the chamber's centre. Where the ducts met they rose up, tangling into a tall column of interwoven pipe work and cables, higher than a lander's dorsal fin. The machine, the core of the artefact, was perched on the top of that column.

It was moving. Parts of it rotated, while others eased back and forth like pistons. Some of the pistons moved through the turning sections, a complex interplay of wheel and peg, shaft and socket. Every section of the device seemed to be shifting into and through every other piece in a dance that made Lydexia's eyes hurt and her mind spin. It was fascinating.

When the helots began burning their way through the column, she had to turn away. She couldn't bear to see that dance fail. "Hirundo? Can you oversee this butchery for me? I need to report back to *Vigilant*, to make sure there is a suitable hold ready…"

She trailed off. Hirundo had one hand to his ear, the other held up for silence. He was receiving a transmission through a secure channel.

Lydexia drew close. He was murmuring into his breathe-mask, using the short-range pickup there instead of a separate comm-linker. "Confirm," he was saying. "No, confirm. Stop babbling, for God's sake!"

She made a questioning face, but he simply raised his hand again. "Very well," he muttered. "Seal the area. No, completely. No one but myself and doctor-captain Lydexia are to know of this."

A second later he straightened up. The call seemed to have ended. "My apologies, doctor-captain. Some of the helots working in the dome below us have discovered something. I believe you should see it."

Lydexia spread her hands. "Can't it wait? Surely this–"

"*Now*, my lady!" His expression gave her no chance to argue.

The fist of panic returned, hard in her gut. "What is it? What have they found?"

"A body."

The corpse lay at the very base of the artefact, in the lower dome. The floor there was almost flat, and carved into a series of concentric channels. Blood, litres of it, had frozen into the channels, gluing the carcass to the rusted metal.

"The throat's been torn out," said Hirundo, kneeling. "And there are scratches. Broken fingernails... Whoever did this bested her in combat, and then ripped her open."

Lydexia felt numb. "Can it be? After all this time, is this how it ends?"

"There are no bio-signs, my lady. Frozen or not, this is a corpse." He stood up. "Fitting, wouldn't you say?"

"I don't understand..." Lydexia took a step back, away from the blood and the slack, open-mouthed face of the carcass. The one undamaged eye had frozen open, frosted and milky. "Who could have done this?" She turned away, back to Hirundo. "We can't tell anyone about this, not yet."

"My lady? Shouldn't the holy Patriarch be informed?"

"No." She shook her head. Gradually, shock was giving way to determination. "We seal this, take the body and the time-core back to Chorazin for testing. When we are sure, *then* we'll tell High Command."

"And the galaxy will rejoice," breathed Hirundo.

"I'm not sure about the mutants," Lydexia replied softly, "but if this is true, then yes. Humanity will mark this day forever."

She would run the tests herself, she vowed, from start to finish. For her own peace of mind, and to still the leaping of her heart, she would be the one to make sure. If it was true, if the icy corpse lying at her feet was who she thought it was, then the nightmare would finally be over.

Humanity's greatest enemy had fallen. Durham Red, the Scarlet Saint, was dead.

2. BETTER DEAD THEN RED

The rumours of Durham Red's death took six weeks to reach Dedanas. In the passenger tender *al-Qirmiza*, shuttling its occupants and their luggage down through the ocean world's soupy atmosphere, it was the only topic of conversation.

"A damned disaster," snapped Marentus Brae, flinging up his hands in disgust. The gesture made the multiple rings on his fat fingers clatter against one another and his chins wobble alarmingly. "If the bitch saint is dead, it can only mean trouble, and trouble on a sector-wide scale. I could be ruined."

The tender was spherical, a globe of brassy metal thirty metres across, and its passengers sat around the inner wall of a circular upper deck. They faced each other from the soft confines of a continuous leather couch.

A pair of mutants sitting across from Brae tilted their heads in unison. "Surely not, honoured Het," they began, speaking as one. They were identical, small and slim under their dark robes, with a fat tube of pulsing, knotted flesh joining their skulls, left temple to right. "If Saint Scarlet is truly dead, won't the Tenebrae rise in anger?"

Brae reddened, obviously unnerved by the pair. "Well, yes. They will. But that's the whole point, don't you see?" He turned to direct his attention to the bearded man on his left. "They'll rise, but without leadership. They'll break themselves upon the Iconoclast ranks."

The bearded man shrugged. He had spoken little on the trip so far. "Since when was war bad business for a maker of weapons?"

Opposite him, a tall, languid man with a powdered face raised one hand in a dismissive gesture. "A short, hot war is worse for business than a long cold one," he opined.

Brae nodded, jowls shaking. "Shantilli has it right," he said. "Once the Tenebrae are broken, Iconoclast orders from my manufactories will drop to a third of present levels. I can't afford that."

"Not with lithium at Accord taxation rates," agreed Shantilli. He settled back into the arms of his two companions. "So, Het Brae, do you hope to stockpile before the Tenebrae rise?"

"I do."

"Curse the Tenebrae." The woman who had spoken was another mutant, slender and smooth faced, clad in a figure hugging leotard of fabric metal. "Their ridiculous crusade has brought us nothing but trouble."

"It's unusual to hear a mutant speak in such a way," said Shantilli, sounding bored. He waved his hand again, loosely. "I'll admit my travels in the Accord have been limited, but most mutants I've met have been all too eager to side with the cultists."

Beside him, the linked pair of twins opened their mouths as if to answer, but the smooth faced woman spoke too quickly. "That's because, Het Shantilli, most of my kind are whining fools. It's perfectly possible to live comfortably in peace with humans, as long as one makes the appropriate payments."

The bearded man turned to her. "Your world can afford its tithe, then?"

"We have that good fortune, yes."

"Pity those that do not," said the twins. "However, we still have no proof that Durham Red was killed. There are only rumours."

"Rumours have to come from somewhere," said Brae. "I say she has to be dead. Why else would the mutant worlds be in such a turmoil?"

"I'm not so sure," said Shantilli. He closed his eyes and yawned. "Not that I'd shed any tears over her death, you understand, after what she did to my home world."

"That is true, then?" The twins had fixed him with their double gaze. "Durham Red destroyed Magadan?"

"Apparently." He blinked lazily at them. "I was away from home at the time."

"But you believe she lives."

"I do. Some diseases are just too tough to cure."

The twins nodded, their faces blank of all expression. "Although we do not share your sentiment, Dominus, we share your opinion. We are sure Durham Red is alive."

"Nonsense," crowed Brae. "My luck could never be so good."

The twins stared at him for a moment, then turned to the hooded, veiled woman on their left. "And your opinion, lady? You have not spoken on this yet."

Behind her veil, Durham Red couldn't help but grin. "Nah," she said finally. "The big guy's right. She's history."

Not long after that, the tender ignited its grav-lifters and began to decelerate. Red could feel herself squashing down slightly into the leather couch, and was glad about it. The sooner she was off this bubble and away from her fellow passengers, the better.

There had been space to avoid them on the clipper from Thaetia. Although the journey to Dedanas had taken nearly three days, Red had been able to spend most of that time away from the others, in her private cabin. Or, to be strictly accurate, in the cabin of the Lady Yalishanna Trier, buyer for the Trier-Hasnek corporation of Chios Secundus. The Lady Yalishanna herself was still on Thaetia, missing her clothes, her crypt-idents and about half a litre of blood. She would no doubt have woken up by now – the drug Red had slipped her was good for about two days of unconsciousness – but it would still be some time before she found her way out of the tavern room, after what Red had done to the locks.

Perhaps, Red reflected, the event would teach Yalis-hanna to act more like a lady in the future, and less like a horny businesswoman going sex-crazy on a corporate freebie. A harsh education, but from what Red had learned about Her Ladyship in the days leading up to Thaetia, a long deserved one.

Now though, it was Red herself who felt trapped and drained. The tender was built for comfort, not speed, and since leaving the clipper had progressed towards the sur-face with agonising sluggishness. After an hour of listening to her co-passengers bicker about whether she was dead or not, she was almost ready to rip open an air-lock and jump.

There wasn't even much of a view to look at. Although the deck was ringed with viewports, they were set well above the spherical tender's widest point. All Red could see through them was the sky, changing all too gradually from black to blue. Occasionally there was a flash of hori-zon, but Dedanas had no landmasses, and so presented nothing more interesting than an uninterrupted stretch of ocean. Besides, to see through the viewports at all required either twisting around in her seat like a bored child, or staring across the deck past one or other of her fellow passengers. And that risked someone mistaking her gaze for an invitation to start talking to her.

Which wasn't something she was interested in at all. Each one of them had started to bug her in the short time they had been forced together aboard *al-Qirmiza*. Brae, the weapons dealer from Fernal, had a way about him that made her fangs itch for his throat, if she could ever find it under all that flab. The mutant twins were quiet enough, but Red couldn't help but find them creepy. Something about their blankly identical faces and their flat, monotone voices speaking in perfect symmetry com-pletely unnerved her. The quiet guy with the beard seemed tolerable, but he'd been looking at her oddly of late, and the woman with the smooth, noseless face was just plain annoying.

The presence of a Magadani dominus wasn't making her feel exactly comfortable, either.

All in all, hardly a fun party to crash. But Red wasn't here for fun. She had serious business on Dedanas, and it didn't involve buying cut-price lithium.

A few seconds after the lifters ignited, a concealed sounder chimed softly, then spoke. "Honoured Hets," it said. "The Mercantile Caucus of Ulai welcomes you."

"About bloody time," growled Brae.

"*Al-Qirmiza* is about to enter final descent vector," the sounder continued. It might have been the vessel's pilot speaking; if it was, Red decided, he had a lovely voice. "The interior of the tender is gravity-damped. You will feel no ill effects. Please remain seated, and enjoy the final stages of our journey."

With that, the voice fell silent, and the ocean beneath *al-Qirmiza* tipped up on its end.

Red was suddenly looking at an expanse of wave-rippled blue racing towards her at an angle of about thirty degrees. It was like seeing the side of a mountain coming right at her, and an instinctive flutter of panic went off behind her ribs. She suppressed a gasp.

None of the others seemed even to have noticed the effect.

The sea wasn't tilting, of course. The tender itself had tipped, angling its rotund hull to let some of the energy from its grav-lifters slip aside, trading lift for forward thrust. Held in place by the deck's artificial gravity, Red was now sitting at the highest point of the couch, looking down past the bearded man at the endless blue seas below.

At long last, Red could see something of interest among the waves. Far ahead, almost lost in the misty sea air, objects marred the unbroken expanse of ocean. Distance made them tiny, toy like, but they were growing as Red watched.

Beside her, the twins were craning their necks to see what she saw, stretching their connecting tendril. "Ulai is in sight," they reported. "We can see the spaceport."

That was the biggest object, a disc of white against the stark blue of the sea. As the tender got closer, Red started to make out imperfections in the disc's surface – pimples and bulges, dark spots and tiny points of light. Then she saw one of the dots begin to rise, recognised its shape, and realised with a start how big the spaceport was. That dot was a bulk hauler, kilometres long.

"Is that where we'll set down?" Brae asked.

The noseless mutant shook her head. "No, Het. That's only for cargo flights. The lithium you buy will lift off from there, but we'll go straight to the Ulai fin itself."

They were close enough to see that the spaceport would pass by on the right of the tender. Red saw another structure over to the left, more angular but equally huge. That was the manufactory complex, or at least the part of it that protruded from the ocean's surface.

Red knew the mining complex would be even further in that direction, but she couldn't see it. The air wasn't clear enough for her to pick out the transfer platform. She could, however, see dozens of white lines crossing the blue between the structures. There were cargo barges down there, each hauling kilotonnes of refined mineral, their mighty paddles churning up wakes dozens of kilometres long.

"There," cried Brae abruptly. "The Ulai fin."

Red offered up a silent prayer of thanks as she followed the fat man's gaze. Sure enough, just coming into view was a titanic wing of gleaming white, rising from the waves like part of a downed starship. It was immensely tall, dwarfing the breakers that battered its flanks, and so slender that it seemed as if a storm or an especially violent sea swell might shear it right off its moorings. To Red, who had never seen such a thing poking up from the sea before, it looked dangerously delicate.

She wasn't the only one who thought so. Shantilli was shaking his head in wonder. "This world must boast an eternally calm sea," he murmured. "I've seen storms that would bend that thing over."

"On the contrary, Dominus," the twins replied. "The winds here can reach five hundred kilometres an hour, and the waves eighty metres high – there is no landmass to moderate such conditions."

"Really?" Red's eyebrows went up. "Bloody hell. Must be built strong, then."

"It is. In addition, the entire structure rotates on its axis."

Red gaped. "You're kidding."

"Not at all." That was the bearded man. "There's an axle running down from the top deck, right through into the sea bed. If the wind gets too high, or the current too strong, the whole arcology swivels to reduce its profile."

"Sneck." Red whistled softly. The tender was levelling out, and the fin filled her view. She was close enough to see its windows, thousands of them, arranged in lines down the glossy white sides of it. If each line of windows was a deck, the fin must have been two, maybe three kilometres high, not counting the section that lay below sea level.

Flat vanes set along its sloping front edge had grown into vast decks peppered with holes. Some of the holes were filled with golden spheres, tenders like *al-Qirmiza*, and Red could see one hole in particular expanding in front of her. The little ship was coming in on final approach.

There was a chime, and the sounder spoke again. "In a few moments," it said, "*al-Qirmiza* will reach the upper dock of Ulai. Once we are socketed, there will be a short delay while the umbilicals are fixed and the atmospheres equalised. This may take a few minutes, so please remain seated and continue to enjoy the hospitality of the Caucus."

So she'd have to endure these people for even longer. "Bugger," Red muttered, sitting back and folding her arms.

The twins snapped a double glance at her. "Excuse us?"

"What? Oh, it's, ah, an expression of joy. Back on Chios Secundus, I mean." Red felt herself cringing back under the linked mutants' piercing stare. "Like, 'Ooh, we get to stay in this lovely tender for even longer, oh bugger.'"

Four eyes blinked at her in perfect unison. "We see."

I'll bet you do, thought Red, glaring at the holo. The sooner she could drop her charade and get away from this crowd, the better.

There was a slight vibration as the grav-lifters throttled up, and Red heard the distant whine of servos as the landing claws engaged, and then the walls of the socket rose above the viewports, obscuring her view. A moment later, the tender settled and the lifters shut down.

There was a chime, and the deck's internal lighting changed from white to a very gentle shade of blue. "Welcome to Dedanas," said the sounder.

Next to Red, the twins stood up carefully. "Bugger," they intoned.

Red smiled. "Couldn't have put it better myself."

After being cooped up in the tender for so long, Red would have welcomed a decent walk in the sea air to stretch her legs and clear the shipboard claustrophobia from her head, but she had forgotten how privileged she was now supposed to be. There was no question of being allowed to walk more than a few steps in succession, a rule that seemed to favour Marentus Brae in particular. Perhaps, Red surmised sourly as she was led towards a monorail car, Ulai's rulers expected their visitors to be corpulent. Maybe allowing one's appetites to run wild was a corporate objective out here among the Periphery.

The car was a blunt-nosed cylinder as long as a ground bus, constructed entirely from thick glass facets in a cage of brass frame. A uniformed servant showed them inside, gesturing each over the threshold in turn. Red glared at him as she went past, considering herself perfectly capable of getting into a monorail without help, but if the man noticed her expression he paid it no heed. Yalishanna's hood and veil was a passable disguise, she had learned, but it was no aid to expression. Most of the time, no one seemed to even look at the face behind the silk.

When the last of them was in, the servant moved to stand in the doorway. "This is but a short journey, Hets," he assured them. "The transit tunnel will take you directly to the arrivals lounge, where you may rest and take refreshment while your luggage and entourages are being offloaded."

"Lounge? Refreshment? For Christ's sake…" Red grimaced. All this was taking far too long, and her left forearm was beginning to itch. She resisted the urge to scratch it. "I thought we were going to do some business here."

"In good time, my lady." And with that the servant stepped back, allowing the glass door of the car to roll down and seal them in.

"Sneck it," Red snapped, and thumped angrily back into her seat. The monorail was already beginning to pick up speed. The tunnel entrance gaped at her, then swallowed the car whole.

There was a light touch on her hand. It was Shantilli, leaning over from the opposite seat, his sylphs sitting wordlessly to either side of him. When she looked up, he smiled. "In a hurry, my dear?"

"You could say that." Red tried to keep the edge out of her voice. Shantilli was as annoying as anyone else on the flight – a rich, powdered idiot trailing his lobotomised sex slaves around like trophies, his clothes worth a year's food to any hungry family, but Red couldn't bring herself to treat him badly.

It was guilt, she knew, pure and simple. She had been indirectly responsible for the destruction of his homeland, and the deaths of untold thousands of his people. Even though she had managed to drive a few Magadani out of the ruins to safety, they were trapped on their encoded world, the gateway between them and the rest of the universe sealed forever. Shantilli could never return home.

If she couldn't feel guilty about that, what would shame her?

"I'm just not used to all this poncing about," she went on. "Go in, get the job done, and get out again; that's how I do things. All this?" She waved her hands about. "This is just wasting my bloody time."

"The Dedani mean no harm, my lady. They simply need to unload the tender. You have an entourage, yes?"

She shook her head. "Nope. Well, there's a couple of guys who help me out now and then, but they're not here right now." She glanced out of the nearest pane as the car began to slow. "They might be along later, though."

"So a few minutes won't make any difference."

"Don't bet on it."

He put up his hands in defeat, the smile still playing about his painted lips. "Ah, I see I will be drinking alone. Forgive my intrusion, Lady Yalishanna."

"No problem," she said, not unkindly. "I'm just on a tight schedule."

"Another time, then. After this tiresome trading is over and done with."

In spite of herself, she winked at him. "You never know."

The arrivals lounge was large, open and airy, the floor strewn with silken cushions, the tables heaving with delicacies. Holographic globes drifted in the air like vast soap bubbles, filled with turning diagrams and schematics of the wares Ulai had to offer. Lithium for power cores, molybdenum for starship hulls, deuterium and tritium refined as pure fusion fuel, even purified seawater by the tanker – their atomic structures spiralled overhead, along with their shipping costs and taxation rates, while recorded voices from hidden sounders followed the bubbles around in a continuous, synchronised sales pitch.

A small army of traders had already occupied the place. Some had paired off and were talking animatedly in a mix of spoken words and complex, arcane gestures, while many more were sprawled around in loose, open groups, relaxing before the hard bargaining began.

Pale skinned young women in uniform robes paced slowly between the traders, moving with an easy, practised grace. They carried trays laden with glasses of wine or mint tea. One came close to Red with a strange assemblage of brass pipes and globes hooked over her left shoulder, a rack of tiny cups in her right. As she passed, Red smelled coffee, sweet and strong, and her mouth watered.

The lounge looked a lot more inviting than she had expected, and it was an effort to deny herself even the least of its pleasures. Her forearm was hurting again, though, and that spurred her on. She grabbed the next servant girl to pass by.

"Excuse me? Look, I don't want to sound rude, but is there any chance I could get on with some business? My boss is going to freak out if I don't start dealing soon..."

The girl nodded and disappeared through a doorway concealed between two wall hangings. Red watched her go, and then saw Shantilli out of the corner of her eye, already languishing amidst a group of buyers. Largely female ones, she noticed with a slight smile. He'd be okay here for a good while, which could save him considerable trouble later on, if things went badly.

In a few moments the doorway opened again, and a tall, white faced young man stepped through. He paced quickly over to where Red was standing. "Lady Yalishanna Trier?"

"That's me."

He drew close to her and bowed. "Oray Abd Durwan, your trademaster." His bow wasn't deep, and it was skewed sideways by the device he carried slung over his left shoulder. This was no coffee pot, but a glass cylinder of greenish, bubbling fluid, capped with brass filigree and terminating in a curled metal tube. The tube was hooked through a small loop, so that its end lay close to Durwan's cheek. It smoked very slightly. "I believe you are eager to begin work?"

"The sooner the better."

"Very well. In that case, allow me to summon a gravity sled."

Red put a hand up. "Let's walk."

"Walk?"

"Yeah. Move forward by putting one foot in front of the other? You remember." She started ahead, leaving him to catch up. "Come on, it'll be fun!"

It felt good to stretch herself out on the walk from the lounge to the trading halls. She moved fast, legs swinging under Yalishanna's robe. Oray Abd Durwan, obviously used to slower customers, almost had to run to keep up.

The journey took them even deeper into the deck, into large, open areas that teemed with life. Within a few blocks of the arrivals lounge, Red found herself in a wide internal street, pushing her way through crowds. The street was roofed with ornate girders and hanging lumes, but in all other respects it might just as well have been in the open. It certainly smelled that way; its air must have been pumped in from outside rather than created internally like it was in so many Accord buildings. It had the tang of sea salt to it.

Before long, stalls began to appear on either side, and soon Red was in the middle of a market. The crowds around her – an almost equal mix of human and mutant, she was pleased to notice – were plainly here for their own kind of trade, a smaller, more intimate version of that taking place in the lounge. This was the kind of bargaining Red could relate to. Not fat businessmen squinting over the shipping costs of refined molybdenum, but a frenzied personal interplay of barter and bargain.

The goods around her were a wonder. Silk sheets hung next to brassware and jewellery, sense-engine parts alongside meat and dried fruit. Red slowed her pace a little, just enjoying the show. Next to her, Durwan seemed quite bewildered by it all. "Forgive me, my lady," he said as they walked. "I usually take a sled or monorail."

"And miss all this?" Someone was trying to sell her live chickens by thrusting them into her face. On her other side, a furred man was offering her baskets of oranges, spiky fruit, hashish. "What is this place, anyway?"

"We call it the Lesser Suq," Durwan told her, waving traders away with each step. "The stallholders set up here in the hope of attracting custom from the traders. There is little of that, of course, but they don't seem to mind."

"I'm not surprised. No shortage of customers, is there?"

"A surfeit, I'd say. Please, lady, follow me. I know a short cut."

Durwan was as good as his word, and within a few blocks Red was being shown into a large, low ceilinged hallway that bore no resemblance to the outside world at all. Durwan took her through a set of security doors at one end, using a small crypt-disc hung around his neck on a gold chain, and into an even larger area. This one was circular, richly carpeted, the lights discreetly low. Around the circumference of this new hall were door-ways, most standing open. "Please," Durwan invited her. "Pick one."

"Any one?"

"The choice is yours, lady."

"Um. Okay, that one." The doorways were all identical, anyway.

Inside was a small room, sparsely furnished. There was a small, round desk, two chairs, and a side table on which stood a pot of mint tea and two glasses. Red could smell the strong mint, mixed with the musky chemical aroma rising from Durwan's shoulder tube. Out in the market she'd not noticed it, but in the closeness of the trading chamber it was hard to ignore.

She sat on one side of the desk, and Durwan took the chair opposite her. As he did, he turned his head and placed his lips around the end of the tube, drawing a long breath of its vapours. His eyes closed for a second or two, and when they reopened, his pupils were very large. "Now," he smiled. "We begin."

"Great," Red replied, sitting back. "Before we start, I'd just like to say what a great place you've got here. I mean, I've been to a whole bunch of planets in the back Accord, but Dedanas is way more fun."

"Thank you, Lady Yalishanna."

"And your prices are really good. You beat anywhere else hands down on refined minerals."

He nodded graciously. "We are fortunate. Taxation rates here in the Periphery are less than half of those on worlds under Iconoclast control." His voice was odd now, strangely cadenced. It reminded Red a lot of the recorded sales pitches in the lounge. "In addition, our mining technology is quite revolutionary, which also serves to keep costs down."

Ah yes, she thought. The mining technology. She wondered if Oray Abd Durwan knew how revolutionary it actually was. "I'll bet. Oh, one last question."

"Yes?"

"That gas you're breathing." He was taking another puff as she spoke. "What is that?"

"It's called Tajar, my lady, or barter musk. It's a neural enhancer."

Red blinked. "What, it makes you smarter?"

"It improves my memory and mental functions, especially in the fields of mathematics and economics. It reduces my reliance on data-engines and electro-abaci during trade."

"Right." She nodded. "So it's not essential to your life, then. If you were asleep or unconscious for a while, and couldn't puff on it, you wouldn't be in trouble."

He frowned. "No, my lady. Why do you ask?"

"No reason," Red replied, and punched him hard in the nose.

Durwan flew over backwards, the impact of the blow flinging him clear out of his chair. He struck the wall, bounced off, and collapsed in a heap.

Red was already out of her own chair. She hauled Durwan up and sat him back against the wall, putting two fingers to the side of his throat. She'd not invested the blow with a fraction of the force she could have, but hitting people was never an exact science. Red was glad to find a steady, if rather brisk pulse under her fingertips.

Blood was threading down from Durwan's swelling nose. He'd be out for an hour, maybe two, which was probably going to be long enough. Red reached under his robes, taking out the crypt-disc and lifting the chain over his head. "Sorry about that," she told him.

It was a pity she'd had to strike him at all, but she'd been searched quite thoroughly before getting onto the clipper. There had been no chance of bringing any drugs or weapons onto Ulai.

Within a few moments the disc was slung around her own neck. She took off the veil, then stripped off Yalishanna's hood and outer cloak, bundling them up tight and shoving them into the teapot. The fabric was fine, strong yet gossamer thin, and she was able to get the lid back on without too much trouble. That just left her in a loose tunic and trousers of black silk, and a pair of boots that were a lot more practical than they looked.

The veil went back around her face, tied on like a mask with a knot behind her head, under her hair. Her face was different at the moment, her hair colour similarly disguised, but there were some things she couldn't cover as easily. The fewer people who saw her fangs the better.

Red stopped for a second and took a deep breath, letting her own pulse slow down. Things had gone well so far, but the plan could go badly wrong at any time. She needed to be doubly careful from now on.

For a moment she was almost tempted to take a sniff of Durwan's trade musk, but she decided against it. There was no telling what the stuff would do to her. Besides, a chemically induced degree in mathematics wouldn't help her now. All she really needed was an elevator, or the local equivalent. A way of getting down to sea level, and beyond, before the trademaster woke up.

She stepped outside, locking the door behind her, and set off to find the quickest way into the oceans of Dedanas.

3. MINE SHAFT

The bearded man, whose name Durham Red had never found out, had been right about the fin and how it turned. The massive flared base of it sat not on the seabed itself, but on a titanic disc of metal and polished stone a full kilometre across. Hundreds of concentric rings were set into the disc, gleaming in the greenish light from underwater searchlights: bearings and gear tracks, on which the Ulai fin would rotate whenever the ocean world's weather got severe.

It was an impressive construction, and slightly worrying. As she tooled the little submersible past the fin's base, she found herself wondering just how far down into the seabed the axle extended, and what might happen should it ever fail. She certainly wouldn't want to be anywhere nearby if it did.

Traversing the disc at one-quarter thrust seemed to take an age, but Red didn't want to attract attention by opening up the vessel's drives this close to Ulai. Stealing the thing had been easier than she had been expecting by a long way, but there was no sense pushing her luck.

So far, things had gone very well indeed. Durham Red, who seemed to attract ill fortune like a magnet draws filings, was beginning to find that just a little suspicious. However, she forced herself to stay positive. Surely there was no reason, she told herself, easing the throttles up a few degrees, why would her luck change. After all the woe she'd seen, why shouldn't things go her way, just for once?

The fin was behind her now, fading into the sea's murk. Within a few minutes it would be invisible to the naked eye, for all its size and searchlights, although the submersible's sonar still showed it with perfect clarity. Eyes were not the best way to see down here, Red knew. Not under two hundred metres of ocean.

Red didn't know if the submersible belonged to Oray Abd Durwan personally, or if it was just one of the vessels he was authorised to use, but in either case his crypt-disc had led her right to it. The coin sized identification wafer had proved amazingly useful on her way down through the fin, getting her through locked doors, giving her access to interactive maps and guides, even getting her into the submersible pen and almost to the mini-sub's hatch. Things had taken a slight downturn at that point, due to a couple of dockyard techs who had spotted her and tried to raise an alarm, but they would be sleeping off that mistake for a couple of hours yet.

In her rear, view holoscreen, the great fin vanished completely into the haze. Red took that as a signal it was safe to speed up, and eased the throttles forward to one-half thrust.

The submersible accelerated smoothly, its impellers powering up with a shrill hum. It hadn't taken Red long to get to grips with the vessel's controls. Although her experience of undersea travel was quite limited, the combination of throttles, pedals and control collective was not a great deal different from those she had used in dozens of different kinds of space vessels. The sonar took some getting used to, and the sub's complete lack of weapons made her nervous, but that was only to be expected. Heading into danger without a gun in her fist was something she had never felt comfortable doing.

Ahead of her, slightly distorted by the sub's domed forward canopy, forests of weed and coral rose out of the murk.

Red pulled back on the collective slightly, lifting the submersible another twenty metres above the seabed before levelling out again. She checked the sonar, using her free hand to extend the range, and the holographic patch of seabed in front of her flickered and smoothed out as its dimensions increased by a factor of ten.

Objects appeared, spun from threads of light.

With the range increased, the sonar now showed Red all the structures within a hundred kilometres. The fin was still there, oddly truncated at the point where it broke the surface, but it was no longer alone. Red saw the pyramidal bulk of the manufactory over to the far right, and ahead, almost at the sonar's limit, a spider of lines and domes that made up the mine complex and its refinery. A slender cylinder extended from the refinery, pointing straight up towards the surface, and Red corrected her course slightly to aim at it, taking the speed up to three-quarters. The sub surged forward, impellers humming madly, and the cylinder – the refinery's hoist tower, designed to carry tonnes of purified minerals up to a transfer platform on the surface – began crawling towards her.

"Not long now," she whispered.

Her left forearm was beginning to itch again, and sent hot needles of pain up to her elbow. She grimaced and waved the arm about a few times to try to ease the discomfort. There wasn't much room to wave anything inside the submersible, but the movement helped somewhat. She hoped that it wouldn't trouble her too much before she reached the refinery. Now was not the time to be distracted.

Chimes sounded from the control board. Red found herself looking up towards the distant surface. There, the instruments told her, something enormous was churning the waves into froth, carving a channel in the water as it passed. One of Ulai's mighty transport barges, laden with goods from the refinery, was on its way to the spaceport.

When Red looked back at the sonar, the hoist tower was drawing close to the middle of the screen. She set the device to threat mode, decreasing the range, but upping the resolution and the rate at which the sonar took soundings. Instantly, the tower's representation dropped back, but began moving more quickly. Red throttled the impellers back as the mine complex began to resolve itself from the blue green haze in front of her.

She saw the tower first, or rather the warning beacons that studded its surface. Then the refinery itself became apparent, first as a random sprawl of lit windows, then gradually growing an outline. It was immense, like everything here, built to a huge scale. The processing towers rose above her like volcanoes, the pipes and gantries were forests, the domed reactor behind it a looming mountain.

Tubes extended from the base of the tower; pressurised tunnels, braced to the seabed with arched steel girders. Red took the submersible down to the nearest, and swung the vessel around to follow it.

She was checking the sonar every few seconds, but there were no other subs in the water.

The tube extended for about ten kilometres before it met the mine. There was little to see above the seabed, of course, just a great cap of metal so wide it went off the edge of the sonar. Next to it, attached by another tunnel, was a cone shaped building of dark metal, its top flaring out into a wide disc.

Red was just wondering how deep the mine went when the sonar outlined that flared roof in crimson.

Instantly the board came alive with chimes and alert lamps. Red cursed and hauled on the collective, swinging the sub over and around. Someone down in that building had locked onto her power signature. If they fired at her from this range she'd be too close to dodge.

Security here, it seemed, was a lot tighter than back at the fin.

Red throttled one impeller up to full, the other into reverse, spinning the submarine about and then dropping it towards the seabed. Sand and grit whirled up into the cones of her forward searchlights, flying behind her as she poured on the power.

The comms board lit up. "Submersible Sumuk Nine. Disengage your power train immediately and await pickup. You are in a proscribed area!"

The board was set to audio only, but Red gave it the finger anyway. "Disengage this."

"We won't warn you again, Sumuk Nine."

"Fine by me."

She was answered by a new chime from the board, a ragged, insistent gonging, rising steadily in pitch. Whoever was on the other end of the comms channel hadn't been kidding. Red slammed both throttles hard and began yanking the collective about, trying to throw up as much seabed muck as she could, and then dragged the stick back. The submersible rose fast, creaking in protest at the pressure changes.

It was a good try, a valiant attempt at escape, but there was no way it was ever going to work. The first torpedo hammered into the seabed and detonated there with a brief flash and an expanding sphere of shockwave, but the other wasn't fooled. It sizzled past Red's submersible, trailing bubbles, and arced around to port. She could see it on the sonar, a bright point of yellow light outlined in threat warnings and velocity markers, homing in on her with awful speed.

The chiming became a continuous tone. Red threw her arms over her head just as the second torpedo detonated fifty metres behind her.

Whoever was in control of the weapon had timed the blast perfectly. The explosion tore into the submersible's rear like a hammer blow, slamming Red forwards in the cabin. She was strapped in, heavy pressure webbing holding her into the seat, but the torpedo's destruction still threw her about like a bead in a rattle.

Blearily, she saw the seabed spiralling up to meet her. Pieces of metal, some of them glowing with heat, were whirling down past her to meet it. That was what was left of the impellers, she realised. The power core was intact, but the drives and control surfaces were history.

Trademaster Durwan would not be pleased about this.

Ulai traffic control sent out two more submersibles to pick her up – big, armoured things, their lumpy hulls dotted with torpedo launchers and sonar pickups. Red's own sonar had been knocked out by the blast, but what was left of Sumuk Nine had come down with part of its canopy facing largely upwards. She saw the other subs dropping through the swirling murk, lit by their own running lights.

They took her back to the refinery, the submersible's twisted frame held tightly in powered grabs. Red could only sit, strapped into the seat, bracing herself against the pressure cabin's walls as the armoured submersibles dragged her up through a horizontal water lock, into a docking area that dwarfed that of the Ulai fin. The lights there seemed blazingly bright after the sub's dim cockpit indicators and the cloudy darkness of deep ocean, and Red winced, shielding her eyes as her captors extended their grabs and dropped Sumuk Nine unceremoniously onto a nearby deck.

The wrecked sub teetered, then rolled over onto its side, bouncing Red around some more. "Hey!" she yelled. "Try being a bit more careful."

"We're done being careful." It was the same voice she'd heard before. "Now unseal the hatch and come out."

"And if I don't?"

"Then we'll open that can up with a fusion lance, and believe me, you *really* don't want to be inside if we start doing that."

He was probably right. Red pondered for a few moments, then retied the veil around her face. "Okay," she muttered. "Give me a minute."

"Thirty seconds."

She unlocked her harness and then, after a certain amount of undignified struggling, managed to open the side hatch and climb out. With Sumuk Nine on its side the hatch was now vertical, so she had to make her way down the slick, sea stinking flank of the battered machine before she could reach the deck.

By the time she got there, a squad of soldiers had already formed up to cover her. She looked into a small forest of gun muzzles and put her hands up, grinning weakly behind the scarf. "Hi," she said.

One of the soldiers lowered his weapons and stepped towards her. She tensed, expecting a blow, but when his gloved hand came up it was only to grab the crypt disc around her neck and pull it free. The chain snapped as he tugged it, tiny gold links flicking away onto the wet deck.

The soldier slotted the disc into a reader. "Well. You don't look like trademaster Oray Abd Durwan to me."

"She's not."

Red glanced about. The speaker was striding up the deck towards her, flanked by a pair of guards. He'd changed his trader's business suit for a set of flowing robes, and wore a tight fitting skullcap over his short hair, but there was still no mistaking the bearded man from the tender *al-Qirmiza*.

He stopped in front of her and took the crypt disc from the soldier's hand. "Trademaster Durwan is still on Ulai, recovering from this woman's assault. As are two dock workers in the submarine pens. This, Hets, is the Lady Yalishanna Trier. And she's a spy."

"Industrial espionage," said the bearded man, "is a crime, and we Dedani take it very seriously indeed. You're in a lot of trouble, Lady Yalishanna."

Red scratched her forearm idly. "More than you know," she replied. Sure enough, right on schedule, her plan had become totally derailed.

The man's name was Utan Bas Loman, and he was a sub-director of Ulai's corporate security division. Apparently he had been warned of Yalishanna Trier's objectives several weeks previously, back when she had made an application to visit Ulai. He'd been tracking her ever since then, even shipping out to Thaetia to keep an eye on her, making sure he was on the clipper to Dedanas, on the same tender down to the fin. The only thing he hadn't done, it seemed, was find out what she'd looked like.

Red's hair was a mousey brown at the moment, and a layer of artfully applied bio-gel had subtly altered the planes of her face, but she still didn't look much like Yalishanna Trier. Loman had only done half a job.

That was fine by her, but how long could the situation last? One decent bio-scan, or a blow in the wrong place, and her disguise would quite literally come to pieces. Her image wasn't as well known here in the Periphery as it was in the Accord, but it could only be a matter of time before someone worked out who she was.

It could happen at any moment. Red couldn't afford to be around for any longer than she had to be.

Loman had taken her to a small holding chamber in the Refinery's security station. She hadn't been bound, but the door was heavily armoured and solidly locked, impervious even to her strength. For the moment, too, she had kept her abilities hidden. It didn't hurt to have an ace or two up her sleeve, and the more of her mutant nature she kept hidden, the less it could be used to identify her.

They'd seen her teeth, of course, while she was being searched. A fashion trend, she'd explained, back on Chios Secundus, and didn't anyone have them here? That seemed to have satisfied her captors, who had declared her devoid of weapons or communications devices, given her clothes back and led her into the chamber to dress. Minutes later, Loman had reappeared.

He sat before her now, on the other side of a desk very much like that in the trading chamber, although there was no mint tea on offer here. Soldiers stood against the far wall, armed with weapons that looked a lot like shock cannon. The guns weren't pointing directly at her, but they were aimed close enough to be uncomfortable. If she tried anything, she'd be full of voltage before she could get over the desk.

Shock cannons were usually non-lethal, unless you kept the trigger down too long.

"So," she said, leaning back in her seat and folding her arms. "What happens now?"

Loman tilted his head. "We have two choices. One, you could tell us exactly why you are here, and who in your corporation is part of this conspiracy. I want to know the names and ident-codes of your conspirators, and I want a full rundown of the operations you've run on other worlds. I know all about Fallaway and Topheth, but I'm sure there are more." He thoughtfully tapped his fingers on the desktop. "If you do that, you'll be detained in one of our security facilities until we see fit to have you deported offworld, and that will be the end of the matter."

"And behind door number two?"

"Excuse me? Oh, I see. Well, option two is that you refuse to tell us anything. In that case, we would have no choice but to inform the nearest Iconoclast garrison of a threat to their production, and let them deal with you. High Command has exclusive contracts with us, you know."

"Do they? Lucky you." Red closed her eyes for a second, thinking hard. She'd screwed up here, and done it badly.

Lady Yalishanna had looked like a sweet bet for getting into Ulai. Her ticket already booked, idents logged, and her sexual proclivities so well documented that Red had only needed to turn up at the same tavern and the woman had been drooling over her like a schoolboy with a crush on his teacher. She'd never seen someone walk into a honey-trap so easily.

How was Red to know that the woman was an industrial spy?

Her options were narrowing quickly. "Okay," she said quietly, opening her eyes to see Loman's reaction. "Here's the prize behind door number three. I say the name 'Trogyllium', and you let me walk out of here and catch the next tender to Chios Secundus."

Lomas, she noticed, had gone ever so slightly pale. To his credit, though, he didn't cave immediately. "Go on."

"In front of the help?" Red gestured at the guards. Loman glanced back over his shoulder, as if noticing they were there for the first time.

"Go," he told them.

"Sir?"

"You heard me. This is a matter of planetary security. So stand down until I tell you to do otherwise."

He waited until they had filed out and locked the door behind them. "Speak."

"Okay, if you want me to spell it out. Lady Yalishanna Trier is locked in a tavern room on Thaetia with no clothes on, unless she's found her way out by now." She fixed him with a glare. "If you'd done any research at all, you'd know I'm not her. My name's Alissa Carmine, and I'm with the Alpha-Wulf sector security agency."

"Never heard of it."

"That's the point, dipstick. But you've heard of Trogyllium, haven't you? That's where the slavers operate out of, the ones you've been buying your mine workers from."

Loman narrowed his eyes. When he next spoke, there was something sly and cold in his voice. "We run a legitimate business here, Het Carmine–"

"Do you bollocks," Red hissed. "You've been running this place on slave labour for a decade, ever since the Grand Council shifted the Accord's border fifty light years in your direction. The Ulai government panicked and decided to cut their labour costs down to nothing. Revolutionary mining techniques? Yeah, if you were putting up the snecking pyramids."

Loman leapt up. "Enough."

She shook her head. "My report's still pending back on Chios Secundus. It'll go public if I don't report back pretty damn soon, so you'd better start powering up a sub to get me back. If I return to Alpha-Wulf in one piece, then maybe, and I mean bloody *maybe*, you'll get enough time to put your house in order before the killships turn up. Say what you like about the Grand Council, but they really don't like slavers."

Loman turned and stalked away from the desk. He was getting his temper back under control; she could see that from the set of his back. She'd touched a nerve or two there, all right.

"Very well," he said finally, his back still to her. "It seems I'm in something of a corner."

"You and me both."

"You know that one report from a security agency won't change anything. And given enough time, we could cover the evidence so well that no one, Iconoclast or not, would ever find it."

"If time's what you need, you can only get it from me." Red grinned at him. "Tick-tock, snecker."

He looked back at her over his shoulder. "Give me a few minutes," he said, "and I'll see what I can do."

"Hey–"

"Don't worry. You'll not be harmed." The door opened for him as he reached it, and closed behind him as he went through.

Red was expecting to hear the locks engage, but they didn't. She knew the sound of them because she'd heard it on the way in – the distinctive thumping of magnetic bolts.

This time, nothing. Loman hadn't keyed them yet.

Red stood up. Had the damned fool left the door unlocked deliberately, expecting her to make a break for it? She took a step towards it, slow and careful.

As she did, it swung open again. Loman stood in the doorway, levelling a shock cannon at her. "I changed my mind," he said simply. "You will be harmed after all."

And he pulled the trigger.

The wall behind Red was cold and wet, the air heavy with the stink of sea water. She lifted her head and saw that she was chained to it by her wrists and ankles. She needed to see that, because she couldn't feel her own body at all.

She blinked, shaking her head as gently as she could. There was a pulsing, pounding ache inside her, sloshing around her nervous system like waves hitting a beach. Loman must have given her a full charge, and kept the trigger down almost long enough to fry her. "Bastard," she mumbled.

Her lips were numb, and her tongue felt like a balloon in her mouth.

The floor beneath her was odd, made of tiles of cracked green ceramic. She could see her bare feet on it as she hung with her head forwards. They had taken her boots away. The rest of her clothes hadn't been touched, which was a bonus, but the floor was very cold, and the water swimming around on it was grimy and tainted.

The next thing she saw was the knife blade.

It was long, and curved, and it glittered. It was being held out for her, so she could see it, and then it rose to meet her face, the point of it pressing into her chin. She had to lift her head again to avoid being sliced by it, all the way level and then higher than that. Her neck muscles protested – a return of sensation that was only partly welcome.

With her head up, she could see the knife's wielder and the smile on his face. "Hello," he breathed.

"Grota?" As soon as she'd said it, Red cursed herself mentally. *Idiot.*

The man shook his head. He was short and narrow shouldered, his thin frame draped in a coat of glossy plastic as green as the tile. His round head was quite bald, save for a bizarre crop of curly hair on the top of his skull, but any humour Red might have found in that was wiped away by the hunger in the man's eyes.

At the mention of the name his smile dipped a little. "Where did you hear that?"

"Around."

"Ah, I see. On the way in, perhaps." He stepped back from her, taking the knife away. "His reputation grows."

Red kept her head up, looking the man up and down. He was a mutant, she realised, although the hairstyle was an affectation. She could see little cuts and nicks in the shaved parts, where his hands had slipped with the blade.

"No," the fellow went on, "I'm Remuel. Grota will be along later."

"After you're done with me?"

He gave a little shrug. "Sadly, no. He wouldn't like that. He prefers his meat fresh. And believe me, he has quite an appetite." He lifted the knife to his mouth, touching the very point of it with the tip of his tongue, licking until a bead of blood formed there. "But when he's done, he usually lets me have his leavings."

"Big of him."

"Big? Oh, you have no idea…" The man gave a lilting chuckle, then paused. His strange head cocked over. "Ah, he's here. Punctual as ever. He always likes to greet his new arrivals."

Red listened too, and past the thumping of her own heartbeat began to hear what the coated mutant heard. Footfalls, heavy and slow, coming closer.

The little man giggled. "Get ready," he said happily. "Daddy's home."

4. MEAT

Grota wasn't alone when he came in. Utan Bas Loman was with him.

It was Loman that came in first, through an opening in the wall to Red's right. There was no door there, just the start of what could have been a tunnel leading away, square in section and clad in the same green tile as the rest of the room. The floor was wet there, too; Red heard his footsteps sloshing through greasy brine.

There were drains in the floor, rusted and filthy, but sea water dripped continuously from the ceiling and down the walls. This place, whatever it was, leaked badly.

She wasn't the only one who thought so. When Loman strode in, his face was set with disgust. "This place is more repellent then ever, Grota," he muttered.

There was a chuckle behind him. "And whose fault is that? The repair budget seldom reaches this far down."

"That's as may be. Still, I'd prefer it if this didn't take long." He gave Red a cursory glance. "Do what you do, then have Remuel get rid of her. She's not for keeping."

"Pity." Grota put his head around the corner of the opening, saw Red hanging there, and smiled. "I'm a little short of playthings right now."

He ducked in through the entrance and clambered into the tiled room.

Red stared. The men in front of her would expect a reaction of terror, and in all honesty such an expression wasn't hard to feign. Grota was huge.

The man was obviously a mutant. No human, even with the most extreme of Iconoclast modifications, could achieve such a size. He was a full metre taller than Loman. His dark, shaven head dipped forward to avoid touching the ceiling. His fists were the size of a man's skull, his shoulders impossibly broad, his neck corded with tendons as thick as industrial cable. He was naked to the waist, and the muscles of his torso were vast, hard and defined.

Durham Red was quite the connoisseur of a well-developed male musculature, but there was nothing to admire here. The man was an aberration, even in the eyes of another mutant. He was a monster.

The look on his face, too, was monstrous. He gazed down at Red with a raw, vile hunger that made Remuel's sweaty need look almost gentle.

His hands clenched and unclenched. "Very nice," he said, his voice a liquid growl. "My thanks."

"It's not a gift." Loman stood to one side, regarding Red steadily, his arms folded over his chest. "She's made certain threats, and I want to know how valid they are. You're going to make her tell me."

"While you stand there and watch, eh, Loman?" Red rattled her chains. "Get your rocks off while he takes me apart?"

He shrugged very slightly. "It's been a dull week. I could do with a good laugh."

Grota chuckled under his breath and stepped closer.

Red found herself backing up, squashing herself against the wall. "Loman, call this thing off."

"And why would I want to do that?"

"Look, I was hasty, okay? I don't give a sneck whether you've got slaves down here or not." Grota's hand was at her face, now, his thumb sliding down the side of her cheek and along her jaw line. "I can be reasonable."

"Hush," Grota whispered. He brought his thumb up to his mouth and licked it clean. "Don't babble so. It's distracting. And maybe, if you don't struggle too much, you might even enjoy it."

Behind him, Remuel snickered horribly.

"You don't have to do this," Red hissed, twisting away from Grota as his hand came up again. In reply the mutant smiled, his lips full, almost feminine.

"I know," he breathed. "If I had to do it, it wouldn't be fun."

"You could keep me. He said something about keeping me."

His great head shook, slowly, side to side. "Not this time. Het Loman was very specific about that, when he called me in. Personally, I think it's a shame. You look strong. You might have even survived this, if I was especially gentle." He stroked the side of her face again, his massive fingertips tracing the planes of her skull. "But it's not to be. I'm sorry."

"So am I," Red snarled, and snapped her head towards his hand. Before he could jerk it back, her teeth were sinking into the flesh of his thumb.

He roared, a high howl of pain, and dragged his hand back. Red opened her mouth at the last moment, letting the thumb out from between her fangs before he pulled her jaw from its moorings, but she'd bitten him down to the bone. His blood was in her mouth, sour and hot. She spat it away.

Grota had balled his other fist. On the far side of the room Loman shouted at him to stop, not to harm her yet, but the big mutant was past caring. He struck.

Red snapped her head to one side, and the fist caved in the wall behind her.

Tile and wet concrete splintered away. Red yanked her right leg up, feeling the soft iron cuff around her ankle dig in for a second before the links parted and spun away. She heard Remuel shout in disbelief – he must have been the one who had strung her up – but she ignored him. Her attention was all on Grota, and the sound he made when her knee came up with blurring speed and hammered into his groin.

He shrieked satisfyingly, and stumbled backwards.

Loman was trying to haul something out of his robes. Red yanked her right arm loose, her foot groping on the floor as she did so. She felt a slab of broken tile, got her toes under it and kicked it into the air, catching it with her free hand and lobbing it at Loman's head. It caught him in the left temple, scoring a track through his scalp, and he fell.

Two more hard pulls, and she was free. Remuel came at her with the knife, but she just punched him in the face, considerably harder than she had hit trademaster Durwan. He slid across the wet floor and slammed into the far wall, blood spouting from nose and lips.

The world went dark. Red snapped around to see Grota bearing down on her, his face a mask of rage.

She took a step back, giving herself some room, and dropped into a fighting crouch. The iron cuffs on her wrists and ankles were heavy, threatening to spoil her balance. In the few instants before Grota reached her, she bounced lightly on her bare toes, assessing the metal's weight, compensating with a fractional change of stance, before she whirled around to send her foot into the side of his head.

The force of that kick should have shattered the man's skull, but he barely seemed to notice it. Instead Red found herself staggering back, her toes hot with pain, and the giant mutant reaching down to her head with both hands, thumbs eager for her eyes.

She dropped and leapt forward between his legs, coming up on the other side of him and shoving him hard. He toppled into the wall, his head breaking more tile.

It didn't even slow him. He spun on his heels and came after her again, pain and anger lending him speed. She put two punches into his belly and another up into his nose, but she had misjudged his height a fraction. She realised that the last blow had made her overreach herself just as Grota backhanded her across the chamber.

There was a split second of smeared green in her vision, and then the far wall crashed into her back. Her head went up with the speed of her impact, slapping through the tiles and into the concrete behind. For an awful moment, the wreckage held her against the wall, and then she toppled forward to hit the floor in a rain of green ceramic and sea water.

A shadow fell across her. Without even seeing what caused it, she darted aside, and Grota's foot put a crater into the floor next to her head. Red rolled over and over across the tiles, splashing, fetching up against something dark that groaned when she hit it.

Grota was almost on her again. He was too strong to take down hand to hand, Red realised, too fast to escape. She needed a new tactic.

Beside her, Loman was trying to get up. Red rammed him back down onto the tiles, then shoved her hand into his robe, reaching in the way he had been when her slab of flung debris had stunned him. She felt the warmth of his hand against hers, then the metallic coolness of the object he had been reaching for. As Grota charged towards her she gripped it, brought it up without freeing it from the man's clothes and tugged the trigger, blowing a hole clear through the fabric.

Above her there was a wet explosion and the sound of damp matter hitting the ceiling. Grota took one more step towards her, his boot coming down against her shoulder, and then stopped. His hands fluttered as he dropped, with the agonising slowness of a felled tree, onto his knees.

Red got up, taking the gun with her. Grota's knees had locked, leaving him frozen in a kneeling stance. Even in this position, his face, had he still possessed one, would have been level with Red's, but the bolt from Loman's plasma derringer had hit him right in the nose. Now there was nothing above his lower jaw but a ring of bone, the sides and top of his thick skull still upright, but robbed of all contents and drooling tissue down his chest.

Blood began to soak down onto the tiles, spiralling into the rusted drains.

Red straightened herself up, stretching the kinks out of her neck and back, shaking the flashing lights out of her vision. She'd hit that wall really hard. Grota's backhanded blow had caught her across the ribs, which at least meant that her disguise was still on. It didn't stop her sternum feeling as though it was knocking loose against her spine, though.

Loman was trying to get up again, his hands slipping in bloody sea water. Red glared down at him, then realised that something important was missing from the chamber.

"Remuel," she muttered. "Sneck."

The knifeman had scampered off somewhere while she and Grota had been fighting. That was a surprise, and a pity. For one thing it meant that the man was a lot more resilient than she had expected. For another, she'd be forced to keep Loman around for longer than she'd like.

She reached down and hauled the security man to his feet. "Get up, you bastard," she snarled, kicking him hard. He yelped and struggled to his feet, an action that brought him up level with the wreckage of Grota's head, a sight that tore a cry of horror from him. Red felt him trying to squirm away, but she had too good a grip on his robes.

"Oh no you don't," she whispered, bringing her mouth close to his ear. "You take a good look at that, okay? And then imagine what I'm going to do to *you*."

He twisted in her grip. "Please…"

Red barked out an incredulous, humourless laugh. "You've got to be kidding. 'Please?' How many times have you heard that in this room, Loman? How many times have you watched that muscle-bound psycho raping some poor snecker to death, and listened to them screaming that word at you?" She threw him back against the wall, then followed him, grabbing him again before he could fall. "How many times did you join in, Loman?"

"It wasn't like that!" He'd stopped pulling now. He must have finally realised how strong she was. "There were security issues, discipline–"

Red snarled, shaking him hard. "Security issues? Slavery's a security issue? Systematic rape and torture?" Suddenly, being in the tiled chamber sickened her. She dragged Loman away from the wall, past Grota's still kneeling carcass and out into the tunnel. "Get out here, you little shit. We're going to have a chat about your security."

The tunnel opened out into a long hallway, the walls bare concrete, the floor more of the same green ceramic. Rusted metal tables were bolted to the floor at regular intervals. Red took Loman over to one and shoved him against it. "Okay, Loman, here's the deal. You're going to tell me everything I need to know, and you're going to do it quickly, or bad things are going to happen to you. Do you understand?"

"I don't know anything." His face was white with shock, his eyes wide. "I'm just a sub-director–"

Red slapped him, hard, a vicious blow that slewed his head around. "Don't even try," she said flatly. "I'll tell you this just once more, Loman. Grota died really quickly back there. His brains were all over the ceiling so fast they still don't know they're not in his skull. But you?" She shook her head. "Ask yourself how much of your own skin you'll be able to eat before you choke on it, and then decide whether you really want to bullshit me again."

He nodded, or perhaps it was a spasm of his neck muscles. Red felt her forearm starting to itch again, and decided it was a nod. "Good lad. Now, cast your mind back. I'm not the first inquisitive soul to come checking out your 'revolutionary manufacturing techniques', am I?"

There was no answer. Red frowned at him. "Let me jog your memory for you. Five mutants: two men, three women? They got into the mine complex itself before you caught up with them, remember?"

"Yes. I remember."

"You killed three on the spot, shot them right there in the mine. One looked stronger than the others, so you put him to work as an example. And one was pretty, so you gave her to Grota. Ring any bells?"

He nodded again, eyes empty.

Red grinned at him as nastily as she could. "Well, here's the part of the story you don't know. The pretty one survived that bastard's attentions, for a while. When Remuel took her back to the mine she escaped. She managed to get all the way up the hoist tower hidden in a mineral shipment, and she sent a signal before she died of her injuries. Some friends of hers picked it up, and asked me to help them out." She punctuated the words with another slap to his face, not as hard this time. She didn't want his head coming off, not yet. "So here I am."

"Yes," he breathed. "Here you are."

Red didn't like the way he said that at all. She spun around and took Remuel's knife right in the face.

It was a vicious, backhanded slash, sweeping across her from jaw to cheek, aimed perfectly to open her up in the most painful, disfiguring way possible. Red didn't have time to jerk back more than a millimetre or two before the blade met her skin. She felt it part, a sudden coolness in the wake of the knife.

Loman had seen him coming up behind her. She'd been so engrossed in the security man that she'd not sensed the mutant readying his blade, hadn't heard his soft footfalls as he brought the knife into range. He'd gotten the drop on her, plain and simple.

On any other day the wound he dealt her would have had her open, agonised, an easy target for the next fatal slice. Today, however, most of the skin on Red's face wasn't even hers.

She snapped a fist out and grabbed Remuel's wrist. "Hi," she smiled.

The mutant howled in fear, realising that he'd sliced into bio-gel, not flesh. He tried to drag his arm free, yanking fruitlessly against Red's grip.

Behind her, Loman was trying to edge away. Red punched him, without taking her eyes from Remuel, sending him flying over the table, then reached over and ripped the blade from the terrified knifeman's hand. "Naughty."

"Bitch!" he screamed, a last moment of defiance.

Red bared her fangs at him. "Oh, you have no idea," she snarled, then flipped him down onto the tabletop, smashing his face with stunning force into the metal. The sound of the impact echoed deafeningly around the hall, almost as loud as Remuel's scream when Red plunged his own knife through his shoulder blade and into the steel below, pinning him solidly to the table.

"Dinner is served," Red hissed, and sank her teeth into the side of his neck.

His howls reached a new pitch. He certainly had energy, this one: she had to hold him still while she drank, for fear that his kicks and his clawing would dislodge them both from the steel. It was a long minute, maybe two, before the lack of blood began to shut his brain down.

Finally, his kicks became jerks, and then random shivers. Red let him free as his heart went into final arrest, the last dribbles of blood from his neck pooling on the steel. There was no pressure left in him to send it further.

She straightened, wiping her mouth with the back of her hand. His blood had been unpleasant, thin and sour, but a meal was a meal, and the effect on Loman had been worth the whole sorry farce.

Red went over to where he lay, slumped against the wall, his face as white as Remuel's. She crouched. "So now you know who you're dealing with, and what I'll do to you if you don't help me."

He nodded spasmodically, beyond words. Red got up, pulling the rest of the bio-gel off her face. She wouldn't be needing it any more.

The hall and the chamber were part of a much larger complex of rooms, which used to be one of the refinery's food preparation areas. Meat had been processed there at one time; butchered and hung on hooks and carried in bloody slabs to the kitchens. Muscle had been carved away from bone amidst all that green tile, loops of gut freed to slap down onto the shining floor; the glistening, shivering workings of animal life separated from the meat they had once powered and kept alive.

That had been a long time ago, before the refinery's kitchen had been closed down and replaced by regular shipments of low-grade rations packs. But despite the constant rain of sea water leaking in through the ill main-tained walls, the place still stank of the cleaver and the saw. Years of butchery – of more kinds than merely the animal variety – had impregnated the tiles. Just being there made Red's stomach roil, her fangs itch.

Despite Remuel's blood in her belly, it was all she could do to keep her teeth from his throat, as she dragged Loman between the racks and the tables.

Awful as the thought was, though, she needed him in one piece. The last of the infiltrator squad was alive when his female companion had made her escape bid, and there was every chance he was still working down in the pit. Loman had already told her in which one – if he still lived, she could find him.

Getting into the mine itself would be a lot easier if she had a member of its security team at her side.

The pressure tunnels joined the refinery at the base of the hoist tower. Loman took her there without event and, with her features hidden under a stolen cowl, got her through the first checkpoint. He didn't hold out much hope for the second.

"You might as well kill me now, monster," he told her, as they made their way through the passenger section of the transit array. "This won't work."

"If it doesn't, I'll do worse than kill you." Red peered around, keeping her face well under the cowl's hood. She wasn't the only person to be wearing one, which made her feel a little more comfortable. There were hundreds of other travellers in the array, mostly technicians or security personnel, and several were cloaked in the same way.

Probably something to do with protecting the clothes beneath, she guessed, if the processing chamber's state of repair had been anything to go by.

"Threats will only get you so far," Loman replied. "Believe me, I know. And I also know that the guards at the other end of the tunnel will want to know exactly who you are, why you want to go into the mine and what you are doing with shreds of bio-gel all over your face."

"I'll worry about that. You just make sure we get into an empty car."

The pressure tunnels were a lot bigger up close than they had seemed from inside the submersible, big enough to contain a number of interior tubes. In the centre were two vast ducts, one set above the other, where rock hewn from the mine walls was transported back to the refinery by the tonne. The passenger transits occupied several smaller channels to either side.

Loman found an unoccupied car, and Red dragged him inside. Only when it was on its way, internal thrusters sending it along a frictionless rail set into the tunnel roof, did she throw the hood back.

"This," she said quietly, "is the bit I've really not been looking forward to."

The security man kept quiet, sitting uneasily across the car from her. Red heard him start when he saw her take Remuel's knife out of her belt, and she gave him a warning glance. "Don't fret," she muttered. "It's not for you."

"What are you going to do?"

"Shut up." She dragged in a deep breath, and pulled back her left sleeve. The long scar down the back of her forearm felt more itchy and uncomfortable than ever. When she put the tip of the knife to it, she winced.

"Oh crap, here we go." And with that, she drew the knife along the scar, slicing deep into the skin of her forearm.

It hurt, a lot. Red clamped her teeth together to avoid swearing, as blood surged out of the wound. The painkillers she had used there had worn off hours ago.

Luckily for her, the first cut had been deep enough. She pushed the knife back into the wound, digging painfully under the skin, and then tugged it back. The long, slim tube of plastic hidden there popped into view, slick with blood and fluid. She reached down and pulled it free.

Loman was looking at her in absolute horror. "Oh, shut your jaw," she snarled at him shakily. "How else was I going to get anything past the scans?"

She set the tube aside, then used the knife to cut a couple of long strips from the cowl, binding them carefully around her arm before pulling the sleeve back down. The wound would heal quickly – Red's rate of self-repair was phenomenal, even to her – but it still burned.

The tube looked worryingly big, now that she had it free. Damn, had she really been carrying that around inside her arm since Thaetia? No wonder she was itchy.

She cleaned it off on the seat, and then stripped the seal, pulling the coating away from the strip of technology beneath. A couple of tiny lumes, blinking away at one end, told her the device was active and awaiting its final command. Red glanced up, judging the speed of the car. "How far along are we, do you think?"

"More than half way."

"That's what I thought." She lifted the device and pressed the "send" key. "I'd find something to hold on to, if I were you."

"What do you mean?" He scrambled up from the seat, his eyes roving wildly. "What have you done?"

"Me? I just pressed this little button. But when my friends get the signal this thing sends out–"

The car jolted, cutting her off. Her last sight of Loman before the lights went out was a face white with sudden terror, eyes and mouth open like holes in a plaster wall. Then sparks surrounded him, showering down from the car's ceiling lumes as every one of them exploded.

Voltage cracked and sparked around the car for a few moments. Red yelped and snatched her hands back as the rail she was holding onto went live. "Bloody hell."

When the sparks died, there was no light in the car at all. Unlike the monorail in the Ulai fin, this was a utilitarian piece of equipment, welded together out of sheet metal and braced with steel frames. There were no windows, because inside the tunnel there was nothing to see. Red was trapped in a metal box, hurtling along its rail, in a mining complex suddenly devoid of all electrical power.

Something had gone badly wrong.

Red got up and made her way to the rear of the car, working by feel, then found a couple of metal braces and held on tight. That rush of voltage through the metalwork had been quite unexpected. She had planned on the lights going out, but not for an electromagnetic pulse to rip through the refinery.

If that had happened, then all bets were off. "Loman? Remember I said that bad things would happen if you didn't help me?"

"I remember."

"Well, bad things are going to happen anyway. Sorry."

That, more or less, was when the car reached the end of the track.

If the power had been on, or indeed any backup battery systems working at all, a series of magnetic brakes would have slowed the car to a halt just as it reached the platform at the entrance to the mine. But the EMP had put paid to that. The car went through the platform, the guard post and the buffers at something close to two hundred kilometres an hour.

Loman didn't even have time to scream, and perhaps that was a kindness he didn't deserve. With her eyes shut, Red didn't see exactly what happened to him, but she could guess.

There was a series of impacts, each one worse than the one before. The first was when the car went through the armoured barriers at the guard post, and Loman probably died then. Everything loose crashed forwards to slam into the forward wall of the car. The entire vehicle compressed by about a metre, the walls and floor buckling horribly.

The second impact was the buffers, which ripped through into the car itself and sent half the seats spinning forward. Red just about kept her grip during that one, but the final crash, as the remnants of the car erupted through the security doors at the end of the tunnel and into the mine's entry hall, tore away the very braces she had her hands locked around. Every part of the car's interior, Durham Red included, went bowling forward in a hail of debris, shattering and bouncing, and rolling to a halt in the darkness, finally silent and still.

By the time Red regained her senses, the slave revolt was in full swing.

The feedback surge had taken out everything: automated weapons, electronic tagging systems, even the magnetic locks that held the prisoners to their chains. The guards must have found themselves in absolute darkness, with no working communications, and surrounded by several thousand angry ex-slaves. They couldn't have lasted more than a few seconds.

Red made her way in through the entry hall, staggering slightly at first, but growing steadier on her feet with every second. She passed Loman's body on the way in. It had been flung a considerable distance into the hall, actually fetching up against the doors at the far end. Red didn't bother to check for the man's vital signs; it was quite obvious he wouldn't have any. Most of the contents of his torso and skull lay in a broad trail behind him, pointing back towards the wrecked car. He was empty by the time he hit the doors.

Inside the mine, the only light was from fires. Red could hear shouts from within, echoing around the cavernous galleries and broad tiers, cries of triumph, of rage, of fear. Old scores were being settled out there in the darkness, and not every slave in the pit would walk free from Ulai.

Red stopped the first group that came past her, asking if they knew the man who called himself Joash. They didn't know him, but they could see by the light of their torches that Red wasn't one of the guards. She didn't tell them who she was. That would have caused more confusion than was already gripping the place, and as far as Red could see the situation was already as confused as it had any right to be. So she told them how best to escape, and that help was on the way. They might not be able to get to the Ulai fin, but with a concerted effort they could take the refinery. What they did after that was their own business.

The next group didn't know Joash either, but the third knew that he worked down on the fourth tier. In this manner, Red gradually worked her way through the chaos and the carnage, until one of the mobs she encountered parted at her question, and Joash stepped forward.

She could see instantly why Loman had set him to work instead of blowing his brains out onto the bare rock. He was tall and powerfully muscled, although the brutal regime had taken a toll on him. The torches illuminated a face that was all hatred and scars, and hands that clutched a guard's rifle as though it was the only thing he had ever wanted to hold.

"I've got a message for you," she told him, "from Ascha."

He stepped towards her, gripping the rifle hard. "Where did you hear that name?"

"From the transmission she sent. She made it up the hoist tower, you know. All the way onto the transfer platform and into the comms bay, before she died. She sent her signal back to your fleet."

At those words, he seemed to sag. The gun fell from his hands. "I knew she was dead," he whispered. "Moon of blood, I could feel it…"

Red put her hand on his shoulder. "You're free because of her. You all are."

He nodded. "What was the message?"

"She said that there was nothing you could have done. That she loved you, and that she was proud to be your wife."

"God," he said simply, and closed his eyes.

Red gave his shoulder a squeeze. "Joash, I'm so sorry. I wish I could give you more time, but you know there isn't any. I've got a ship waiting to take you back. We have to go now."

His eyes, when they opened again, glistened in the torchlight. "I can't go back. I failed him."

"Joash, Commander Sibbecai asked me personally to come and find you." Red chuckled. "What, you think he's going to abandon his own son?"

5. FURY

By the time *Omega Fury* left the orbit of Dedanas, it was already part of an exodus. Red sat in the weapons throne and watched dozens of starships ripping their way up through the ocean world's atmosphere, desperate to escape. Yachts and luxury cutters were swooping up on their grav-lifters, accelerating past haulers and bulk transports like minnows darting past whales. Passenger clippers spiralled into the air at speeds that must have terrified those inside, and Red even saw a stream of tenders rising from the Ulai fin like brass bubbles, climbing into orbit in the vain hope that something would be there to latch onto them and carry them away to safer worlds.

Most of the ships had come from the fin. News of the slave revolt must have spread through its communications network in minutes. Red could only imagine the panic that must have caused, but she couldn't bring herself to feel much sympathy for the Dedani. No one on that world could have remained totally ignorant of what was going on in the mines; it was too big an operation. And if there were people on the fin who didn't know exactly where their profits were coming from, it could only have been through a lifetime of very carefully looking the other way.

Not any longer. The slaves had been culled from all races and all walks of life. Captured Iconoclast shock troopers had broken stone along with Tenebrae clerics, humans and mutants suffering side by side. If Red had been expecting that to turn them into a unified force, banding together against a common enemy, she would

have been fooling herself, and she wasn't that stupid –
most of the workers had turned on each other as soon as
their chains came off. The mix of slaves, though, meant
that as soon as the first distress calls were sent out both
human and mutant ships would have been on their way
to help. Dedanas wasn't technically within the Accord,
existing as it did within the sprawling border area known
as the Periphery, but that wouldn't stop the interested
parties flying in with all guns blazing.

High Command would want their troopers back. The
Tenebrae would want to pick up agents they might have
had in the mines before the humans arrived, along with
any disgruntled mutants who might be turned to their
cause. The sector authorities would send ships to collect
unaffiliated citizens from both species, while hospital
vessels, freelance chroniclers, Harvesters and even pirates
would be powering in at maximum speed factor too. No
wonder *Fury* left Dedanas space among a swarm of jump-
points and drive flares.

Red was quite relieved when *Fury* went to superlight.
There were so many ships in the sky she was beginning
to worry about colliding with something.

When the deck had stopped shaking, Red hit the release
on her control board. The throne slid backwards, out of
the workstation, and then turned ninety degrees as it
reached the end of its track. The safety harness unlocked
automatically, but for the moment Red stayed where she
was.

"That," she said brightly, "didn't go badly at all."

She saw Godolkin's head turn slightly towards her,
although he didn't take his eyes off his screens. "Considering your recent operational record, Blasphemy, I have to
agree. So far all our objectives have been met with the
minimum of injury, humiliation and personal abuse. A
date worthy of note, I feel."

"Yeah, all right. I won't mention the bit when you sent
an EMP through the entire facility. How many missiles did
you put into their reactor anyway?"

"Just one," said Judas Harrow from the sensor workstation. "But it was a big one."

"No shit." Red stood up and suppressed a groan. Her companions might have had a relatively uneventful time of things, but she had taken some serious physical punishment in the past couple of days. Now that she had stopped running and her adrenaline levels had dropped, her body's complaints were finally making themselves heard. "Okay, I'm going to go and check on Joash. Godolkin, it's time to give Sibbecai the good news. I'll let you do the honours."

"Thy will be done." Godolkin touched a control. The message was preset, a coded quantum signal narrowbanded to one specific crypt-key. It wouldn't go directly to Sibbecai's flagship, but instead to a relay buoy he had left for her. "Transmission sent, Blasphemy."

"Good lad. That should cheer the toothy old bugger up." She stretched, hearing clicks as her spine straightened, and then headed to the rear hatch. "Right, I'm off to the infirmary. Let me know as soon as you hear anything."

"As you wish," Godolkin replied. Then, very quietly: "Be gentle with him."

Red grinned at the back of his head, but said nothing.

Fury's three decks were circular, stacked one on top of another like plates in the centre of its egg shaped pressure hull. The control deck, which housed the bridge, systems monitors rooms and comms hub, was the middle deck of the three. To get to the infirmary Red had to go up a level.

She left the bridge and paced around the inner corridor, the plain steel mesh of the deck cold under her bare feet. The boots she had worn on Dedanas were in the cleaning unit along with the rest of her outfit, and until all the bits of Utan Bas Loman had been ultrasonically scrubbed from the soles, Red had decided to go without them. Ever since she had been forced to leave the wrecked *Crimson Hunter* back in the forests of Ashkelon, she had only owned one decent pair of boots.

Her present outfit was uncharacteristically plain, too – just a pair of leather trousers and a vest of black fabric-metal. After the excesses of Ulai, and everything that had brought her to the Periphery, she felt like dressing down for a while.

The access tube between the decks had no closable doors. Red just ducked around to the nearest opening and stepped through. Instantly she was weightless, her stomach flip-flopping at the sudden change in gravity. The tube was kept at zero g; even if the ship landed and shut off its own artificial gravity, anyone stepping into the tube would find themselves in free fall.

She grabbed a handhold and shoved down on it slightly, letting the motion carry her up to the hab deck, hitting the deck already walking. *Fury*'s pressure cylinder was so small – each deck was barely twenty metres across – that every compartment was pretty much right next to every other. She was at the infirmary hatch in seconds.

Joash was lying on one of the medical pallets, wearing nothing but a pair of shorts. He'd discarded most of the rags he'd been wearing down in the mines and cleaned himself up while Red had been on the bridge. For a moment, before he noticed she was there, Red found herself looking with some appreciation at what his lack of clothing revealed.

"Well, hi there," she said finally.

He started, his eyes snapping open. When he saw her he immediately swung himself off the pallet and dropped to his knees. "Holy one," he gasped

"Come on, Joash, none of that." She stepped forward and took him by the elbow, helping him up. He wasn't entirely steady on his feet yet. "You should know I don't do the Saint Scarlet thing these days."

"My father said as much."

She watched as he leaned back against the pallet. He must have been a man of ferocious strength, both physical and mental, to survive as long as he had in Grota's mines, but he had been at his limits when *Fury*'s missile had shattered the refinery's power plant. After the lights had gone out he had fought his way to freedom on sheer rage, but that had faded long before Red had gotten him to the docking chamber and onto the ship. She'd had to drag him the last few metres by his ankles.

He was looking better now. *Much* better, Red decided, and then realised that her eyes were fixed on his naked chest again.

She tore her gaze away. "No problem. How are you feeling?"

"Unsteady," he replied. "The deck feels as if it's moving."

Red came over to sit on the pallet next to him, hopping up onto it and swivelling around to put her back against the wall. "It *is* moving," she told him. "The dampers are set really low. Sneck, if you think this is bad, wait until we drop out of superlight. I'll make sure Godolkin gives you a yell, so you can grab hold of something."

He nodded. "Holy one, you know I can't begin to thank you for this–"

"Joash, don't even go there. Your dad saved my bacon back at Irutrea, and a lot of other people owe him their lives too. Humans, mutants... There was no way I wasn't going to help."

"I'm surprised he asked you." Joash folded his arms tightly across his chest. There were scars there, whip marks, by the looks of them, and Red wondered if he was trying to hide them from her. "My father ran covert operations for the Tenebrae before he joined Xandos Dathan. Back then, if a team was captured they were considered dead."

"Well, maybe he's lightened up since then. Anyway, he didn't ask me – he didn't even know I was in the Periphery. I heard Ascha's message too."

He looked around at her sharply. "How? It was–"

"Encrypted, I know." Red spread her hands. "What can I say? Tapping into the comms network is pretty much essential these days, if I fancy staying alive." She smiled. "And it's one of the things I'm very, very good at."

He raised an eyebrow. "I'm sure there are many others."

"Oh," Red purred. "You'd be surprised…"

Joash started to speak, but was instantly drowned out by a crackle of static from the internal sounders. *Fury's* internal communications net had been jolted badly when the ship had first crashed on Ashkelon, and had never quite recovered. It always spat out a second's white noise before a new call came through.

Harrow's voice followed it. "Holy one?"

"Christ," she hissed under her breath. "I really wish people stop calling me that…" As far as Red was concerned, she was about the least holy person she knew. "What is it, Jude?"

"We have an answer from the relay buoy. Commander Sibbecai sends his most heartfelt thanks and a set of co-ordinates. Godolkin is setting the jump computer now."

Red took a deep breath, then slid down from the pallet. She shouldn't have been flirting anyway, not with a man who had just lost his wife, and who probably still worshipped her as a saint. "Thanks Jude, that's great work. Where's Sibbecai now?"

"Haggai, holy one. The broken planet."

There had been a time, many centuries earlier, when Haggai had been a very pleasant world indeed.

It was a small planet back then, yet dense enough to provide a healthy gravitational field. It rolled around its sun at a distance that made its surface temperature exceptionally comfortable for human life, and an axial tilt of less than ten degrees gave it calm, even seasons. There was life there, both plant and animal, but nothing very dangerous or toxic, and all the living matter on Haggai was based on chemicals and proteins that could be safely ingested by humans and mutants alike. In a universe of harsh extremes, it was a rare jewel, a little paradise rimward of the Fornax Wilds.

That had been a long time ago, before the Bloodshed. When that awful, genocidal conflict had erupted across the galaxy, Haggai suddenly found itself in the terrible position of being strategically valuable.

No world wants to be valuable in a war. Especially a war which, in its last days, had escalated to the use of extinction level weaponry. Haggai had paid the ultimate price for being useful: according to what few records survived from that turbulent time, someone had decided to reduce its strategic value with a planet cracker.

Nobody remembered who. In the end, it really didn't matter. Haggai was left a ruin.

Red had been warned about what it was like, had read the data files from *Fury*'s database. Still, she couldn't help but curse when it first appeared on her forward holo. She'd seen worlds razed before, their populations slaughtered, their biospheres irrevocably wrecked. While these worlds had been destroyed in terms of their ability to support life, Haggai had been physically shattered. When *Omega Fury* decelerated from superlight, it did so alongside a globe that had been split entirely apart.

Great shards of stone hung in space, unmoving, their ragged tips still pointing inwards towards the lost core of Haggai, their flattened outer ends still forming a nightmare jigsaw of lifeless, desiccated crust. The planet had been reduced to a storm of shattered rock by the cracker's detonation, millions upon millions of fragments held by their combined gravity into a sickening parody of the world's original shape. It was as though a globe of delicate porcelain had been dropped onto a hard floor, with the very moment of its destruction frozen on camera: a split second capture of dissolution on a planetary scale.

Fury was drawing closer to one of the crust fragments. Red brought up a close view on her holo and saw mountains, and the rough edges of what must have once been oceans, scanning beneath her. If she wore a vacuum shroud, she realised, she could walk on that wreck of a planet, kick over the dusty bones of the billions who had been living there when the cracker hit the equator, and began, with a series of shaped antimatter charges, to blast itself right down into the core.

She sagged back into the weapons throne. "What a snecking mess."

Judas Harrow was still in the sensor station on the far side of the bridge. "I'm not picking up any hard returns," he reported. "Actually, that's not entirely true. *All* I'm picking up is hard returns, swarms of them. The debris is overloading our sense-engines."

"That," growled Godolkin, "leaves us vulnerable. We will not be able to detect an enemy until they either engage their drives or launch weapons. In either case, this is a perfect spot in which to be fatally ambushed."

"No one's going to ambush us." Red leaned back in the throne, trying to ease a crick out of her neck. "Sibbecai said he was going to be here, and he will."

"Shall I engage the shadow web?"

"Nah." The web was *Fury*'s stealth system, a layer of specialised armour that rendered it almost invisible to every kind of detection, up to and including visible light. "You used it so much on Dedanas it almost drained the power core. Besides, we don't want to go skulking around – we're here to meet an old friend, and you don't do that in disguise."

Godolkin made an unhappy sound, but kept his council. Red decided not to say anything else until it became really necessary – while the Iconoclast was piloting the ship in the midst of this frozen maelstrom, she didn't want to break his concentration.

It was Godolkin who normally took piloting duties now that *Crimson Hunter* was gone. It made sense for him to do so. For one thing, although it was heavily modified by its previous owners, *Omega Fury* was technically an Iconoclast ship. Despite Red's innate skill with space vehicles of any kind, it was Godolkin who was most qualified to fly this particular vessel, and Red was usually happy to let him get on with it. Besides, the pilot station was bigger than those on either side of it, and probably the only one which could accommodate Godolkin's massive frame with ease.

After the spacious, open plan bridge of *Crimson Hunter*, Red found *Fury*'s command area quite claustrophobic. Its three embedded workstations weren't much bigger than fighter cockpits, accessible only by sliding the thrones back and away from the controls. Once she was strapped in, though, Red could see the logic behind the control arrangement: *Fury* was a fast warship, designed to be thrown around the sky in a way which would have caused *Hunter* serious structural damage. Even the dampers were set low to facilitate high speed flight, letting the pilot manoeuvre without having to fight an anti-inertia field. The cramped, narrow command stations were built to safeguard the crew while the ship was executing high g burns and brutal changes in vector. A little claustrophobia was a small price to pay for the protection they provided.

But that, of course, made things highly uncomfortable for the people inside the vessel. It meant that she could barely see her companions, even though they were right next to her. Most of the time she kept a couple of postcard sized comms holos open on her board, showing the faces of the two men as they worked. It stopped her feeling so isolated.

Both screens were active now. Harrow's youthful features were creased in concentration as he tried to interpret the sense-engine returns, while Godolkin's face was relaxed, almost meditative. His eyes were half closed, the altered right one showing as a pale thread between his lids. Red knew enough about the big Iconoclast to recognise when he was in a state of complete concentration, totally attuned to the ship's controls, the vibration from its manoeuvring thrusters, the faint shifts of gravity through its decks.

She looked back to her forward views, where kilometre high bergs of grey stone slid past.

"There's a lot of terrain down there," Harrow ventured. "Perhaps we should land."

Godolkin shook his head. "I'd advise against it. These shards may look solid to you, but they are rife with fractures from the planet cracker's concussion. If we attempted to set down we could end up shattering an entire segment."

Red didn't like the sound of that. The space around *Fury* was already filled with debris, more than she had ever seen in one place. In a normal asteroid belt this much rock was spread around an entire planetary orbit – the general rule of thumb was that if you could see one asteroid, you wouldn't be able to see another. They would all be too far away.

The broken world's gravity was, somehow, in equilibrium with all the other forces acting upon it. Maybe in a few thousand years all the bergs and spars and drifting mountains would begin to dissipate, but for the foreseeable future they remained horribly close. Any false manoeuvre on Godolkin's part could see one of those razor like, stone edges slicing *Fury* open like a knife cutting fruit.

Abruptly, one of the holos sprang up in front of its fellows; *Fury* had picked up a beacon signal. Seeing it, Red practically cheered. "There." she yelped. "Guys, have you got that?"

"I see it," Godolkin reported. Harrow was already slaving more detailed returns onto his board. Red felt *Fury* tip over, a shudder in the deck as the drives fired in tiny, staccato bursts.

She wondered if Joash, still up in the infirmary, had managed to grab something.

On Red's primary holo-screen, a crack in one of the biggest segments of planet began moving towards her, widening like a jagged black maw. Immediately, *Fury* started yelling. "Proximity alert." it screeched nasally.

"Recommend vector change to zero-one-five! This is a priority command."

"Shut the sneck up," Red snapped. She had hated the voice alert system as soon as she had heard it, and her feelings towards it hadn't mellowed. "Jude, haven't you been able to turn that bloody voice off yet?"

"Apparently not," grated Godolkin.

Between holographic views of rock strata rising past her, she saw Harrow shake his head. "I'm sorry, Red. There's a series of overrides I can't access. The Omegas must have really liked it."

"Further proof," Godolkin ventured, "that they were all mad."

The beacon signal was getting stronger. Holos on Red's left and right showed titan walls of frozen magma crawling past, great spars and nodules and solidified waves that had once been the molten interior of a world. At times those chaotic surfaces seemed as if they were barely moving, but it was a trick of scale: the wedges of planetary material *Fury* was passing between were thousands of kilometres long, and the features she saw were the size of towns, of starships.

The shadows were deep here. This far into the ruins, sunlight that had once warmed the faces of this world's children could only cast planes of solid darkness.

The beacon's chime was rising in pitch as *Fury* moved closer to what was once the core, and the terrain of the chasm was changing again. Instead of a frozen ocean of leaping, molten stone, great voids were now appearing – first cracks and fissures, then gaping caves. Red had a sudden flashback to the surface of Lavannos, that awful planetoid that had once been Earth's moon. There were voids in that glassy, fused surface that had been kilometres deep, dozens across, their bases forever lost to the light. The largest of them, named the Eye of God by those that lived and worshipped there, might have matched the smallest of those sliding past her now.

Finally, as *Fury* passed before an open void the size of a major city, the beacon's chime became a solid warble, then a shriek. Red stood it for about a second before she switched it off. "Godolkin, hit the brakes."

Fury shuddered as the manoeuvring thrusters brought it to a halt relative to the chasm. Red looked at her starboard holo and saw points of light appearing in the darkness, tiny specks of glare deep within the cave. "What the–"

"Warning." The voice alert system, bellowing its complaints across the bridge, sounded even more hysterical than usual. "Multiple weapons systems have acquired this vehicle. Initiate evasive action."

Godolkin's hands were hovering over his controls. "Mistress?"

"It's okay," she said, staring at the patterns of light glowing out there in the cave. "It's them. We've found the fleet."

Red had last been aboard the battleship *Persephone* almost four months earlier, in those dark days when the mutant warrior called Xandos Dathan had tried to convince her to fight for him to bring about peace in the Accord. Peace, however, had never been Dathan's intention. Instead, he had been planning to ignite a new war between humans and mutants, at a time when the Iconoclast forces were in disarray. Had Red not discovered his plans and persuaded some of Dathan's warriors to fight against him, billions would have died.

One of the men she had turned was Sibbecai, Dathan's commander of marines and one of the most capable tactical leaders Red had met. Along with the fleet commander Jubal, Sibbecai had helped Red turn the tide of battle around on the world of Irutrea, giving her just enough time to board Dathan's planet killing super cruiser and end the madman's plans once and for all.

That was a debt she could never spend enough time repaying, although Sibbecai didn't see it like that. Despite

Red's protestations, he merely regarded it as a duty to his Saint. The man had been a soldier of the Tenebrae before Dathan's Umbrae Nova had recruited him.

He was there to meet her on *Persephone*'s hangar deck after *Fury* had set down, with a full honour guard at his heel. As usual, he was dressed collar to boots in glossy uniform armour and a flexible carapace in dark burgundy, and he bowed low as she drew close.

"In the name of the crimson light," he rasped, "it's true. Our Saint lives."

That certainly wasn't what Red had expected him to say, and it caught her slightly off guard. "Come again?"

"Forgive me, holy one." He straightened, bringing his face level with hers. Or rather, she thought, he would have done if he'd had a face. Sibbecai's mutation had robbed him of any recognisable features, save a double row of horribly exposed teeth. He had no lips, no nose, no visible eyes, just a ragged mass of scar tissue above the gape of his mouth.

In terms of looks, Joash definitely did not take after his father.

"You have not heard the rumours?" he asked. His voice was a harsh, lusty bark, but his lack of lips didn't seem to affect his pronunciation. Red had never worked that out. "I never wanted to believe them myself, but when my own people claim to have seen the proof..."

"Rumours?" Red made an exasperated sound. "Proof? Sibbecai, would you mind just telling me what the sneck's going on?"

"They said you were dead."

"Lots of people say I'm dead. Wishful thinking, usually, or some smart arse trying to claim the bounty. What, are people starting to actually believe it this time?"

Sibbecai opened his mouth to answer, but then a change came over him. It was subtle, little more than a fractional change of posture, a relaxation of the rough skin of his face. His head tilted, just slightly, towards *Omega Fury*.

"I'll tell you later," he breathed.

Red glanced back over her shoulder to see Joash emerging from the hatchway, and she smiled to herself. The answers could wait a while.

She stepped aside, and let the father greet his son.

Persephone had been eviscerated by Dathan's fusion lances during the battle of Irutrea. The entire port side had been laid open, and fires started there that had burned for days, even in the vacuum of space. Eventually, more to stop the ship's atmosphere processors ripping themselves apart to feed the flames than to save lives, Sibbecai had simply ordered the wrecked half of his vessel to be sliced off and flung away.

Parts of the battleship had been replaced, but the view from the observation deck still showed a scene of devastation. Red looked out over what should have been a vast, delta shaped hull of armour, but much of what she could see was just gantry, lit by the hundreds of running lights she had seen from outside the cavern. *Persephone* was holding together, but it was in no condition to fight a battle.

She turned away from the view, leaning back against the transpex wall. "So what happened to Jubal?"

"We split our forces," said Sibbecai. "The last I heard he had raided a tithe fleet en route to Kassatta, so if his ships are half Iconoclast next time you see them, don't be surprised."

"His fleet must have been in better shape, then."

Sibbecai shrugged. "He had the experience to use them. And this fleet is gaining strength, my Saint. For now we watch and wait, but we'll be plaguing the enemy again before long."

"I don't doubt it," Red replied, but she knew her old ally would have a long job getting his forces back up to strength. On the way into the cave she had seen six, maybe seven capital ships, including the stricken *Persephone*. And three of those had been frigates. If *Omega*

Fury had been dropped into the middle of Sibbecai's fleet with murder in mind, the stealth ship could have done the Umbra Nova serious damage.

Joash had been taken to *Persephone*'s infirmary and was doing well. While he was being tended, Red had left *Fury* to Godolkin and Harrow. The Iconoclast didn't feel entirely comfortable aboard a ship full of mutants, and Harrow had wanted to get back to hunting down the voice alert's command chain. He was convinced he could still that nasal drone eventually, and Red wished him the best of luck. The sooner *Fury* stopped shouting at her the better.

Sibbecai had invited Red to the observation deck, but so far they had done nothing but make small talk. Whatever the commander had to tell her, she realised, was making him intensely uncomfortable.

There had to be a way of working around to the subject, or they would be here for a week. "So, have you heard anything about Dedanas?"

"I have. Ulai is in chaos, as you can imagine, and High Command was not happy to discover captured Iconoclasts among the enslaved. As far as I can tell, most of the freed mutants have been extracted by Tenebrae procurement teams, and the humans are on their way. The Ulai fin has shut down all its borders in fear, and well they might." Sibbecai had begun to pace, his big arms folded. "Their goods and chattels will be forfeit to the Patriarch from this point on."

"That's going to be tough on them," muttered Red. "Ulai's valuable, turns out a lot of gear, so my guess is they'll brush any mention of me under the carpet. But some people are going to find life a bit less comfortable from now on."

"They built their comforts on the backs of slaves," Sibbecai replied, still pacing. "I rejoice in their downfall. I'm just sorry it cost Joash his squad." He stopped mid-pace and turned his eyeless face to the window. "And his wife."

"Sibbecai? Where was the other squad?"

There was a long silence. Finally, without moving at all, Sibbecai said, "Chorazin."

"Chorazin is a rock," he told her later, in one of the mid-deck elevators, "a worthless piece of stone so close to its sun that you could melt iron on its surface, but the Archaeotechs have a temple-lab there."

"And your people snuck into an Iconoclast base on a red-hot planet?" She whistled. "They must have had some balls."

"It was necessary. There had been reports, rumours. Items on the Iconoclast data networks that demanded investigation. I was hunting for any information on the Dedanas mission, as you might imagine, but it was Chorazin that kept rising to the top of the pile."

"Must have been something big." The elevator slowed to a halt. As the doors opened, Red caught sight of an indicator board next to the controls. "Hey, this is an infirmary sector. Are we visiting Joash?"

Sibbecai shook his head as he strode out of the lift into the corridor beyond, glancing back to make sure Red was following him. "This is a hot zone."

"A what zone?"

"A quarantine area for those with highly infectious diseases."

Red stopped walking so quickly that she almost overbalanced. "Snecking hell."

Sibbecai laughed and beckoned her forward. "Don't fear, Saint. There's no plague here. We thought that's what we'd found, at first, so we had this set up in a hurry, but we needn't have bothered, as you'll see."

"Blimey, you sure know how to make a girl feel comfortable." She started on again, trotting to keep up with Sibbecai's long strides. Her boots had been cleaned by the time she reached *Persephone*, and she was doubly glad of that now. Whatever the commander told her, she wouldn't have felt comfortable walking around this particular deck barefoot. "So what were they doing down there? Bio-weapons?"

"It was a possibility. Believe me, Saint, Lord Tactician Saulus wasn't the only Iconoclast working on anti-mutant weapon systems, not by a long way. Such things are supposedly banned under the auspices of the Accord, but it continues." He snorted. "On a hundred worlds, it continues."

"So it was a weapons lab."

"I'll show you." Sibbecai had reached a heavy, armoured doorway set into the corridor wall. He held a crypt-disc against the locking pad until Red heard magnetic latches slam back into their housings, and the doors hissed aside. Air rushed past her as it opened.

Negative pressure, Red realised. The hot zone must have been kept at a lower pressure than the corridor outside to prevent germs from escaping.

She followed Sibbecai inside and moved past him as he stopped to speak to a pair of medics. "He's sleeping," one of them said to him. "We've done everything we can."

"Who?" Red asked.

The medic who had spoken raised a hand and pointed across the chamber. The room wasn't large, and most of its interior space was taken up by something that looked very much like a high-tech coffin. Like much Accord technology, it was massively built, riveted together from plates of dark metal, and studded with a forest of feed tubes and cables. Fat pipes emerged from it at each end, snaking away into the walls. If Red listened very carefully, she could hear it humming.

She stepped forwards and peered over the coffin's edge.

There was a man inside. He looked human, but the very fact that Sibbecai's people were looking after him told her that he probably wasn't. There was a bio-dressing on one side of his face, some bruising to his scalp, but these were minor injuries. Nothing that would necessitate such a complex life support system.

The reason that he was held in the machine, however, was obvious to Red. The man was indescribably old.

His face was sunken back over his skull, his closed eyes nested among flaccid wrinkles, his toothless mouth slightly open as he breathed. There was no hair on his scalp, just swarms of liver spots. The skin of his chest looked like damp parchment draped over bone. His fingers were like claws, his limbs like sticks. There was no muscle on him at all.

Pulses ticked beneath the translucent skin of his neck, but they fluttered as Red watched.

"Poor old bastard," she whispered. If she raised her voice above that, she feared the sound of it would shatter the old man's bones like china. "Did you find him on Chorazin?"

Sibbecai came up next to her, shaking his head. "No."

"Then where?"

He puffed out a long, sighing breath from between his teeth. "The team I sent down to Chorazin consisted of three men and two women. One came back. This warrior, Nerichau."

"Warrior?" Red stared at him, then turned back to the man in the coffin. "But he's–"

"When he left *Persephone* he was twenty-four standard years old. By the time he got back he was closer to seventy. Now the medics can't even gauge how old his body has grown."

Red gaped. "Holy sneck…"

Sibbecai moved away from the device. "Before the years overtook him, he told me that he'd found the lab, the chamber where this great weapon lay. But the Iconoclasts were in the middle of an experiment, and Nerichau's team was caught in some kind of backwash. Whatever effect this weapon produced, it did this."

Red rubbed a hand down her face. She could see what was coming. "What else did he see, Sibbecai?"

"You seem to know already."

"Just a wild guess," Red said thickly. "My corpse."

6. CHORAZIN

There was a blood chapel aboard *Persephone*. It dated from the days when the ship had been part of a Tenebrae fleet stationed near Iricos, or so Sibbecai claimed. A relic from the days before Saint Scarlet rose from her thousand-year slumber, and told the Tenebrae at Pyre that they'd been getting it wrong all these years.

"It's been sealed, Saint, I assure you." The faceless commander was using a series of crypt-discs on the locking panel as Red watched, breaking the code sector by sector. "The original discs were smashed after Pyre. We abandoned that part of our faith just as you decreed."

"Which makes you the exception, Commander," said Godolkin. "Most Tenebrae still embrace the shedding of blood in her name."

"Old habits die hard," replied Sibbecai. The locking panel gave a final chime, and the door ground open.

Red watched the panels slide rustily aside, and grimaced. "I didn't decree a bloody thing, Sibbecai. After what I'd seen on Pyre, I didn't give a sneck about the Tenebrae or anything they did, and that's what I told them. Just to leave me out of it." She sniffed. The chapel certainly smelled unused, reeking more of dust than blood. "Whatever. As long as it's secure."

She stepped past Sibbecai and went in, looking around the gloomy place as she did so. It was mainly dark beyond the door; a few lumes were blinking on in the chapel's corners, but some seemed to have failed over the years, and even those that were working didn't look to be set very high. Then again, Red reflected, the rites that had taken place here weren't the kind that were best seen in strong light.

The chapel was hexagonal, like many compartments on this class of ship, its six walls curving up and narrowing as they rose, meeting in a point many metres above her head. A spiked brazier hung down from that point at the end of a long chain, swaying very slightly, and below it was a ceremonial dais, carved with ancient runes and curving channels. That, she knew all too well, would be where a chained human sacrifice would be bled, his throat ripped out by Tenebrae adepts wearing fake vampire fangs.

It was a sickening thought. Considering how she was already feeling about things, she began to wonder if the chapel was really the best place to conduct this briefing, secure or not.

She found a bench seat at the edge of the chapel and sat down, leaning back against the dark metal wall. Godolkin had already entered; she could see him padding forward around the dais, warily checking the corners, glaring into the shadows. He plainly didn't want to be here, or even away from *Fury*, but this was important. Red wouldn't have subjected him to it if it hadn't been.

To an Iconoclast, walking into a Tenebrae blood chapel must have been like sitting down for tea in Satan's dining room.

Judas Harrow, of course, had seen it all before. Red sometimes forgot that the young mutant had been an active member of the Tenebrae before he had revived her on Wodan. He'd only been a novice adept, but she knew he'd participated in rites. He'd even offered her the use of a pair of those steel fangs to bleed him with, before he discovered that she had the real thing.

She saw Harrow sit down on the bench next to hers and noticed the way Godolkin watched him from the shadows. The two men would never be friends, but they had been getting along reasonably well in the last few months.

Just being here, though, could set all that back a long way.

The sooner she had them out of here, the better. "Sibbecai, where's this lieutenant of yours? This place is freaking me out."

"A moment, Saint." He was still at the doorway, peering out into the corridor. A second later Red heard footfalls, and looked up as a shadow fell across the dais.

"You're late," she said.

"Forgive me, holy one." The man walked in, carefully skirting the dais with an expression of slight distaste.

Red looked him up and down. He was a solid, compact mutant, neatly bearded, dressed in a long coat of black fabric-metal over a Tenebrae officer's uniform. Like Harrow and Joash, he could easily have passed for human, and probably had biomorphic implants to make sure he could get through Iconoclast detection. If Sibbecai went back to running covert ops, more and more of his agents would end up with those.

He stopped in front of her and gave her a slightly languid bow. "Lieutenant Cormoran, my lady. I can only apologise for holding you up, but this is a difficult part of the ship to get to. The way isn't as easy as it once was, especially when one is forbidden to ask for directions."

"I think the Saint's request for privacy is a valid one, Lieutenant." Sibbecai touched a control, and the door slid closed again. Blinking in the gloom, Red found herself hoping that it was easier to get out of the chapel than it had been getting in. "These rumours have already done untold damage."

Cormoran stiffened. "Sir, I take full responsibility. Nerichau has always been a reliable and observant operative, but whatever happened to him on Chorazin must have addled his wits. I should have edited his report."

Red shook her head. "Don't be hard on the old guy, Cormoran. He saw what he saw."

The Lieutenant frowned, puzzled. "But my lady, he swore that he saw your corpse. Was it some kind of fake? A clone?"

"No," Red sighed. "It was mine."

It had all started on Vauvus, a colony world on the Accord's coreward edge, some weeks after Red had escaped from Magadan. She had stopped there for sup- plies – *Fury*'s previous owners had been a crew of Omega Warriors, the enhanced Iconoclast troopers created by Lord Tactician Saulus. The Omegas might have been able to survive on a few mealsticks and some lukewarm water, but Red and Harrow couldn't. Even Godolkin was looking out of sorts by the time *Fury* set down.

Red had left the two men to work on the ship while she explored the settlements around the starport. She was gone little more than half a day, but by the time she came back her companions were missing.

The ship was still on its landing pad, undamaged, but Godolkin and Harrow were nowhere to be found.

Red made swift enquiries, and before long was on the trail of a ship that had joined *Fury* on its landing pad shortly after she had left. The other vessel had made no attempt to mask its ion wake, and Red was able, after a few minutes getting to grips with piloting *Fury* alone, to track it all the way back to its home world.

It took about fifty hours. On the way, she started getting violent headaches.

Red had suffered pain before, but nothing like this. Each burst, although only seconds long, was liquid fire scorch- ing a track through her skull. As if that wasn't bad enough, she could feel the source of the bursts, could taste it like blood on her tongue. Again, there was no attempt at concealment. Whoever had taken her compan- ions was torturing them, and somehow beaming their agonies through space, directly into Red's brain.

It was a brutal, insane thing to be doing, and it really hurt.

Red had followed the ion wake all the way back to a gas giant planet that *Fury*'s database had called Salecah. There, on a bizarre orbital platform that seemed to be made entirely of rust, she had come face to face with the woman who had been ritually electrocuting Harrow and Godolkin for the past two days.

"She called herself Brite Red," she told Sibbecai. "But it was me. A version of me, from the distant future. I don't know how far – one minute she was talking about a thousand years, the next a thousand lifetimes." She shook her head sadly. "I dunno. She was mad. Totally insane."

"Impossible," muttered Cormoran. He was standing by the dais, a look of complete incomprehension on his dark face. "No one can travel in time."

"I could. I did." Red sighed. "Back in my day we could do it, in a limited way. I guess Brite learned how to do it all over again. She had a lot of time to work it out, I suppose."

"You're certain?"

"Take a look at Nerichau, then ask me again. Anyway, I just had to look into her eyes to see she was me. I tried to tell myself that it was a trick, but it wasn't. My future self was standing right in front of me."

"She had built the orbital platform to house a time engine," said Godolkin. "She used us to lure the Blasphemy into a trap. *Omega Fury* was shot from the sky."

Cormoran looked horrified. Red couldn't tell how Sibbecai was looking, but he spoke first.

"She tried to kill you?"

"That's why she came back. She didn't like the life she'd led for all those years, and had decided to wipe it all out by travelling back in time and killing me."

"That's deranged."

"I think I told her that." Red got to her feet. "Look, people try to kill me all the time, okay? It wasn't that much of a stretch to imagine some barmy version of me travelling back in time to sneck me up."

Cormoran was walking away around the dais as if Red's revelation was too much for him to hear. Sibbecai watched him for a few seconds, then turned back to her. "And what happened?"

"Oh, nothing much. We fought, I killed her, I grabbed the boys and bugged out. End of story."

"The corpse," Cormoran was muttering. "It was frozen, awaiting dissection. The throat was–" He broke off. "And you did that?"

"Oh, will you people forget about her?" Red put her hands on her hips. "You're kind of missing the point here. If the Archaeotechs have got Brite's body, that means they went to Salecah to get it."

"The Archaeotechs aren't working on some kind of anti-mutant weapon," said Harrow, getting up. "Not directly. But if your people were aged by a failed experiment, it can only mean that the humans have salvaged Brite Red's time engine."

"Give that boy a lolly," Red nodded. "A dead version of me isn't any use to anybody, but a working time machine? Just imagine the Iconoclasts being able to travel in time, maybe all the way back to when mutants were first created, or to critical points in the Bloodshed, or when Jude woke me up on Wodan. And then tell me how safe you feel."

"I should have seen this coming. I shouldn't have just left her there, or that snecking base of hers. I should have fragged it from orbit, poured flayer missiles into the bloody thing until it came to bits."

Red was in *Fury*'s refectory, slumped over a table. She, Harrow and Godolkin had retreated back to the ship while Sibbecai and his lieutenants decided what to do. The stealth ship had been berthed aboard *Persephone*, in one of the battleship's sprawling hangar decks. A space had been cleared for it among the Vampyr assault craft still docked there.

Godolkin had gone back to the bridge, while Harrow had stayed in the refectory with Red. He'd tried to make coffee, but the galley facilities aboard *Fury* weren't really up to it. The lukewarm, brownish liquid he had been able to produce still sat at her elbow, untasted.

"You weren't to know," Harrow told her. "We were all injured, the ship damaged. There was no reason to do anything other than escape."

Red peered up at him from under one arm. "Thanks, Jude, but that's bollocks and we both know it. Just because the bomb doesn't blow you up doesn't mean that you should leave it for someone else."

She straightened up, arching her back to ease the tension in her neck muscles. "And now look. The bloody Iconoclasts are trying to build a time machine, and it's all my fault." She saw the way he was looking at her, and spoke before he could. "No, really. Brite Red's me. So either way you look at it..."

"She's not you. You said yourself, there's no way you'd turn out like that."

"Is there not?" Red wasn't so sure. So far she'd only lived a perfectly normal lifetime, albeit with a twelve-hundred year hiatus, but she already knew that her body's powers of repair were quite phenomenal. If those powers extended to the regeneration of damage due to aging, as well as from people hitting her, then it was perfectly possible that she wouldn't age at all.

She'd be immortal.

The idea horrified her. To never grow old, never die, while those around her faded away. While even the stars themselves grew dim... Given that, she could quite easily see Brite's madness on her own horizon.

Maybe the woman had been trying to do her a favour by sparing her the future.

Red cursed under her breath and rubbed her eyes. "Well, right now I'm halfway to going bananas just waiting. How long does it take to make a decision like this?"

"If Commander Sibbecai had the forces he'd commanded at Irutrea, it would already be made."

"Maybe I should go up to the bridge." Red pushed her chair back and stood up. "Jolly them along a bit."

Harrow made a face. "I wouldn't advise it."

"Drink your coffee," she grinned, then started as a blast of static filled the refectory.

Godolkin's voice followed it. "I have word from Commander Sibbecai, Blasphemy. Your presence is requested."

"Thank sneck for that. Did they tell you what they are going to do?"

"They did not, but the fleet is redeploying. All ships are moving out of the debris field and charging their light-drives."

That could only mean one thing. Sibbecai and his damaged, depleted battlegroup were going to attack the Archaeotechs.

Sibbecai called a briefing as soon as the fleet went to superlight. *Persephone*'s main briefing hall was gone, ripped away by weapons fire during the battle of Irutrea, so rather than use facilities on any of the other ships in the fleet he had instead opened up a secondary tactical chamber at the base of the battleship's bridge tower. It was smaller than the original hall, about the same size as the blood chapel, but it wasn't crowded. Even with two representatives from each ship in the fleet, there were several benches left unoccupied.

That, more than anything, gave Red cause for concern. Sibbecai was proposing a full-scale attack on an Archaeotech stronghold with six capital ships and two packs of Vampyrs.

Cormoran had put together a holographic model of the Chorazin temple-lab. As soon is it appeared, Red realised that her mental picture of the place was way off: she had expected it to be one single structure, a vast Iconoclast cathedral raised to the worship of ancient technologies and forbidden science. The hologram in front of her showed a complex sprawl of buildings, a circular mass of towers and ziggurats that looked more like some vast industrial facility than any temple Red had seen.

"This," Sibbecai barked, "is the main structure of the temple-lab. As you can see, the humans have decentralised its construction. There's no clear pattern to it, which makes a tactical strike impossible. We can't be sure exactly where the time engine is being kept, or whether it might have been moved. So, to be certain of destroying the correct lab, we would need to vaporise the entire base."

"Impossible," hissed a woman to Red's left, her head a pallid fusion of squid and serpent. "We don't have the firepower. Besides, the humans know they have been infiltrated – their protection fleet will be on full alert–"

"That's more correct than you know," said Cormoran glumly. "As Commander Sibbecai told you, this is the main structure of the temple-lab, but far from the only structure."

He touched a control icon, and a broad dome blinked into life above the model. It wasn't quite a complete disc – there was a low, crescent shaped segment missing from one edge, making it look like a biscuit with a bite taken out of it.

A moment later another feature appeared – a ring of jagged material completely encircling the structures beneath the dome.

"Chorazin is dangerously close to Ochaos, its parent star. The planet isn't tidally locked, as you might expect, but instead has a ferocious spin. Basically, you are looking at a world with a two hour rotational period, and a mean surface temperature of over fifteen hundred degrees.

"As you might expect, this necessitates considerable shielding. The lab is built inside a crater almost two thousand metres across, with a rim wall over a hundred metres high." He pointed at the dome. "This is the heat shield. It's cast from bonded duralloy and coated with a three-atom layer of neutronium in continuous suspension.

That doesn't sound like a lot, but a teaspoon of neutron-star material weighs about a hundred million tonnes. Even in such a fine coating, the shield has an incredible mass."

"A heat-sink?" Red asked.

There was a moment's silence, in which Red noticed that everyone was looking at her. She'd spoken without thinking, as she often did. To her, the statement had seemed obvious.

"Really, it's not as daft as it sounds. Neutron-star material isn't a solid; it's more like soup, and they have to hold it in suspension or it would run down off the dome and puddle round the crater wall. Or maybe it would go up – it's bloody weird stuff. In either case, all that mass will soak up the sun's heat like a sponge." She put her face close to the model, poking the hologram with her finger. "I'm just wondering how they get rid of it again."

"Here," said Cormoran. A protrusion on the dome's surface, just above the cut-out, flared to attract her attention.

Red looked up at him. "You're kidding."

"No." The protrusion grew downwards, through the dome and the structures beneath, extending into a series of rods and rings, and finally a spherical structure that could only have been buried several hundred metres under the crater floor.

"This ball here is the temple-lab's primary reactor. From what we've been able to extrapolate, roughly a tenth of its output goes towards powering the base itself. The rest is for this." He indicated the protrusion again. "A cooling laser."

Red whistled. The laser must have been huge, and insanely powerful. In terms of raw energy transfer it would outstrip the fusion lances mounted in *Persephone*'s bow, and those mighty weapons could only fire for a few seconds at a time. To keep the temple-lab from melting, the cooling laser would have to fire continuously, pumping heat from the shield out into space.

No wonder the other Iconoclast divisions looked on Archaeotechs with distrust. Even to Red, this looked halfway to devilry.

Cormoran rotated the view, letting the shield's opening move past those watching. "This is the only weak point. It's the entrance to the starport, which is here, under the lip of the dome. It's also the place with the highest concentration of defensive firepower, so please don't start thinking about flying under the shield for a strafing run. Oh, and there's a very good chance the humans will be able to direct the output of the cooling laser, at least partially."

"So what you're saying is," the squid headed woman muttered, "that we have to attack something that we can't find and can't reach, on a world that will immolate us if we so much as set foot on it, while being fired on by a weapon that rivals the fires of Hell itself."

"Indeed," replied Sibbecai. "And with only six ships."

"Seven," said Durham Red. "And right now, I reckon *Omega Fury* is the most important weapon you've got."

"A most typical display," Godolkin told her after she'd related the briefing's outcome. "Your arrogance, Blasphemy, is without limit."

They were in one of the equipment stores on *Fury*'s lower deck. The Iconoclast was sorting through the ship's meagre supply of guns, but Red could see that he wasn't happy with any of them. He'd lost his holy weapon and silver blade a while ago, on Magadan, and it was clear that the Omega warriors who had once owned this ship didn't favour such devices. All the man had been able to find were cut down bolters and plasma derringers.

Red, on the other hand, was more than happy with what she had. Most of her original arsenal had been lost when *Crimson Hunter* had been abandoned on Ashkelon, but Sibbecai had been happy to provide her with some replacements. She now had a matched pair of particle magnums on her belt, slab-sided pistols as long as carbines, with extended power cores. She wasn't sure where the mutant commander had found the guns – most Tenebrae weapons fired frag-shells – but she was glad he had.

"Flattery will get you everywhere," she told Godolkin, watching him checking the charge on a plasma rifle. "And anyway, I didn't say I was the important thing – it's *Fury* that's going to get the job done, if anything can."

Harrow was off to one side, poring over a dataslate. Lieutenant Cormoran had downloaded a tactical map of the temple-lab onto it. "Holy one, all our efforts will be wasted if the Archaeotechs have moved the time engine."

"I know." She stepped out of the equipment store and back into the staging area to give Godolkin more room. "I'm hoping it's too big to move around easily. And it's been a few days since Nerichau and his team were down there, so maybe the heat's died down a little."

"It's possible," said Harrow. "I'm unfamiliar with Archaeotech doctrine. They are rumoured to operate very differently from other Iconoclast divisions."

Godolkin emerged, clutching the plasma rifle and fixing spare charge packs to his battle harness. "They do. Still, I would council that our mission to Chorazin is suicide. Waiting for Jubal to rejoin Sibbecai's fleet would be more prudent. Then we could make a conventional attack and have some chance of success."

"There's no time," said Red. "And anyway, that would just get a lot of people killed on both sides, and I'd like to avoid that if possible." She scowled at him. "All I want to do is scrap that time engine. Wholesale slaughter's not on my agenda for today."

"Of course," began Harrow, "we may have already prevailed."

Red glanced around at him. "Say what?"

The mutant finished checking his map and clipped the dataslate to his belt. "There is a school of thought, holy one, in which one must assume that we succeed in this task. The Archaeotechs will never make the time engine functional, because if they do so in the future they would have already travelled back into the past and destroyed us. The very fact that we are alive tells us that Chorazin falls."

"A temporal paradox," said Godolkin thoughtfully.

Red snorted. "Jude, that makes my head hurt even worse than when Brite was zapping me. Besides, I don't think Sibbecai would go for it."

"Almost certainly not."

"Anyway, this is going to bloody work. As long as no one screws up, we could be in and out before anyone notices." She hauled the magnums from her belt, spinning them around her fingers to test their balance. "Don't give me that look, Godolkin. I know what I'm doing. We've got a couple of things going for us."

"Which are?"

"One, nobody likes Archaeotechs. From what I hear, even other Iconoclasts think they're untrustworthy, so they probably won't be able to rustle up much of a protection fleet. Nothing Sibbecai can't handle for a few minutes, as long as he doesn't get too heroic."

Harrow looked quizzically at her. "And the second thing?"

"You're standing in it," she grinned. "Come on, we'll be making the first drop soon. Better get Cormoran and his people onboard."

7. SHOW TIME

Aura Lydexia was in the dissection chamber, a sampling blade in her hand, when the alarm sounded.

She had managed to retrieve one of the mutant infiltrators from the Custodes stasis tubes so she could run a series of tissue samples, although the officer in charge of the facility insisted that a full autopsy could only be performed if he, or an officer of equal rank, present. Lydexia wasn't happy about that, but there was nothing she could do. The mutant wasn't a test subject, but an agent of the enemy, and thus came under the jurisdiction of the Custodes. Any autopsy performed on him would be for the purposes of security.

Lydexia had decided to keep the Custodes officer out of Chronotech for the moment, and do everything she could by non-invasive means. To really find out anything she would need to open the carcass – of that there was no doubt – but there were tests that could be done on a subject and leave no marks.

Especially when he was already dead.

The mutant was lying on a drain table; one of four Lydexia had set up in the dissection chamber. The Chronotech facility was a small structure, off to one side of the primary complex, and didn't have the facilities of the less esoteric disciplines. In fact, Lydexia had built it almost from scratch by commandeering a redundant high-energy testing plant that had been due for demolition. The dissection chamber had originally been a small chapel, built into one of the plant's two laboratory blocks, until Lydexia had refitted it at considerable personal cost. In contrast, some of the Bio-weapons chapter boasted vast arrays of surgical equipment, capable of dissecting hundreds of bodies at a time, and direct access to a fusion furnace so the remains could be disposed of easily. Chronotech was a far more modest affair.

Lydexia could understand that. Her primary chapter was Xenotechnology, the study of alien devices, and thus well respected and equipped. Her own specialty of Chronotechnoloy, however, was a branch of the main chapter that seldom saw any advance. Most Archaeotechs regarded it as a waste of effort. Before the Salecah object, Lydexia had spent most of her days on pure theory.

It was hardly surprising. Time travel was a rare occurrence; so rare that it was debatable it had ever really happened. It gave Lydexia little to work on, and the Savants in charge of her chapter had few reasons to divert resources her way.

That, she knew, could change. But at the moment the Salecah artefact was just an alien device of unproven purpose. The chapter Savants would take a lot of convincing before they would believe Lydexia had a time machine in her lab.

An autopsy on the four mutants who had felt its effects would be a start, but that was clearly out of bounds. Lydexia leaned close to the pale, frost rimmed body with the blade held steady, and told herself that tissue samples would be as good a place to start as any. If the results were good, perhaps she could petition the Custodes to let her take the corpse apart properly.

As the point of the blade touched skin, the alarm gonged into life.

Lydexia cursed and straightened up, dropping the blade onto the drain table. Her comm-linker was already buzzing, so she snapped it free of her belt and flipped it on. "Gyor, what's that infernal racket?"

"Forgive me, doctor-captain, but it's starting again."

Lydexia cursed and bolted for the ladder.

Gyor and the other researchers would be in the observation chamber one level up. There were cargo elevators, but Lydexia was young and quite capable of clambering up the caged ladder in less time than it took to get into the lift. She was in the observation chamber within half a minute of the alarm.

As soon as she got there she could see what was causing the panic through the great transpex windows that faced out onto the lightning vault. The time engine, bolted into its frame at the apex of the tower, was spinning furiously.

The last time this had happened, five unauthorised helots had been in the vault. One had just managed to get free of the chamber, but the others hadn't been so lucky. It was only when their desiccated bodies had been examined in more detail that anyone realised they were mutants.

Far more than helots were in the vault now: a researcher team had been checking the power feeds when the engine had started up. Lydexia could see them scattering from the base of the tower, students and helots running with them, battering at the armoured hatches sealing them in.

There was a noise coming through the transpex. A sibilant murmur, like a million voices whispering at once. It was getting louder, the voices growing enraged.

Lydexia dropped into a vacant seat at the main sequencing board, quickly scanning the icons flashing there. "Gyor, slave full control of primary power to me at this board. And someone tell those poor beggars down in the vault that panicking won't do them any good – I'm working as fast as I can."

The board came alive under her hands. Lydexia had designed most of its systems, so it didn't take her long to make sense of the alert icons. The time engine had indeed started up on its own again, and it was dragging power through the feeds faster than the vault's cabling could supply it. There were lines melting out beyond the transpex – something was going to give way, and soon.

Not soon enough for the researchers in there with it.

Lydexia began tapping icons, redirecting the tower's inputs. There was no point trying to shut off the power; that hadn't worked last time, leading only to a catastrophic backwash from the engine, flooding the vault with chronoplasts. This time, she was going to let the machine do exactly what it wanted to. Up to a point.

The vault was a cone shaped structure twenty metres high, and flattened off at the roof. Another truncated cone extended from the ceiling, far smaller and flatter. It housed a huge array of sensing and control equipment, most of which protruded downwards towards the tower in a forest of spines and dishes. Lydexia opened up the control sequence for the array, dropping every damper she had and bringing up a forcewall. In moments, the spinning time engine was surrounded by a hazy cylinder of liquid green light.

The dampers and forcewalls were exactly the same devices used by starships. Lydexia had requisitioned parts of dreadnought class or higher when she was designing the vault; ordinarily, the haze of energy surrounding the tower would have been proofing killships from Tenebrae antimat fire.

Alone, they probably wouldn't stop the chronoplasts, but with the dampers at full charge...

Lydexia cut the power.

The vault went white. A sphere of raw power had appeared at the centre of the time engine, impossibly small, but bright enough to fill the entire chamber with glare. Distantly, Lydexia could hear the researchers screaming.

The dampers were filling with energy discharge. Lydexia could see their readouts on her board; eight bars of green light, turning scarlet in front of her eyes. As she watched, the fourth damper went offline, filled with excess power until its circuitry melted. The energy discharge would be vented into the cooling laser, but the damper itself was history.

Another failed, and another. Two more.

The last three were on the verge of collapse when the light went out.

Slowly, the bars began to shrink back to green. Lydexia turned off the forcewall and ordered a medical team to the lightning vault.

None of the Researchers had been injured. Just to be on the safe side, Lydexia ordered all connections to the time engine severed while the ruined dampers were being replaced. It was a brutal decision to take, and reconnecting the cabling would take days, but she couldn't compromise the temple-lab's safety. If the engine started up again before the dampers were installed, anything could happen.

She requisitioned a secondary set of dampers as well, and was surprised at how readily her request was approved.

Not long after that she received a priority message from her chapter Savant, suggesting the two of them take tea in the refectory. Lydexia had been an Archaeotech long enough to know that such suggestions were not designed to be refused, and given the amount of trouble she was probably in already, she didn't think it prudent to start bucking tradition now. She changed quickly into a set of uniform robes, made a small devotion at her private chapel, and then headed across the temple-lab towards the Xenotech refectory.

On high days, the refectory was capable of feeding a thousand Archaeotechs at once, but when Lydexia entered it was very nearly empty. A small squad of Custodes ushered her in, their armour adorned with the closed eye symbol of their order, and two more led her through the ranks of benches to the high table. There, flanked by elite Custodes guards, sat Eucharis Gemello, savant-colonel of the Xenotech chapter.

Gemello stood as Lydexia approached the table. "Well met, doctor-captain."

"Savant-colonel." Lydexia bowed, and then sat where she was bidden. The two Custodes who had led her in moved silently away, leaving her alone on her side of the long table, and very much aware of how she had been positioned. Her back was to the door and the open vastness of the refectory.

Gemello was a wily leader, she knew that, but sometimes her psychology was a little obvious.

The savant-colonel raised a hand, and a helot scuttled forward with a tray. "Tea?" she asked.

Her voice was high, musical. Lydexia nodded silently, and watched while the helot poured black liquid into two tall glasses. When the servant was done he stepped away, moving into the shadows as if he had never been there.

The savant-colonel took a thumb-sized crystal of sugar and dropped it into her glass. She was dressed head to foot in her robes of office, cream and gold, with a tall headdress. When she reached for the glass she had to hold one trailing sleeve out of the way, in order not to sweep Lydexia's from the table.

"There was," she began, her voice a liquid purr, "an alert in your laboratory this afternoon."

Lydexia nodded silently.

"It was not the first."

"That's right, savant-colonel. There was another when the mutant infiltration team was there."

Gemello lifted her glass and sipped. "Hmm. I've read Captain Hirundo's report on that. He thinks it was a coincidence. Do you?"

Lydexia remained silent for a moment, and then shook her head. "I can't say for certain, but I don't think so. There's no record of what they did in the vault immediately before the artefact activated itself, but it's possible they triggered it."

"And it triggered again when Researcher-Lieutenant Septimus was close by. So is he a mutant in disguise, or just a fool who goes about pressing buttons at random?"

"Neither, savant-colonel. Septimus is..." She trailed off, staring at her glass of tea. "I'm sorry, I don't know. The artefact's control chains are so complex I could spend years mapping them. I can't say why it initiated when it did. Maybe it was coincidence, or maybe it has some intelligence and is actively trying to escape through time. The vault should be shielded against all forms of communication, but chronoplasts don't follow that kind of rule." She sat back. "I've yet to rule anything out, I'm afraid."

"I see." Gemello stroked her chin thoughtfully. She was old, Lydexia knew, but pure gene reclamation had regressed her body to that of a smooth skinned young woman. It was a fad popularised by the holy Patriarch himself, although rumours abounded about the extremes to which he had taken the process.

"Doctor-captain, there are those in the chapter that regard your specialty as an expensive folly. I've heard the word 'sinecure' bandied about more than once. However, you'll be pleased to know that I don't share these views."

Lydexia, unsure of how to react, lifted her glass and gulped down a mouthful of black tea. It was vile.

"In fact," Gemello continued, "I've forwarded a copy of your initial report to Ascension."

Suddenly, Lydexia's tea was trying to go down into her lungs. In her shock, she'd managed to breathe some of the awful stuff in, and had to clamp down hard over a coughing fit. "What?" she croaked.

"Are you all right?"

"Fine." She cleared her throat and settled back, forcing herself to ignore the leaping tickle behind her sternum. "I'm fine. Ascension, you say?"

"Indeed. Admiral Caliban has already expressed an interest, and sends his personal congratulations. Lydexia, if you play this right, your star could be rising very fast indeed."

Something inside Lydexia soared, but she kept her expression calm, her voice level. "Thank you, savant-colonel. Of course, my loyalty is to the chapter and the division. I have no personal ambitions in the matter."

"Bullshit." Gemello's old young face creased in a smile. "Don't play yourself short, girl. This toy of yours could be a worthless trinket, or it could be the saving of mankind. But whatever it is, be aware that it's *your* toy. Don't let Ascension take it from you if it turns out to be a winner, and likewise have no surprise if it all goes wrong and the axe falls. You brought it here."

"I understand, savant-colonel. And thank you."

"Nothing to thank me for, doctor-captain. For good or ill, this is on your head. Just make sure it stays unplugged until those new dampers are in, yes?"

After the meeting, Lydexia went straight back to the dissection chamber. While she'd been away, one of her helots had activated a stasis shell on the occupied drain table so that the mutant she was working on wouldn't start to rot. Even with the massive refrigerating power of the cooling laser, the temple-lab could still get warm during Chorazin's hour long day.

While she was deactivating the shell, she put a linker call through to Commander Hirundo, asking him to contact her as soon as he was free. The reply came before the mutant was even defrosted. "Doctor-captain. It's good to hear from you."

"Thank you, commander."

"Although I've been hearing quite a lot *about* you, these past few days. Your new toy is turning some heads."

"It's doing more than that." Lydexia opened her surgical kit and began laying out the bright, steel devices within. "I'll tell you all about it as soon as I get the chance."

"I look forward to it. So, doctor-captain, what can I do for you?"

"Just a small thing. How would you like to watch me cut up a mutant spy?"

There was a slight pause. Then: "Is it dead?"

"Regrettably."

"A pity. But I'd be happy to anyway. It's been a long watch, and I could do with a good laugh."

"There," Lydexia said later, pointing out a series of small grafts nestling at the base of the mutant's skull. "Biomorphic implants."

"That's how they were able to get through our entry scans." Hirundo sucked in a breath through his teeth, a long hiss of disgust. "The filthy scum must have secreted themselves among that last influx of helot workers. And what happened to the ones they replaced can only be surmised."

"I think I can guess." Lydexia stepped back from the table and turned to check on the tissue series. As she had expected, the samples she had taken from the corpse showed the effects of a massive overdose of chronoplasts. Not all of the man's organs had suffered the same exposure, though. Cutting the power to the time engine early had resulted in an unstable burst.

Parts of the mutant lying on the table had aged a hundred years in those few nightmarish seconds, others only fifty. If the time acceleration hadn't killed him, Lydexia had no doubt that the shock of the imbalance would have.

"So," Hirundo said, folding his arms. "I hear you're off to Ascension."

"I am no such thing." Lydexia gave him a look, feeling the slight start that she always did when seeing his face. She was far more used to seeing him carapaced in Custodes armour, everything below his eyes covered by his breathe-mask. "Gemello said that Ascension had expressed an interest, that's all."

"Still, it would be a big step."

"It would." Lydexia stopped where she was and took a deep breath. "It frightens me, though, I don't mind saying. I mean, Ascension is the holy grail of anyone engaged in temporal research, and God knows there are few enough of us, but it could be too far, too fast."

The Custodes smiled grimly. "The idea of being on the edge of the Manticore Gulf holds no terror for you?"

At the sound of those words, Lydexia's heart bounced, a mixture of fear and need. The laboratory station lay at the boundary of an area of space so dangerous that an entire battle fleet was on permanent station to surround it. At its heart lay something of devastating power, a nightmare from the past that had laid waste to worlds.

Ascension was there for a purpose, and that purpose was pure research. If Lydexia ever set foot there, it would be because she was acknowledged as a prime in her field.

"It holds terror," she breathed. "Yes, but if I was asked, I'd go today."

"Then let's hope Admiral Caliban knows a prime when he sees one." Hirundo nudged the corpse. "Shall we continue gutting this creature, or have you done with him?"

Lydexia reached over to the table and lifted a powered bone saw. "A few more cuts, I think. If Gemello smiles on me I might get to do this to our frozen Blasphemy, and I'd like to hone my technique."

She was partway through slicing away the top of the mutant's skull when Hirundo's linker went off. He stepped away to answer it, as he always did, speaking quickly and precisely into the machine without ever once raising his voice loud enough for her to hear.

When he put the linker away, he was frowning. "I have to go."

"What's wrong?"

"Long range sense-engines have picked up a series of hard returns at the edge of the system. Not many, but it looks like they're closing in. I have to ready the Custodes just in case."

"I understand."

He nodded at the eviscerated mutant. "Keep going with this. No security issues now; just take it apart and find out how it works." With that he turned away, heading for the stairs.

"Thy will be done," she called out, and watched until he was gone from sight.

The Ochaos system wasn't large. Ships detected at the edge of it could be at Chorazin within an hour or so, even without making any superlight jumps.

Lydexia continued working on the mutant for a while, reporting everything she found, until the carcass was nothing more than an empty shell. Then she activated the stasis cover again and sat down at her workstation. Even though the gross anatomy was done with, she still had hundreds of samples to test.

As the brain series began to run, Lydexia brought up a supplementary holo and set it to the temple-station's general alert channel. She would occasionally do this to warn her of events or meetings that she needed to attend, and leave the channel running while she worked. That way, no matter how engrossed she became, there was a chance that she would see the alert in time.

Tonight, though, the channel had more to tell her than when her next chapter meeting was due.

The killship *Lamarion* had been scrambled from its position in Chorazin's shadow and was heading out to engage the incoming vessels. The other two Custodes dreadnoughts, *Gatianus* and *Ugento*, were closer, as they had been patrolling Chorazin's orbit. They had been able to slingshot around Ochaos, giving themselves a boost in speed before changing vector to meet the intruders. *Ugento* had already released its daggership shoals.

The Chorazin temple-lab was on level three alert. Non-Custodes personnel were being advised to stay in their quarters or places of research, and some system lockdowns had taken place in vulnerable areas. Nothing, Lydexia told herself, to worry about unduly.

The intruder ships might be lost, or a surprise inspection force from High Command imminent. Even if they were hostile, there were three fully-armed killships between them and Chorazin.

Even so, Lydexia got up from the workstation, crossed the chamber to the small weapons locker and took a plasma derringer from the rack inside. She pushed the gun into her robes before going back to the test series.

Minutes passed, flowing seamlessly together as Lydexia lost herself in the data. The mutant's brain had been altered by the chronoplast overload, but to form a complete picture of what the alterations had been she had to first discover which abnormalities were the result of the time engine, and which were natural to the man's corrupted physiology. The massive haemorrhages he had suffered made the tests even more fraught. Lydexia found herself having to repeat each series, blind testing herself, running gene reversions and mutation simulations in order to lay down a baseline.

She was close, with a few more series, when the alert status went up to level two.

Lydexia looked up as she heard the warning chimes, then quickly scanned the holo. Daggerships from *Ugento* had engaged the enemy, and antimat fire was being reported from the intruders. *Lamarion* had increased velocity, hoping to assist the other killships. The intruder fleet had started to disperse.

As Lydexia read this, her comm-linker chirruped. She flipped it on. "Speak."

"Doctor-captain, it's Commander Hirundo. Where are you?"

"Where you left me. Why?"

"Stay there, and seal the lab. Do you have a weapon?"

Lydexia felt herself go cold. "Yes, yes I have. Hirundo, what's going on?"

"I'm not sure yet." The Custodes sounded grim. "It may be nothing, but be careful."

The linker went dead.

She stared at it for several seconds, then stood up. The results of the tests she had done were still in the workstation holos, so she saved them to data-crystal before shutting the machine down. Then she drew the pistol and padded across the lab towards the door.

As she neared it there was a noise from outside. Something like a heavy, metallic impact, although it was hard to tell through the closed door. It made Lydexia start, though, as she did when the noise came again.

She froze, listening hard, but there were no further noises. After half a minute she stepped back and locked the door with her crypt disc. It wouldn't stop a determined attacker – the hatch was made from little more than plate steel and locked with a simple magnetic catch – but it made her feel slightly better.

She moved back to the workstation, then to the mutant corpse beneath its rapidly cooling stasis shell.

There was another sound, louder this time. Moments later alarm chimes began clamouring in the observation chamber. Somebody had opened the door to the lightning vault.

Lydexia bolted to the ladder and scuttled up, drawing her derringer as she reached the top. As soon as she did so she looked through the transpex windows and saw figures below her, moving across the floor of the vault.

She dropped to the floor and flipped her linker on. "Hirundo," she hissed.

"Doctor-captain?"

"Hirundo, there's someone in the lightning vault. I can see them through the transpex."

She heard him draw in his breath. "For God's sake, Lydexia, stay out of sight. I'm on my way."

The linker fell silent. Lydexia kept hold of it, the derringer held tight in her other hand, and began crawling on her hands and knees towards the windows. There was a row of secondary workstations there, used mainly for running observational tests while the vault was in use, and she crouched behind the nearest.

The intruders were nearing the tower.

They were moving quite slowly, looking around them, readying weapons. Going with stealth, not speed. Lydexia saw one of them point up at the time engine.

For a moment she felt herself relaxing. These were not intruders, but some of her own people. The man who had pointed was an Iconoclast shocktrooper, unmistakeable in uniform trousers and battle harness.

Then Lydexia saw the woman standing behind him, and her heart misfired in her chest.

She was quite tall, slender, dressed head to foot in a fig-ure hugging costume of matte black leather. Her hair was long, crimson streaked with black, and she carried a pis-tol in either hand. Lydexia realised, with the part of her mind that wasn't shrinking back in terror, that whatever lay frozen down in the Custodes stasis facility was most definitely not Durham Red.

The Blasphemy was alive, and she was here.

8. ONE FROM THE VAULT

Red should have known that her luck had to run out sometime.

Things had gone badly from the start. One of Sibbecai's ships, the frigate *Needlefang*, had begun to suffer damper failure partway through the superlight jump to Chorazin. Without functioning dampers, the ship would have been prey to every physical force from the stresses of vector change to the impacts of weapons fire. A starship engaged in battle might routinely make manoeuvre burns of a hundred gs or more. If *Needlefang* tried that with the dampers down, it would fly apart only seconds after its crew had been reduced to pulp.

There was no way to repair the frigate in superlight, and even returning to realspace partway through the journey would delay the operation by days. Reluctantly, Sibbecai had ordered *Needlefang's* captain to alter course and head back to Haggai, then execute a very gentle deceleration from superlight when she got there. With luck, the stricken ship would be able to get back into the cavern without breaking up or killing its crew in the process.

It was a bad omen, and everyone knew it. Durham Red, quite rightly, considered that she had enough to worry about just keeping her side of the plan together. She had reached the stage of refusing to let herself even think about what she had to do, because to consider it in any detail would be to realise just how many things could go wrong. There were parts of the operation that she hadn't even discussed with her companions. If she had, they would have mutinied there and then.

The fleet decelerated to realspace at the edge of the Ochaos system. As soon as the fires of jumpspace faded away, Red had Godolkin pilot *Omega Fury* out of *Persephone*'s landing bay, engaging the shadow web as he did so. That was when things almost fell apart for a second time: two killships from the Archaeotech protection fleet were patrolling between Chorazin and the deceleration point. Red's plan to fire up the main drives and let *Fury* build up some speed had to be thrown away immediately. The killships would have spotted her drive flare in moments if she'd tried it.

Fury had left Sibbecai's flagship with Cormoran and his strike team already aboard. The four mutants had been on the lower deck, strapped into crash seats in the staging chamber, but Red had practically forgotten about them as she watched the killships closing in. An Iconoclast dreadnought was heading right towards *Fury*, their courses so near to intersecting that Red was on the verge of pouring on the power anyway. Better that than collide with the monstrous vessel.

The range between *Fury* and the nearest killship was down to less than five hundred kilometres when Cormoran leaned into Red's workstation. "Is there a problem?"

Red started and yelped in surprise, then turned to glare at him. The man moved like a ghost. "What makes you say that?" she snapped.

"I thought there should have been a vector burn by now."

"Change of plan." She nodded towards her forward holo.

Cormoran followed her gaze and drew in a sharp breath. "Just how magnified is that image?" he whispered.

"Not much. Range three hundred clicks and closing." On the holo, the killship was a wall of metal, its forward section gaping like a maw. Weapons, some so vast that

Fury could have flown right into their barrels, filled her view. "They were half way between us and Chorazin when we came out of superlight, and I can't even warn Sibbecai."

The dreadnoughts would pick up any communication at this range. Sibbecai might have noticed the lack of a drive flare and worked out Red's dilemma on his own. But with two killships bearing down on him, he might well have had other things to worry about.

"Blasphemy?" That was Godolkin. "Either authorise me to fire the drives, or prepare for collision."

"Give me a moment."

"I don't have one."

"I said–" She stopped in mid-sentence. Jets of searing flame were erupting from the killship's hull. For a horrible moment Red felt certain *Fury* was being fired on, but then the dreadnought began to slide across her holo.

"Course correction," said Cormoran. "Bringing their spinal weapons to bear. They'll release the daggerships soon."

Red sagged back and let out a relieved sigh. "Thank sneck for that."

The killship *Ugento* had a complement of almost two hundred daggership interceptors. All of them fired their main drives as they raced ahead of their mother ship, and Red took that opportunity to get *Fury* back on course. One drive flare wouldn't be noticed among all those others, even if it was heading the wrong way.

For the next hour, all she could do was wait. Behind her, the dreadnoughts engaged Sibbecai's battlegroup, which immediately began to split up and take evasive action. Their task wasn't to defeat the Iconoclast ships – it was unlikely they could have done so anyway – but to keep the killships away from Chorazin while *Omega Fury* neared the temple-lab.

Fury, however, was late. The mutant ships were already in full retreat before Red reached orbit.

As the ship entered Chorazin's orbit, the hull temperature was already beginning to rise. Red could only keep her fingers crossed as the gauges began to climb. She had hoped to come in at night, when there was less chance of the shadow web being cooked clean off the hull. Another part of the plan gone wrong.

Her holoscreen were stuttering, the view they showed brightening, then darkening, and growing bright again as the pickups strove to compensate. Ochaos was already blindingly close.

Fury dipped lower, racing over the glowing surface of Chorazin. Red saw a point of light appear on the horizon, growing into a hazy line and brightening until it became a thread of pure white brilliance lancing upwards into the airless sky.

"Blasphemy, the cooling laser is ahead."

"I see it," she replied. "Godolkin, drop your speed. They won't have any visual pickups at the entrance, they'd never last. Let's not give them anything else to key on, okay?"

The Iconoclast grimaced. "The longer we stay under this inferno, the more chance of losing the web altogether."

"Yeah, and if we go in hypersonic they'll pick us up on Doppler and frag us before we even land, so put the bloody brakes on."

Godolkin did as he was ordered, dropping the ship even lower as he fired *Fury*'s manoeuvring thrusters. Thankfully, that was one emission that the Archaeotechs wouldn't be able to detect. The heat from the thrusters was nothing compared to the temperature of Chorazin's surface.

The holo had stopped dimming and was simply getting more and more uncomfortable to look at. Just when Red thought it couldn't get any brighter, the cooling laser's beam reached vertical, and a star appeared at its base. A second later, Red was looking at a blank screen – the sense pickup had been burned out, fused by the reflection from the heat shield's mirrored neutronium surface.

She saw nothing more until the ship flew in under the lip of the shield, its final thruster bursts masked entirely by the searing heat outside, and then settled into the most remote docking cocoon in the spaceport.

The docking cocoons were heat shielded and linked directly to the cooling laser. As long as the spaceport staff didn't check their records too closely, *Fury* would be safe there, hidden until the strike team needed to leave. When that time came they would all be relying on Judas Harrow - much to his disgust, Red had ordered him to stay on board. She would have been more than happy to have him along, mostly as a welcome contrast to Godolkin's malevolent sarcasm, and the murderous intensity of Cormoran's strike team, but she needed someone to stay with the ship and keep the drives warm. If things went badly wrong, and there was every chance they still might, the young mutant might be their only ticket to freedom.

Once inside the temple-lab, things started to go well once more. Red's passage through the facility was less eventful than she had anticipated, thanks to the running battle taking place at the edge of the system: the appearance of Sibbecai's ships had triggered an alert, and most of the Archaeotechs had voluntarily confined themselves to quarters. Those they did see were quite easily avoided – hooded men and women who walked with their shaven heads down, their gaze turned inward.

Many appeared drugged. Red thought of Oray Abd Durwan back on the Ulai fin, and the barter musk he'd sniffed as a neural enhancer. Maybe these Archaeotechs were taking a similar substance, snorting mind altering chemicals to amplify their intelligence. Certainly there were those that must have come close enough to see her, but they'd just walked past muttering, as if engaged in some furious mental exercise.

There was no sense tempting fate. Red found some lockers and broke into them, stealing some heavy, hooded robes for herself and the team. As long she and her companions kept their heads down, and muttered occasionally in the right preoccupied tone, Red hoped they would form an effective disguise.

The number of wandering Archaeotechs lessened as Red led her team inward. Before long, most of the humans they saw were soldiers, wearing an ornate variant of the classic shocktrooper armour. "The Custodes Arcanum," Godolkin explained, as a squad of them rounded a corner and marched out of sight. "Keepers of the Secret. They are the elite fighting order of the Archaeotechs, and not to be underestimated."

"What's that on them?" Red whispered. "That curved thing?"

"The closed eye, Blasphemy. A symbol of their order. They are sworn to never reveal anything discovered by their Archaeotech masters." He glanced quickly right and left. "Should they ever do so, they are publicly blinded before execution."

"Nice," Red replied. "Which way?"

Godolkin had the dataslate Harrow had prepared. The map it contained wasn't complete, but the big Iconoclast's knowledge and enhanced senses were, so far, filling in the gaps. "Follow me."

She fell into step behind him. The passages in the temple-lab were narrow and dimly lit. "Just as long as you know where you're going."

"And what makes you think that?"

"You're the one with the map, dipstick."

He snorted. "In case you had forgotten, Mistress, it is a map with no names. I am directing our search toward likely areas, nothing more."

Red resisted the urge to kick him. "Why didn't you tell me that before?"

There was an obvious answer to that, but if Godolkin had intended to say it he never got the chance. Three of the Custodes Arcanum had appeared in front of him, bolters at the ready.

"Ah," said Red, very quietly. "Bollocks."

One of the Custodes moved slightly ahead of his fellows, eyes narrowing above his filigreed breathe-mask. "Didn't you hear the alert chime, student?"

"I did not," replied Godolkin, keeping his head bowed. "I was lost in contemplation."

"Admirable. However, you are in violation of an alert curfew. Return to your halls now, and your chapter savants need never know."

Red saw Godolkin tense, and quickly put her hand to his shoulder. "Heed him," she breathed, trying to sound as much like an Iconoclast as she could. Her accent didn't make it easy. "We don't want to get into trouble. Not yet."

"Of course." Godolkin relaxed, moving slightly away from the trio of Custodes. "My thanks."

The man frowned. "Wait, student. What's your chapter?"

"Time travel," Red blurted. "I mean–"

"Chronotech? In this block?" The Custodes turned to share a glance with his colleagues. "You must have been thinking hard, girl."

"Try looking at your chapter plan next time," said one of the men behind him. "Now go on, back to your halls. This is no time to be skulking around. Play your games when the alert is over."

He turned, chuckling, and the three of them strode away.

When they were out of earshot Red finally let out the breath she had been holding. "Sneck, that was close."

Godolkin rounded on her. "Blasphemy, we could have taken them. Why did you restrain me?"

"Because, you great lummox, firefights are loud. If we start blasting away in here we'll be swarmed, and there's a lot more of them than there are of us. So just keep your head down and stay quiet until we get what we came for, okay?"

"This still leaves us no closer to the time engine." One of Cormoran's strike team, Helsa, had thrown back her hood. She was a small woman with an angular face and rather wild blonde hair. "Time is running short. Maybe Commander Sibbecai can hold off two dreadnoughts, but a third is approaching. We have to end this now."

Cormoran put a hand on her arm. "Be still, Helsa."

"At least we know what we're looking for now." Red took a comm-linker from her robes. "Jude?"

"Still here, holy one."

"Good stuff. I'll keep this short, because I don't want anyone picking up the signal, but can you get into some kind of info system for this place?"

There was a pause filled by the sound of keys being rapidly pressed. "Some outer command strings and basic information. That's all."

"Just what I need. Get into the student resources and hunt down a chapter plan. Then tell us how to get to Chronotech."

The temple-lab, in addition to being a seat of Archaeotech study, was also a training facility with a sizeable population of students.

The very idea that anyone would have a university on a world as hostile as Chorazin made Red's mind spin, but she had long ago given up on trying to make sense of life in the Pan-Species Accord. Sometimes she felt as though she was living in a system of societies that had, probably as a result of the brutality of their great war, gone utterly insane.

If the Iconoclasts got Brite Red's time engine up and running, she could see it getting rapidly worse.

From what Harrow had been able to read in the chapter plan, Chronotech was a sub-section of Xenotechnology housed in a structure to the east of the temple-lab. It was based around a high energy testing facility commonly known as a "lightning vault", a nickname that Red found slightly chilling, given that she was going to be wandering around inside it before long.

She, Godolkin and Cormoran were poring over the map while the rest of the team kept watch. Cormoran had pointed out the four blockhouses that surrounded the vault. "These may have access," he said. "The main entrance will be guarded, but the labs might only be staffed by academics. They wouldn't put up much resistance."

"I don't know," Red replied, gnawing a thumbnail. "I never thought I'd say it, but the idea of blasting my way through rooms full of students doesn't really appeal. If there's a way to get into that vault without going through the labs I'd prefer it."

Godolkin sniffed. "This newfound respect for life is laudable, Blasphemy, if misguided. We have greater concerns."

She glared at him. "Keep your opinions to yourself, and do as I bloody tell you: we're going in through the front door or not at all."

Godolkin could sneer as much as he liked, Red thought sourly as they made their way towards Chronotechnology, and if he thought she was going soft then so be it. He'd been with her in the Grand Keep on Magadan, when the entire structure had begun to collapse around them, and all he'd seen was the danger. At the time Red had too, but the difference came afterwards. She knew that hundreds of thousands of people had died in that catastrophe, pulped in their homes because they were too afraid to leave the Keep or just because they had no way of getting out. Men and women, children and babies, the old and the sick; there was no distinction. She had saved a few, convinced the mad creature that ruled them to let them leave, but it could never be enough.

Godolkin had seen genocide before, and thought nothing of it, but Red would hear the screams of the Magadani until she died.

Remorse was one thing, survival another. When the strike team finally got to the Chronotech facility, Red could see that just going in through the front door with all guns blazing would be a quick way to meet her maker. At least forty Custodes Arcanum had been stationed there.

"Sneck," she said, ducking back around the corner to join the others. "It's a convention."

"There has already been one attempt to gain entry into this vault, Blasphemy." Godolkin had taken the plasma rifle from beneath his robes. "It is only natural that they should anticipate another."

"Natural, but bloody annoying." She took the dataslate from him and checked the map again, scanning hopelessly for a secret tunnel or air shaft that she might have missed before. She failed, of course. "Okay, plan B. Who's got the demo charges?"

"I have." That was Malak, one of Cormoran's people. He reached into his robe and took out a palm sized slab of plastic. "Where do you want it?"

"Just give. And two more." She took the charges from him and turned them over in her hands. "Integral detonator?"

"Here." He showed her. "Timer, motion sensor or remote. I have the initiator."

"Remote will be fine." She took the initiator too, then handed two charges to Godolkin. "There you go."

He regarded them calmly for a moment. "What, exactly, should I do with these?"

"Put them somewhere middle-of-the-range vital. Secondary power cabling, water supply, airscrubbers. Nothing that's going to take out half the base, but enough to cause a diversion." She waggled the initiator at him. "I want as many of those troopers out of the way as you can get."

Godolkin turned without a word and stalked off, cradling the charges. If he thought there was any chance of Red setting them off while he was still holding them he had obviously come to terms with it. Perhaps, she thought idly, he would welcome the release.

Lesham, the third member of Cormoran's team, was scowling after him. "Can he be trusted?"

"I'm sorry," Red replied, feigning politeness, "who did you say you were again?"

The mutant lowered his head, but his expression didn't change. "Forgive me, holy one. But he is a human, and an Iconoclast. Hardly the most reliable of allies."

"As a matter of fact, I'd trust Godolkin with my life." Red fixed Lesham with a stare. "More to the point, I'd trust him with yours."

The man said nothing, but appeared to shrink slightly into his robes.

A few seconds later Godolkin returned, padding quickly around the corner. "The charges are placed, Blasphemy."

"Good work, Godolkin." In the face of Lesham's distrust, Red suddenly felt protective of the Iconoclast. "Shall we dance?"

"An excellent suggestion."

The charges were on separate crypt-keys. Red pressed the activation stud twice, and each time was rewarded by a massive hammer blow of sound from somewhere off in the base. After the second blast, she ducked around the corner again to see the Custodes ranks in turmoil. Their rigid formations had gone, replaced by milling confusion. An officer was shouting orders, trying to make himself heard while dust from the explosions drifted past. Moments later he was leading a detachment of soldiers away, two dozen or more of them sprinting from the vault hatch.

"Nice going," Red muttered appreciatively, moving back around the corner. "What did you blow up?"

"There was a communications node not far from here," Godolkin replied. "And a Custodes ready room. It was largely empty, but the effect seems to be as desired."

"I'm not surprised, you evil bugger," Red barked out a laugh. "You fragged their canteen."

"Fifteen troopers remain," Cormoran reported. "Holy one, if we are going to do this, it should be now."

Red held up the demolition charge she had kept back, then leaned around the corner and flung it at the vault hatch. She saw it skid to a halt against the boots of Custodes soldier before she scrambled back into cover.

Panicked shouts erupted. Red waited until she could hear people running, then hit the initiator stud again.

The demo charge exploded with a deafening whiplash of sound and an impact Red felt like a physical blow through the deck. A solid cloud of smoke and debris washed around the corner, enveloping her, making her duck and turn her face to the wall. "Bloody hell, Cormoran. What's in those things?"

"It's a shaped detonex charge." The man drew alongside her, and she heard the metallic sounds of a frag-carbine being primed. "Normally we fix them to something before setting them off. Their effects can be a bit unpredictable in the open."

"A bit," she muttered. The smoke had cleared a little, enough to see a few metres. Red drew her pistols, gestured to the others to follow her lead, and charged around the corner.

The scene, or what she could see of it through the dust and smoke, was one of utter devastation. The demo charge had scoured the corridor; any Iconoclast who hadn't fled had been scattered by the force of the blast. Armoured figures lay on the deck and against the walls. Many weren't the right shape any more. A couple of them were on fire.

The walls around the vault hatch were burning, curtains of greasy flame licking up at the scorched ceiling. Red skirted the blaze and stopped in front of the hatch, wiping the locking controls free of soot. "Who's got the data-pick?"

"That's my honour, Saint." The woman, Helsa, moved past her, taking Harrow's data-pick from her robes. Red stepped aside to give her space as the pick began to sequence the vault's lock.

Harrow had once told Red that the data-pick had cost as much as *Crimson Hunter*, and had been far harder to acquire. Red, watching the way it chewed through the billions of crypt-combinations protecting the vault, found no reason to doubt him.

Something was moving at the end of the corridor, partly concealed by smoke. Red turned to it, and as she did heard the unmistakeable hammer-on-anvil slamming of a bolter, followed by a metal scream as a staking pin caromed off the wall close to her head. She yelped in surprise and brought her magnums up, but Cormoran was faster. A burst of frag-shells ripped back down the corridor, carving holes in the dusty air, and in the distance someone screamed and fell.

"Whenever you're ready, Helsa," Cormoran said flatly.

"Done." Red saw Helsa disconnecting the data-pick and shoved past her, guns held high, shrugging off the robes as soon as she was in. She went left, knowing that Godolkin would go right, that the pair of them could cover the whole circular floor of the chamber.

She could never convince him of it, but she and Godolkin made a damned good combat team.

There was no one in the vault to challenge them. Red turned her aim back to the hatch, covering the rest of the squad as they came through. When they were all in, Helsa closed the doors and began using the data-pick to scramble the lock, leaving Red to lower her guns and look around.

The lightning vault was smaller than she had expected, but still impressive, a tall room the shape of a flattened cone. It was narrow for its height, taller than it was wide, and at the centre stood a slender construction so tall it reached almost to the spiny, cable strewn ceiling.

The tower was ornate, its faces delicately curved, like a vast perfume bottle. At the apex of it, resting in a steel cradle, lay the most bizarre, confusing piece of machinery Red had ever seen. It was like a half solved puzzle, a partly melted labyrinth, a chaotic fusion of wheels and rods that seemed to pass both around each other and through each other simultaneously. Red had never seen anything like it.

But somehow, she recognised it. "That's it," she breathed. "That's the time engine."

Godolkin discarded his own robe, then pointed up at the cradle. "The weak point is there. With enough fire-power we could bring the engine down to the vault floor, and then fix demolition charges directly to it."

"Sounds like a plan." Red raised her magnums.

Godolkin moved further around the tower, aiming his rifle, and the strike team took up positions closer to the base of the tower. "At your command, holy one," Cormoran called.

And that was when Durham Red's luck ran out.

Although there was no one in the vault with them, someone had been watching. Before Red could speak, a blinding wash of green light snapped down from the ceiling in a looping, roiling wave that spiralled down to strike her full in the face. The force of it slammed into her, kicking her clean off her feet and sending her sprawling backwards. She rolled, guns flying from her grip, feeling the rough metal of the deck scrape at her until she finally fetched up against a cable duct, her vision full of flashing lights, her skin livid with residual voltage.

The vault was echoing with sound, a throbbing hum that made Red's teeth try to turn around in her jaw. Voltage crackled and sizzled around her, snapping in fat sparks from her hands as she tried to right herself, to stand up and see what this awesome power was.

There were screams, too.

Red staggered upright. The light hadn't just come down to hit her; it had encircled the entire tower. It was still there, rippling like a liquid, a steady, stable column of glassy light that stretched from the ceiling to the floor. The tower was completely enclosed by it.

"Sneck," Red moaned. "A bloody forcewall."

Godolkin appeared from behind the tower, his shape sent leaping and swarming by the forcewall's ripples. "Blasphemy, we have casualties."

"Shit." She limped around to meet him, and saw Cormoran kneeling on the floor halfway between the tower and the far wall. He was clutching his left arm to his chest, a broad stain of crimson spreading across the fabric of his robes. Helsa was lying some distance away, quite still.

The other two members of the team hadn't been so lucky. Malak was slumped at the base of the tower, inside the forcewall's shell. The light had torn into him, sent his skin one way and his blood another. It had taken him apart in an instant.

Red stepped closer to the tower and looked down at the deck. There was something there, a blackened mass, transfixed by the edge of the forcewall. There were shapes in the mass that reminded her of a man – a twist of spine here, a row of teeth somewhere further up, a tangle of bent sticks that could almost have been ribs – but nothing more.

Lesham had been standing right on the spot where the forcewall touched the deck, and it had pulverised him.

She turned away, sickened. Godolkin was helping Cormoran, easing the man's hand away from his chest. It was missing fingers. "Blasphemy, that is a dreadnought class forcewall. No weapon we have will penetrate it."

Red tried to speak, found something warm and coppery in her mouth, and spat blood. "Someone switched it on," she snarled. "We'll just find them and convince them to shut it down again."

"No time," whispered Cormoran, his face white with shock. "They're here."

As he spoke, the inner vault hatch shuddered, and a spot of searing orange light appeared near one edge. Molten metal started to drool down the inner surface.

The Custodes Arcanum were cutting their way in.

9. AVENGING ANGEL

The data-pick had completely scrambled the lightning vault's locking codes. It would be simplicity itself for Red or her team to decode the new sequence and open the doors again, since they had the pick. Anyone else would have about a trillion icon combinations to sort through.

The Custodes Arcanum, ever practical, had simply decided to burn their way though the hatch instead.

Red had retrieved her guns, and now watched the spot of orange light crawling down the right-hand edge of the hatch. Molten metal was already starting to pool on the deck beneath it. "What do you reckon, Godolkin?"

The Iconoclast was with Cormoran, spraying bio-foam over the man's injured hand. "The hatch is strong, built to withstand the outputs from high energy experiments. They will not cut through in less than three minutes."

"Three? To chop out the whole door?"

He shook his head. "They will cut a hole roughly half a metre square, Blasphemy, and use that to throw in grenades and toxin bombs."

Red muttered a curse. Of course the Archaeotechs would throw in enough ordnance to pulp them without ever getting into the line of fire. They weren't stupid, and their precious time engine had a forcewall around it.

The lightning vault had no other exits, and the big transpex observation windows were near the ceiling, out of reach even if she could blow a hole in one. In terms of engineering, the vault was supremely practical, a sealed bottle in which to unleash the deadly forces of high energy physics without risking the rest of the base. It also made a very effective trap.

She took her comm-linker from her belt. "Jude?"

There was no reply, just a warbling pulse of static. She tried again on another crypt-key, but met with the same result. "Are they jamming us?"

Godolkin got up, handing Cormoran his frag-carbine and picking up another. One of the dead mutants must have let it drop when the forcewall came down . "It seems likely."

"So we're stuck."

"Yes."

"Bollocks."

Cormoran was turning his hand, examining the foam coating. "Nice work, human. A pity it will all be wasted."

"At least you will die holding a weapon, and not your own bloodied limb." Godolkin dropped his trauma kit onto the floor, and then padded over to the hatch. There was already an L-shaped slot in it at head height.

"Predictable," he muttered darkly.

"That's Iconoclasts for you," Red replied, watching the cutting beam's path. The molten spot began to move upwards, slowly turning the L into a U. "All right, people, here's the deal. If they can lob stuff in, that means we can fire out, and the corridor's as confined as in here. Let's do as much as we can to make life miserable for them." She checked her pistols, making sure that their yield was set high. "If anything comes through that hole, we bat it right back out again. Okay?"

"Fiendish," said Godolkin, holding a rifle in each hand. "How long do you think we will be able to keep that up?"

"Until we miss one."

As she spoke, there was a shifting sound behind her, accompanied by a soft moan. Red turned to see Helsa getting up. The woman was tangled in her robes and clasping the side of her face with one hand.

Red trotted over and helped her up. "How are you doing?"

"I'll let you know when my brain stops trying to crawl out of my head." She squinted up at the forcewall. "Sacred rubies."

"Yeah. Whatever that means." Red motioned her over to the hatch, noting as she did so that the square was almost complete. "Bad stuff's going to start coming out of that in a second, Helsa. I need you to stay by the lock with the data-pick, and open it up as soon as I give you the nod."

"There's an emergency escape protocol. I can activate that." Helsa frowned, glancing behind her. "Where are the others?"

"They won't be coming with us," said Cormoran, whirling as the spitting whine of the cutter died away.

The square dropped away from the hatch and landed heavily on the vault floor, a slab of metal as thick as it was wide.

Red leapt towards it and shoved a magnum though the opening, tugging on the trigger. The gun bucked in her hand, emitting a wasp like snarl as it pulsed a bolt of energy into the corridor beyond. Someone outside the hatch screamed in pain.

She got two more shots off before somebody fired back.

The staking pin slapped into the magnum's barrel and sheared the gun clean out of Red's grip. She cursed and fell back, clutching her wrist, her hand singing with pain, but as she did so Cormoran leapt forward with his frag-carbine held in one hand. He jammed the muzzle through the hole and tugged on the trigger, holding it down as he tilted the weapon left and right. Red winced at the thought of the corridor filling with a million razored fragments, a tornado of shrapnel washing out from the hatch. Anyone caught in that maelstrom would be shredded.

This time, fire washed back in reply. There must have been an Iconoclast out there with a holy weapon, Red realised: he had taken out her magnum with a staking pin, and was now hosing the hatch with cleansing flame.

Jets of greasy fire, stunningly hot, roared in through the square. Cormoran fell away, dropping the carbine, and before anyone else could take his place a fist sized ball of metal sailed through the opening.

Godolkin swung the plasma rifle backhanded, swiping the grenade right through the hole and back into the corridor. It bounced once, a dull sound of metal on metal, and then blew up with a solid thump. Fire blowtorched through the opening for a second or two, then died away.

"Helsa," Red snapped. "Get us out of here."

The hatch had opened slowly when they had first entered the vault, sliding on powered rails. This time, explosive latches slammed the two halves of it aside, their speed dragging in a great cloud of hot smoke. Red jumped through, ducking under a shot from a Custodes on her left, slewing around as she moved to fire point-blank into the man's face. The magnum took off his head and ripped open his chest, sending the spurting carcass flying over backwards. On her right, warriors running around the corner met a stream of frag-shells from Cormoran and Helsa, while Godolkin opened up in both directions, somehow tracking targets at either end of the corridor simultaneously.

Staking pins whined back along the passage, bolters chattering in the smoke. Red felt one breeze through her hair behind her neck and another carve a track across her left forearm. "Guys, this is way too exposed."

Godolkin fired off another burst, ripping an armoured figure in two. "I agree, Blasphemy. But our options are limited. There are Custodes at every junction."

"Have we got any more demo charges?"

"Malak had the last of them."

And Malak was lying dead on the other side of the forcewall. "Nuts," Red growled, firing into the smoke. "And it was all going so well."

That was when the lights went out.

For a moment, Red found herself in pitch darkness. It was so sudden, and the air in the corridor so thick with smoke and vaporised blood, that her night vision barely kicked in. For a moment, all she could see were muzzle-flashes, but even they died away as everyone found themselves as blinded as she was.

Shapes moved around her, some close, some further away. She snapped a shot off at one of the distant ones and missed completely. "What the snecking hell's going on now?"

A greenish glow was emanating from the open hatch, the forcewall still in place and blocking her off from the time engine. Nothing else seemed to be operating. Even the hum of the air system, so faint and pervasive that she hadn't even known it was there, had died to a whisper.

She could vaguely see the outline of Godolkin's head as he peered about. "Blasphemy, if there was ever a time to leave this place, it is now."

"Lead the way," she replied breathlessly, watching flashlight beams bobbing from around the left-hand branch. "You're the one with the map."

They started away, Red and Godolkin in front, Cormoran and Helsa behind, basically scuttling along backwards. They had almost reached the right-hand branch, where Red had stood when she'd thrown the demo charge, when her comm-linker chirruped.

She snatched it up. "Jude, is that you?"

"Holy one, I feared the worst."

"Takes more than a forcewall in the chops to put me down." She ran a few paces ahead, peering around the corner to make sure there were no Custodes lurking around it. As it turned out, there were two, so she shot both of them. "Where are you?"

"In flight," Harrow replied. "I've created something of a diversion, but I don't know how long it will last. Start heading for the spaceport, the way you came in. I can monitor your progress from here."

"Jude, you're a bloody marvel. What did you do?"

There was a slight pause, during which Red heard rumbling sounds, and a woman's voice, shrewish and high. The voice alert system, she realised. Then Harrow spoke. "I fired a nuclear torpedo at the cooling laser."

Red almost tripped over her boots. "You did what?"

"Holy one, I'll explain later. Use the power drain to your advantage, but use it swiftly."

The rest of Red's time in the Chorazin temple-lab was a nightmare. The closer she got to the spaceport, the hotter it became and the more still and stifling the air. The lack of power seemed to have affected the Custodes communication systems, leaving their attacks uncoordinated and sporadic, but even cut off from their leaders and wandering in isolated groups, they were ferocious fighters. They fought by torchlight, or encumbered by heavy sense enhancers, or even, in one bizarre case, by the light of burning books.

That was the one who got Helsa, a staking pin slicing between Red and Godolkin to strike the woman in the back. Red heard her scream, and Cormoran's curse, and had to duck aside as the he swung his frag rifle around to kill the man who had fired.

The Custodes was caught in the face by the burst of frag shells, the concentrated blasts of shrapnel chewing his skull apart. Red watched him collapse, then darted back to Helsa.

She was on the floor, but still moving, one hand reaching round to scrabble at the staking pin in her back. It had caught her off-centre, halfway between spine and shoulder. Blood was slicking down the back of her shirt.

Cormoran reached for the pin, but Red grabbed his hand. "Leave it. Just get her up."

Helsa moaned through gritted teeth. "Not like this," she gasped. "Not with this filth in my back…"

"You can pull it out back on the ship," Red snapped. "Where we can stop you bleeding to death. Cormoran, can you help her up?"

He nodded. "I'll carry her if I have to."

"You won't. Not alone."

• • •

The power came back as they reached the spaceport hub, the fan of connecting tunnels that led to the docking cocoons. Lumes in the arching braces above their heads suddenly flickered back into life, and within a moment Red found herself squinting and blinking in full light. "Crap," she muttered. "Someone found the fuse box."

There were Archaeotechs in the hub with her, probably curious students or more senior types trying to get to a ship and escape the failing base. For a long moment there was silence, a few shouts of relief, before the first Archaeotech noticed who was standing next to him, and the quiet erupted into panic.

The hub emptied in moments, howling students bolting for their lives, robes flapping. Red swung around as she heard a heavier tread in one of the access corridors behind her, and saw two Custodes taking cover there. She brought the magnum up, but there were still too many people in the way. She couldn't get a clear shot off.

Luckily the two troopers were faced with the same dilemma, but the hub was already clearing, and the stand-off could last a second or two at most.

"Get into a tunnel," Red bellowed. "Quick."

"Which one?"

"Any one!"

Helsa was slowing Cormoran up. Red got between him and the two troopers, holding the magnum in both hands, aiming along the top of the barrel. "Back off," she snarled at them.

There was no chance they were going to see sense, she knew that. They were Iconoclasts, sworn to destroy her at all costs, brought up in a universe that considered her the greatest possible threat to human existence. She was their Satan, their nightmare, the blasphemous arch-mutant who would destroy them all. She was Saint Scarlet of Durham.

It wasn't a reputation she deserved, or had ever wanted. But it would dog her until she died.

The Custodes fired. A student next to Red shrieked and fell, a staking pin stapling her robe to her thigh. Another fell with two more buried in his chest. Red dropped the magnum and hammered forwards, shoving the last remaining Archaeotechs out of the way, and barrelled into the two troopers.

She grabbed the head of one, slamming it with massive force into the wall, caving in his skull, and then grabbed the second one by his chest armour. His bolter went off, a deafening chatter that sent staking pins flaring past her and into the ceiling as she used her momentum to drive him over backwards onto the floor.

Red screamed her anger into his face. He snarled back, bringing his knee up into her belly, slamming the bolter into the side of her head, but he was too close to get any swing behind it, too restricted by his armour. Red shoved his head aside and opened her mouth, letting him have a good view of her fangs before she sank them into his throat.

He was tough, even if he was a murdering fool. He kept trying to kill her right up to the moment his heart stopped. When Red sagged back onto her haunches, blood slick on her chin, his dead eyes still held a trace of defiance.

"Sneck," she whispered. "I'm never going to get away from you people, am I?"

More footfalls sounded in the passageway. Red darted up and dived out of the way as another barrage of staking pins carved the air towards her, then ran back into the hub. Godolkin was waiting for her at the entrance to one of the tunnels, both rifles raised. "Blasphemy!"

She reached down to retrieve the magnum, skidding to a halt next to Godolkin. "Is Jude there?"

"On his way. He has been tracking us by listening in to Custodes battle reports."

Armoured forms appeared at the end of the passageway, then ducked back as Red fired across the hub, keeping her aim high as the injured Archaeotech tried to crawl out of the line of fire. "He'd better hurry. We're going to have company really soon, and we've run out of places to go."

Godolkin snorted. "Blasphemy, this mission has been a disaster. Harrow's paradox theory has been disproved."

"Not yet it hasn't." She snapped off a shot, sending a Custodes spinning away with half his skull gone. "We can't give up."

The Custodes she had bitten hadn't given up. He'd fought her to his last breath, not just trying to get away, to live, but actually to kill her. She couldn't let the time engine remain in the grasp of people like that. They'd do anything to wipe her out of history.

"No," said Godolkin, looking back over his shoulder. "But we can retreat. Now."

Red turned. The end of the tunnel had opened, the interior of *Fury*'s primary airlock behind it. Cormoran was hauling Helsa across the threshold.

"Thank Christ for that." She fired off another couple of shots, purely for effect, then bolted, Godolkin on her heels.

The Custodes weren't far behind. She heard staking pins hit the outer hatch as she climbed in through the inner doors. "Jude, the natives are getting cross. Better punch it."

"With pleasure," he replied over the ship's internal comms.

Red turned to Cormoran, hearing thumps and bangs from outside as the airlock disengaged. "There's an infirmary on the upper deck. Godolkin, go with them, make sure they're both stable for the trip back to Haggai."

"Thy will be done. Are you going to the bridge?"

"Yeah. Can't let Harrow have all the fun, can I?"

Judas Harrow was in the pilot throne when Red got there, surrounded by a dizzying array of holoscreens. He had reconfigured the ship's controls so he could fly with one hand and use the weapons and main sense-feeds with the other.

"Bloody hell, Jude," Red gasped, leaning in from the back of his workstation. "You've everything but the kitchen sink up here."

"It's nothing you haven't already done," he said, not looking around. Several holos ahead of him were showing views from different angles around the ship, but not in visible light. The spaceport around them was wrought from strings of light and planes of shadow. This would be his view until *Fury* was away from Chorazin's blinding day, and the video pickups could be used again; the world as seen in terms of gravity, radio waves and neutrinos.

"When?"

"You flew *Fury* single-handed when you rescued Godolkin and me from Brite Red."

"Flew, yes," quoted Red. "Landed, no. Besides, I didn't have the weapons online."

"Really?" Harrow blinked at her, looking startled. "I thought–"

"You're doing fine," she grinned, then moved to the weapons station and slid into the throne, letting it lock her in and slide forward. "Godolkin's playing nurse, so we'd better get out of here."

Harrow nodded. "Would you like control of the weapons, holy one?"

"Now when would I ever say no to that?"

Targeting holos appeared in front of her, weapons selectors to her left, ship status diagrams to her right. "You used the other eviscerator?"

Fury had fallen into her hands with a complement of two eviscerator missiles, heavy nuclear torpedoes with a starship killing yield. The first had destroyed the Ulai refinery's power plant back on Dedanas.

"I did," Harrow told her, tapping keys. "The cooling laser was protected by a forcewall."

"I'm not surprised." A holo on her right flared. "Jude, they've got their weapons back online."

Phalanx turrets were turning to track the ship. Blind in the ranges of visible light, Red could see the ripples they made in Chorazin's gravity as they moved, the flare of neutrinos growing in the heart of each firing chamber. The shadow web was still engaged, making it hard for the temple-lab's phalanx turrets to target the ship accurately, but at this range they wouldn't need to be accurate.

"It's all right," said Harrow. "We're not staying."

Fury leapt forwards, edges of acceleration slipping past the dampers to shove Red hard into the throne. There was no atmosphere to clog the ship's drives, no need to launch using clumsy grav-lifters. The interceptor surged up and out of the spaceport on a column of plasma fire.

In her forward view, the opening in the shield was a narrowed eye, heavy lidded and glowing with heat. It raced towards her, past her and shrank in her rear holos as *Fury* blasted up and out into the black, searing skies of Chorazin.

Antimat fire fountained out of the opening.

Harrow stood *Fury* on its tail, spun it clear around and then powered towards the ground in a swooping dive that made Red's vision grey at the edges. Her forward holo filled with Chorazin's cratered ground, which dropped away at the last second, leaving the ship skimming the surface with scant metres to spare, streams of antimat bolts ripping past from the temple-lab.

Chorazin was a tiny world, its horizon always close. In seconds *Fury* was too low for the phalanx turrets to track, their shots slamming into the surface in geysers of molten stone. Others tore away into the sky, hot neutrino flares dwindling in the altered holofeeds.

A shadow fell across *Omega Fury* as they passed onto the dark side of Chorazin.

Red puffed out a long breath as she sagged back into the throne. "Nice flying, Jude. I just hope Godolkin and the others were holding on tight."

"With the dampers this low it can be something of a bumpy ride."

"So, what now? Back to Haggai?"

Harrow shook his head, very slightly, not taking his eyes from the holos. "We have one small matter to deal with first."

"Hmm? What's that?"

In answer, Harrow tapped a key, slaving one of his views to Red's holo bank.

Over the fractured horizon of Chorazin, a shape was rising towards them. It was a vast, vertical blade of metal, its forward section gaping and studded with weapons mounts, its flanks and top bristling with enormous spines. It looked like a fish, a steel angelfish five kilometres high, its tail pouring out plasma exhaust and its guns hungry for harm.

It was a killship, an Iconoclast dreadnought.

"The *Lamarion*," Harrow reported. "It was closer to Chorazin than the other two, and as soon as your presence was reported in the temple-lab it swung about."

"Must have thought two would be enough for Sibbecai." Red scanned her holos. "Bloody hell, he's close. Can we jump away?"

"He'd be right after us."

"We can't lead him to the others. Sibbecai wouldn't stand a chance." Her warning holos flared again. "Oh shit, Jude, he's got tone on us."

The space between *Fury* and *Lamarion* became a sea of light.

The dreadnought had opened up with every weapon it could bring to bear. Hundreds of hunger guns, partly sentient antimat cannon, had swung about to unleash bolt after bolt of raw energy in *Fury*'s direction. Multiple laser cannons hammered out vast poles of coherent light, and fusion beams the width of roads scythed out in parallel streams of destruction. Had *Fury* been directly in the path of any of the dreadnought's spinal weapons it would have been incinerated in a heartbeat.

Red felt the ship being battered as antimat fire caromed off the forcewall. "How the sneck did they manage that, Jude? Is the shadow web still on?"

"They must be tracking our exhaust emissions."

"Well shut the bloody drives down," she yelped. "Don't give them anything to key on."

"I already have, holy one. We're coasting." Harrow tweaked a thruster control, and Red felt the ship change vector. "But we'll coast in a straight line until we fire a vector burn. They can work out where we'll be."

Red nodded. They could keep jinking, feathering the drives to hide from the dreadnought between burns, but sooner or later *Lamarion*'s gunners would get their sums right. It wasn't a game they could play for long.

She thought furiously. "Okay, we'd better try something else. Jude, when you hammered the cooling laser, all the power went down."

He nodded. "Of course. They drew power from all the other systems to keep it running while they switched to back-up wiring."

"Great. Just keep these bastards off my back for a few seconds more, okay? I need some thinking time."

"I'll try."

There had been something on the chapter plan that she hadn't really looked at before. She'd been too busy finding a way to the Chronotech facility to worry about secondary cooling systems. Now it could be the only thing that might save them.

She brought up the plan again, stared at for a few seconds, then switched it off. "Jude, turn us around. Get us back to the temple-lab."

Harrow turned his head to her, looked at her for a long moment, then angled the collectives. "Don't tell me. I don't want to know."

"You trust me, don't you?"

"Against my better judgement, I do, yes." He eased the throttle forward, and the ship surged ahead.

Lamarion followed, still firing, the shots getting closer as *Fury*'s drives gave them something to aim at. Red started tapping at the weapons board, bringing up a cascade of firepower. "Okay, get us on a course that will take us hundred metres over the roof, right past the laser, then shut the drives down again. I've got to time this just right."

"They'll have us by then."

Red checked her holos and saw that Lamarion was still turning. "Maybe, maybe not."

The dome and the cooling beam were right in her sights again. Red looked at it now in diagram form, radar and heat and power output, rather than open the video pick-ups again. In a way, it made her job easier.

"Just like a game," she breathed.

"Holy one?"

"Never mind, Jude. Just hold your course for a few more seconds…"

A counter on her board reached zero. Red triggered the cascade, sending a wave of flayer missiles towards the cooling laser, following them with streams of antimat fire from her forward cannon. She felt the launch impacts through the hull and watched the missiles streak away across the craters. They left no smoke trails in Chorazin's airless sky, just the brilliant flares of their drive emissions, shrinking into stars as they raced away. With their target set, all she had to do was wait for them to strike.

Her job would have been easier if she'd had one more eviscerator, but flayers would have to do.

The sky above the dome grew a constellation of stars, green sparks as the antimat bolts struck the laser's protective forcewall. Moments later the missiles struck, hammering further into the protective screen until finally one made it through.

As *Fury* raced over the roof, the laser beam faltered for the second and last time.

"Come on, you son of a bitch," Red muttered, palms slick on the controls. "Don't make me look like a bloody idiot again today, come *on!*"

A hundred laser beams lanced up from the crater edges.

Red whooped, jumping in her seat. The main cooling laser was down, shattered once and for all by the barrage of flayer missiles. But the builders of the temple-lab were too clever to trust their lives to one system, even if it did have backup wiring. Scores of smaller lasers were now doing the same job, pumping heat away from the shield and back into space.

Smaller they might have been, but when *Lamarion* followed *Fury* over the dome they carved into its armour like knives.

Red saw the killship falter, its drives stuttering, as the beams ripped into its belly. Manoeuvring thrusters belched flame along the sides, desperately trying to vector away from the lasers, but detonations were already sparking inside the hull. Great pieces of armour were falling away, cut free by the mighty beams, and Red could see fires starting in the open forward section of the ship.

Killships were tough. *Lamarion* would survive, but as a cripple. Red leaned forward in the safety harness and put her forehead against the coolness of the weapons board. "Okay Jude, that's it. Get us back to Haggai. I've got some explaining to do."

They were halfway to Haggai when Sibbecai made contact. "It was a valiant effort, Saint, and a brave fight, but too much for us, I fear."

"My fault," Red told him. "I bit off more than I could chew, and I got a lot of people killed."

"No one blames you."

"They should. I'm the one who cocked it up." She sighed and stretched in the workstation. "Helsa's going to make it, but Cormoran's going to need some new fingers. As soon as we get back to Haggai we can drop them off. How did *Persephone* get on?"

Sibbecai dipped his faceless head. "Not well, Saint. Two killships was one too many. We scored some hits, but they could survive theirs. *Persephone* is a wreck."

Red groaned. "I'm so sorry..."

"All things have their time. Speaking of which, holy one, I have news."

"What kind of news?"

He shrugged. "I suppose that depends on your point of view. Chorazin is now considered too great a security risk by High Command, and is to be shut down immediately.

Inspections of all Archaeotech facilities will be taking place over the next standard year."

Red frowned. "So if they're shutting Chorazin down, where's the time engine going?"

"It took some considerable digging to discover that, Saint. But even if I could not assist you as you deserved on Chorazin, at least I can tell you this. The time engine is being transferred to the lab-station Ascension, on the edge of the Manticore Gulf."

10. ASCENSION

Caliban was in the Chapel of Sight when he received the report, standing below the great circular viewport and gazing silently up into the centre of the Gulf. It was a view he never tired of, even though there was very little he could actually see with unaided eyes. The nearest Bastion vessel was a hundred kilometres away, close enough to see as a definite shape, but little more. Those circling it were just splinters of metal in the darkness, the rest invisible. Thousands of vessels, their formation always shifting, changing, but each holding fast on the perimeter.

And each aiming every weapon and sense-engine they had at the Gulf's heart.

"I know you're there," he breathed. "I can't see you, but I know you are. Do you know I'm here?"

"Lord Heirphant?"

He turned his head, looking back over his shoulder. One of the station's helot-workers was at the Chapel's portal, holding a dataslate.

Caliban returned his gaze to the viewport. "I left orders that I was not to be disturbed, helot. If they did not reach you, there must be a serious fault in my chain of command. What do you think?"

There was a faint whirring of servos from the helot. It was obviously in conflict, unsure of whether to leave or approach. That meant that it was in receipt of conflicting orders.

Whose, apart from his own? Caliban raised a hand. "Come on, then. Let's see it."

The worker paced forward, its footsteps measured and unhurried over the Chapel's tiled floor, and handed the dataslate to him. He glanced at its face as he took it, and saw that it had been a woman once, quite small, her white face smooth and unlined. One of her original eyes remained, looking up at him with a liquid stare, while the other was obscured by a sensory prosthesis. The dome of her hairless skull was more metal than skin.

Caliban frowned. The worker was little more than a girl.

He turned his attention to the slate, but couldn't help wondering what crime this creature had committed to have been subjected to alteration in such a brutal way. "A priority order from High Command," he said, mainly to himself.

The helot tilted her head slightly, servos in her neck whining. Caliban found himself looking at her again, the tip of one finger tapping at the slate's screen. "What is your name?" he asked finally.

"Eighty-seven A."

"What about before? What were you called then?"

The eye blinked, the prosthesis rotated. "I do not remember."

"I see." He tapped the slate again. "I need to read this in private, Eighty-Seven A. Return to your duties."

The helot turned and began to walk away with the same mechanical pace as before. Just before she got to the hatch, Caliban called out. "Helot, wait."

She froze, steadied herself, and waited. Caliban wondered if she was nervous, if there was still room for fear in that eviscerated mind. "Helot, I am likely to be busier than usual in the next few days, and will require assistance in certain tasks. I may call on you again."

"I understand, Lord Heirphant."

"If I do, I shall refer to you as Elu. Now you may go."

Caliban watched her leave, watched the portal slide shut behind her. "By God," he muttered, his eyes still on the door. "What kind of people are we, that we do that to our daughters?"

He turned back to the viewport. "What is it you have made us?"

As soon as he'd read the report, Caliban returned to his quarters. He had offices a few decks below the observation platform, with a small residence attached to them. The walls, under his own orders, had been extensively sound-proofed, mainly so that he could have the peace he required to study or pray. This was also useful, of course, when there were likely to be noises inside his quarters that he didn't want heard by his guards.

Swearing, for example.

Caliban had spent a long time in the Iconoclast forces, and had joined Archaeotech division relatively late. His decades of soldiering had taught him some impressive language, blasphemies and epithets from a dozen separate worlds, and there were few that he didn't use in the minutes after he closed and locked the hatch to his private office.

After the foul language was done, Caliban took a calming breath, mentally reciting the fourth cognitive catechism to calm his mind and still his anger. Then he sat down at his desk and read the report again, just to make sure he had all the facts.

Security inspections he could just about handle. There were procedures he would need to follow, to make sure certain data wasn't openly available, and maybe even a few lies that would need to be told. With care and suitable preparation, the scheduled arrival of Prefect Tullus and his entourage would not cause him undue concern.

Now this. As if being considered a security risk wasn't bad enough, his station now had to play host to the very woman who was the focus of the breach in the first place. Doctor-captain Aura Lydexia was bringing her accursed time engine to Ascension.

Caliban leaned back in his seat and tossed the slate away. Before the intrusions at Chorazin, he had been quite interested in the woman's research, in an abstract manner.

Certainly there were elements of her work on the Salecah
artefact that touched on some of the projects taking place
in Ascension's laboratories, and Lydexia's thesis on
chronoplast emissions was confirmed by much of the
work Caliban oversaw. But to be told by High Command
that she and her technical crew were to be transferred to
Ascension and given the highest priority in terms of lab
space and resources... It was intolerable. Not to mention
extremely inconvenient. Caliban needed to be careful
around Tullus, but the man was an Iconoclast security
officiator, not a scholar. Most of the time he would have
no real idea of what he was seeing on Ascension. Lydexia,
however, was quite a different matter. Caliban would have
to rework most of his data-storage protocols before she
arrived.

She was done in four days, just a week ahead of Prefect
Tullus.

Caliban opened a drawer in his desk and took out a
sheaf of parchment and a long, silver tipped quill. It was
an archaic way of working – most Archaeotechs preferred
to work directly to data-engines Caliban could see the
worth of that, but when there was serious thinking to be
done he really needed a wide desk, some good-quality
parchment and a pen.

He held the pen over the first page for a moment, pon-
dering the first heading, and then slowly put the pen
down. He couldn't, in the time he was allotted, do this
entirely alone. And who aboard this floating construction
could he really trust?

There was a comm-linker built into the desktop. He
pressed a concealed key. "Operations, this is Lord Hierophant General Malchus Caliban."

"Yes, my lord?"

"The helot-worker Eighty-Seven A. What function does
she– Does *it* serve?"

There was a pause, filled with muttering and the tapping of keys. "Menial duties on the observation platform
and sensorium, my lord."

Caliaban steepled his fingers. "Recall it."

"Do you want the helot terminated, my lord? Has it displeased you?"

"On the contrary. Have Eighty-Seven A reworked for administrative duties and sent to my quarters."

The ops manager's reply sounded slightly surprised. "Thy will be done, Lord Heirophant."

"Oh, and one more thing. There may be sensitive information involved. Have it fitted with a data-lock, gold level security."

That would cost, but Caliban could afford it. And, if his suspicions were correct, he would need it badly in the next little while.

The procurement clipper *Vigilant* arrived at Ascension on the morning of the fourth day, just as scheduled. Caliban went down to the docking ring to meet Lydexia as she disembarked. He took Elu with him, partly as an education for his new assistant, but mainly to gauge Lydexia's reaction to the helot. Caliban had always believed that he could tell the most about someone in the shortest time by seeing how they treated their servants.

There were viewports on the ring, big slabs of synthetic diamond set into the walls. Caliban moved close to one as *Vigilant* made its final approach, and motioned Elu to join him. "There," he said to her, pointing. "See that vessel? That's Lydexia's ship."

Elu nodded once, the servos in her neck whining softly. "I understand."

"Remember, say nothing unless addressed directly, but record everything. You may see what I miss, so I'll be relying on you."

"I will not fail you, my lord." The helot's voice was more flowing now, less mechanical. Some of the damage to her brain had been reversible, although much had not. She would never again be truly human, but Caliban had been assured that she was no longer in a state of perpetual suffering.

The clipper slowed to a halt and edged sideways, nudging itself closer to the ring with bursts of its manoeuvring thrusters. Elu saw the ship's flank approaching the window and flinched.

"It's all right," Caliban told her. "They won't hit us."

A series of metallic sounds issued from the wall as the two airlocks met. Caliban listened for the hiss of equalising pressure. "Here she comes. Be ready."

The lock opened, and Aura Lydexia stepped out, flanked by four Custodes guards.

The doctor-captain was a striking woman, slender and fine-boned, her shaved scalp a network of circuit tattoos. She wore full uniform armour and a long coat of soft black leather. As she stepped onto the deck she stopped, saluted Caliban and bowed. "My Lord Heirophant."

"Welcome aboard, doctor-captain. I've heard so much about you."

Lydexia straightened and ran her hand back over her scalp. A nervous gesture. "I can only apologise, my Lord. I know how irregular this is, and how much you must have sacrificed to make room for me. If there had been any other way..."

"High Command was insistent, as was your chapter savant. The lady Gemello is a formidable woman."

"I believe the correct word is 'terrifying'." Lydexia turned to the Custodes on her right, a very tall man with long hair swept back in a tail. "My lord, this is Commander Iamés Hirundo. He'll be my bodyguard while I'm here."

"Of course." Caliban gave the man a nod. "And this is my assistant, Elu."

There was a moment's hesitation, and then Lydexia nodded to the helot. "Pleased to meet you, Elu."

"I am pleased to meet you, doctor-captain," and Elu herself gave a little nod in return.

Inwardly, Caliban smiled. Elu was learning, and Aura Lydexia had passed her first test, although she didn't know it.

The next few days were going to be very interesting.

Lydexia was quartered on the habitation deck. The cell Caliban gave her wasn't large, but it was probably slightly more spacious than what she'd had on Chorazin. Archaeotechs, for some reason, always seemed to find themselves short of space.

Caliban had also managed, at extremely tight notice, to make a laboratory module available for the time engine. The research that had previously gone on in the module was plainly coming to nothing, so Caliban had closed it down: the scholars there would be returning to their temple-lab on Tripolis, their progression through the Archaeotech ranks stalled. The equipment they had been using would follow them a few days later, once it had been properly inspected and any data-crystals wiped clean. At the moment it was stashed in the docking ring's cargo area.

Lydexia brought her belongings over from *Vigilant* personally, everything she owned packed into a small carryall. It would take a small army of helots and technicians to move and install the time engine, but Lydexia and Caliban would only need to supervise the last stages of that process. For the moment, there was little reason for either scholar to stand and watch the packing crates being emptied.

Instead, he decided to show her the observation platform.

Commander Hirundo took it upon himself to thoroughly inspect Lydexia's new cell while she was away. In turn, Caliban had left Elu in his quarters, cataloguing some papers, and Lydexia commented on that when they met. "Won't you require her?"

"She has duties elsewhere," he replied, gesturing towards the open elevator. "Menial tasks of a technical nature, but vital nonetheless. You'd be surprised how much of what I do here is paperwork."

"I'm sure I wouldn't," said Lydexia rather ruefully. She had her share of administration too. She stepped into the elevator, moving to one side as Caliban followed.

The woman was tense, almost on her toes. She wanted to say something, he realised, ask some delicate question, but was afraid to. Her body language was obvious.

Caliban was heartened that his reputation reached far past Ascension's walls.

He reached out and touched a control, sending the elevator on its way. "Speak, doctor-captain. No matter what you've heard, I'm actually quite difficult to offend."

"Forgive me, my lord. But Elu…"

"What about her?"

"It's… It's unusual for someone of your rank to have a helot as a personal assistant. Especially one with a name."

"I gave her the name, just before I had her upgraded." He folded his arms. "It means 'full of grace' in one of humanity's ancient tongues. I thought it apt."

"I see."

"Never underestimate the helots, Lydexia. They were human once, and many retain qualities from their previous existence, even if it does require a trauma-spider to retrieve them. Did you know Elu was just eighteen when she was converted?"

Lydexia shook her head. "I could see she was young."

"She lived on Senprad's Planet, a human world with mutant enclaves. Apparently, her parents discovered her consorting with a mutant. One that was very nearly human, but that made no difference to them. They handed her over for the process themselves."

The doctor-captain gaped at him. "What? My God, their own child?"

"Makes you proud to be human, doesn't it?" The lift chimed and slowed to a halt, its doors parting. "Ah, here we are."

He stepped out and led Lydexia onto the observation platform.

Her reaction was rather as he had expected. As far as his research on her could discover, she had lived most of her life on Chorazin, cooped up in the halls and chambers nestling beneath the heat shield. To find herself on an open deck almost half a kilometre across must have been something of a shock.

He gestured her forwards, and together they began to walk into the centre of the platform. The outer rings of workstations were on raised decks above their heads, but there was little that she should see there. Everything that she needed to know about Ascension would be found in the centre.

Even from here, halfway between the core stations and the outer wall, the main holo-displays were vast. They filled the air above the platform's centre, huge globes of gridded light orbiting the cylindrical data-core, and each with dozens of smaller holo-displays orbiting them. It was like a compressed solar system, each world wrought from hazy threads of colour, attended by fleets of tiny moons.

Caliban pointed at the nearest globe. It was filled with a single holographic model, a misshapen dumbbell bisected by a flat circular shield and topped with a huge parabolic dish. "As you can see, this is the main monitoring station for Ascension itself. The docking ring you arrived at is down here, just above the reactor block. Those spines at the far end are the sensorium."

"Amazing," Lydexia breathed. "My lord, correct me if I'm wrong, but the upper part of the structure is familiar. A monitoring station?"

"That's right. When the Bastion was first deployed, thirty long range sensor stations were installed just outside the perimeter. Most of them were decommissioned in later decades, but Archaeotech division petitioned High Command to have one modified for our own uses. We added the spindle, moved the reactor block and the docking ring to the end of it, and built the shield between."

"To protect the sensorium."

He nodded. "Emissions from the reactor were always going to be a problem with a sensorium as sensitive as ours. Even docking starships can force a recalibration."

Lydexia began to move around the core, looking sometimes at the circling globes above her head, sometimes at
the screens and holopanels on the workstations below.
Caliban followed her, watching carefully, seeing where
her attentions lay.

She stopped, indicating another globe. "This is the Bastion itself."

"Well observed." The globe was empty, but for a single
indicator at its centre. But its surface was studded with
icons. "Ten thousand vessels, spaced evenly over the
perimeter of the Gulf. We monitor their formation
changes from here."

"Do you communicate with them?"

Caliban shook his head. "It's proscribed, by Patriarchal
decree. No one's spoken to them in a hundred years. They
are only ever re-supplied by helot ships, and they are
vaporised the moment their duties are complete."

Lydexia looked aghast. "What about the crews? How
long have they been in there?"

"No one knows." He spread his hands. "We are forbidden to make any kind of contact with them. As far as we
can gather, they still have active crews, because the formation changes always occur as scheduled."

"That's horrible." The woman had gone even more pale
than usual. "My Lord, the Gulf is half a light-year across.
At such a range, how could the Bastion be contaminated?"

"Ask High Command. Or His Holiness, if you could ever
get his attention." Caliban sighed. "This is a forgotten
backwater of the universe, doctor-captain. The Accord
has spread away from the Gulf like water from grease. The
only reason we are tolerated at all is because we get
results."

"I see."

"No," Caliban told her. "Not yet, you don't."

He took her to the Chapel of Sight. The elevator that took
them there was faced with panels of transpex, and the
gantry that held the Chapel had been left mainly open. It

gave a perfect view of the interior of the sensorium as they rose through it, a vast forest of towers and spines, some a hundred metres high or more.

"I've been reading up on you, doctor-captain," Caliban told her when they were halfway up the gantry. "Your body of work is quite impressive."

"Thank you, Lord Heirophant." She dipped her head demurely. "I'm sure that's simply because there are so few others working in this field. Chronotechnology is a less than a lost art, even to other Archaeotechs. Most regard it as superstitious folly."

"Well, that's not how it's seen here." Caliban gazed out through the sensorium. The elevator was already above the lowest spires, and more of the open blackness of space could be seen between those that remained. "We pick up chronoplast emissions every day. Your work and ours goes hand in hand."

"My Lord, there are very few who see this chapter as you do. After Xystus, I'm surprised they even gave me a room, let alone a place to work."

Caliban glanced across at her. "I noted a mention of an incident on Xystus. What happened?"

"Nothing." She shook her head sadly. "There was a massive emission, and I persuaded a senior scholar at Chorazin to run a procurement there. When we arrived, there was nothing, just a chronoplast wave, and nothing to account for it."

"No signs?"

She shrugged. "Very little. An imprint in the sand, just a square about a metre and a half on a side, and some footprints. I have scans of the site, of course, but they reveal nothing."

"And yet here you are..." The elevator was above the highest sensorium spire now, and Caliban caught a fleeting glimpse of pure, uninterrupted space before they reached the Chapel.

The doors parted, and they stepped through the portal and into the Chapel of Sight.

"I come here often," he told her. "Sometimes just to look at this place with my own eyes." He pointed upwards, stretching his arm towards the ceiling. "There, in the centre of the viewport. That's the closest Bastion ship. I can see its drive bells from here, but I don't even know its name."

"And the Manticore?"

"Ah." Caliban lowered his arm and grinned. "For that, you need better eyes."

There was a bank of video panels ranged against one of the Chapel walls. He strode over to them and keyed them on with his crypt disc. Each brightened with a burst of static, followed by a clear picture.

The largest, a metre wide hexagon in the centre of the array, showed the Manticore.

It was a dark, glossy globe of black metal, strangely faceted, as though it had been built in layers, with each surface slightly less complete than the last. Light showed through the fissures and chasms in its shell, myriad points of blue glare, and facing slightly away from Ascension was a vast, shallow crater, glowing dull orange from within, smoothly complex like a series of concentric lenses.

The Manticore looked like a mechanical eye, gazing up and away.

"Two hundred years it's been there," Caliban breathed. "It just appeared, destroyed a fleet of Iconoclast warships without even trying, devastated twenty worlds... and then just stopped. It's been here ever since, and so has the Bastion."

"My God," Lydexia muttered. "What manner of devilry is that thing?"

"Whatever it is, it's our reason for being here, doctor-captain. I've been studying that bastard for thirty years, and my father before me, and just when you think it's dead, that it's got no more to tell you, it twitches. Moves a few hundred metres, turns itself around, and our research goes into overdrive once more." He left the screen and paced back to gaze through the viewport ceiling once more. "It's a treasure box, the greatest source of temporal technology in the universe, and all we can do is sit out here and listen to it snore."

He left Lydexia to go back to her quarters while returning to his own. Elu was there, diligently sorting through parchments and data-crystals, just as he had left her.

He went to the desk and sat down. "Elu, you may stop and rest. Aren't you tired?"

"I will not need to feed-recharge for six hours, my Lord."

"Stop anyway." He put his elbows on the desktop and rested his head in his hands. "She's dangerous, Elu."

"The doctor-captain?" Elu stood up carefully, the servos in her hips and knees whining faintly in the silent office. "Is she a threat to your safety?"

"Very probably. We're going to have to bury those files deeper than I thought. Her research is going to come worryingly close to mine."

"Command me, my lord."

Caliban didn't speak immediately. He lifted his head and sat back, steepling his fingers thoughtfully. "What do you know," he asked after a time, "about Saint Scarlet of Durham?"

"The Blasphemy, my lord. The arch-mutant, enemy of all humankind."

"Do you fear her?"

Elu had to think about that one. Caliban tried not to hear the soft clicking of relays under that metal scalp as she interrogated her own brain. "Yes," she said finally. "I fear her."

"Well, thanks to Aura Lydexia, she's here. A version of her, anyway." Caliban scowled to himself, thinking about the frozen corpse she'd brought onboard. At the moment it was being held in a hazardous waste store down on the lab deck, but if Caliban had his choice he'd feed the thing into the nearest fusion furnace and be done with it.

And what of the real Durham Red? By the sound of things, she had an interest in the time engine too, just as her dead duplicate must have done.

It was an intriguing mystery, but right now Caliban needed no such thing. People with mysteries to solve tended to go digging in dangerous places.

He would have to watch Aura Lydexia very carefully indeed

11. OVERLOAD

"He's late," said Durham Red.

"He's an Iconoclast Prefect," replied Godolkin. "Of course he's late."

They were on the bridge of *Omega Fury*, along with Judas Harrow. As usual, Godolkin was in the pilot's throne, while Red took the weapons station and the sharp-eyed Harrow handled the sensors. It was an arrangement they had become used to since taking control of the ship, with each of the three companions playing pretty much to their strengths.

Any one of them could have swapped, as Harrow had so ably proved back at Chorazin, but it felt comfortable to fall into a pattern, and there were times when Red would take any comfort she could find.

"According to the schedule," said Harrow, "he should have decelerated just over an hour ago. Could he have changed course?"

"There're other supply dumps," Red muttered glumly. "He could have gone to any one of them. I think we've missed him."

"Should we leave?"

"And go where?" Red glared at her forward holoscreen, willing it to show the flare of a jump-point. "We'll never get near Ascension if we don't do it like this. I mean, it took us two days just to get next to this place, and Ascension's one big listening post."

"Stationed next to the biggest Iconoclast fleet in history," said Harrow. "You have a point."

Thanks to some very careful flying by Godolkin, *Fury* had managed to approach the Quadrata supply dump without being detected, but it had been slow going. The dump was a town sized amalgam of fuel refinery and ammunition store, studded with weapons turrets, and constantly patrolled by a small fleet of killships. Even with the shadow web engaged, Quadrata's controllers would have picked up any hint of a drive burn, so Godolkin had been forced to decelerate from superlight well out of detection range and then coast in. Only when the ship had been a mere hundred metres from the dump's flank had he risked using the manoeuvring thrusters to slow down.

It had been a long, tense flight. Now all they could do was sit and wait, while killships circled just a few hundred kilometres away.

Godolkin sighed. "Remain calm, mutants. Tullus is an Iconoclast Prefect, which tells us several things about him. He will not change his course, because to do so would mean deviating from his original plan, and he lacks the imagination to make such a decision. He will be late, because he will consider it his privilege to make others wait for him. And he will decelerate to re-supply, even if it is not strictly necessary, because he lives in mortal terror of running out of anything."

"Blimey." Red raised her eyebrows. "Sounds like the people I used to work for."

Harrow nodded. "I think most people in the Accord have worked for someone like that. Hello, what's this?"

Red checked her holos. "I'm not picking anything up. What are you looking at?"

"That," said Harrow, as a jump-point billowed into existence ahead of them.

It looked like an explosion at first, a crimson fireball expanding into the blackness, but as Red watched, the centre of it inverted, twisted and sucked itself back like the eye of a tornado. And from the midst of that storm came a starship.

A slab of grey metal two kilometres long erupted into realspace, racing as it left the jump-point, but instantly slowing, its speed dropping to nothing in seconds. That was an illusion, Red knew, a by product of the way light behaved in jumpspace. If the ship had really slowed down that fast the crew would have been smeared over the forward bulkheads.

"Okay, we're good to go." Red checked her instruments as the Iconoclast ship edged close to Quadrata's flank. "We'll move when they start taking the supplies across."

Tullus's ship, the *Phaselis*, wasn't all that big by Iconoclast standards, and Quadratas was an efficient installation. It took only an hour to restock *Phaselis* and top up the fuel load.

Not long after that, the ship opened up another jump-point and accelerated towards Ascension. When it did so, it was carrying somewhat more in the way of crew and equipment than Prefect Tullus might have expected.

Red had spent a productive two days while *Fury* had drifted towards Quadrata. She had spent the time poring over Iconoclast histories from the ship's data engines, learning as much as she could about Ascension.

Although she was no history buff, there was a lot in the story of the lab station that she found interesting.

Ascension's history had begun a little under two hundred years earlier, back in 627YA, when an alien object of tremendous destructive power had appeared, without warning, in orbit around the planet Kentyris Secundus. An Iconoclast fleet had been issued to deal with it, thinking it was some new mutant weapon, but the object had despatched them with ease. It then proceeded to devastate Kentyris Secundus and twenty inhabited worlds around it, killing over eight billion people, before retreating to an area of open space.

Apart from minor changes in position, it had been there ever since.

The object had been codenamed "Manticore" by the fleets that had first engaged it – just a random word used to designate a target. The name had stuck, to the point that the empty, lifeless area of space around the object was now known as the Manticore Gulf. A fleet of ten thousand Iconoclast warships surrounded the Manticore, watching continually for any sign that it might be ready to move into further inhabited areas and slaughter their peoples too. Although it was debatable that even that enormous fleet could do anything more than slow the object down.

Over the years, the Manticore had been forgotten by most of the Accord. It was left to sleep behind its wall of starships, invulnerable, implacable, utterly mysterious. If any ship or probe passed within a thousand kilometres of the Manticore, it was instantly destroyed. Any further, and it was ignored.

Just to be safe, the Bastion ships remained one-quarter of a light-year from the Manticore at all times.

If it hadn't been for the Archaeotechs and their obsession with lost technologies, no one but the Bastion would be in the vicinity at all. There was something about the Manticore that they were interested in, interested enough for them to rebuild an old sensor-station into a fully equipped research base, and leave it in the middle of nowhere for fifty years.

Of all the other Archaeotech temple-labs in the Accord that was where High Command had sent the time engine.

It could only mean one thing. Somehow, the Manticore had a link with time travel.

Omega Fury rode *Phaselis* all the way to Ascension, latched under its port drive nacelle with the shadow web running. By the time she got there, Red was beginning to get very worried about the amount of continuous time the web had been on. "It wasn't built for that kind of treatment," she told Harrow as she was putting the vacuum shroud on over her clothes. "You're going to have to give the thing a rest, or it'll burn out and take the power core with it."

"It's not the shadow web I'm worried about, holy one." Harrow was with her in the staging area, checking the shroud's seals. It wasn't something he needed to do – the shroud was built so that one person could get in and out of it quite easily on their own. Red was going to end up doing that on the way back anyway, should everything go according to plan. "We should be with you."

"Jude, the last time I went after this thing I went in mob-handed, and messed up badly. I've got to do this on my own."

"It's suicide."

"I'm not the suicidal type." She put her gloved hand on his shoulder. "Come on, remember your own paradox. If the Iconoclasts got the time engine working in the future they would have wiped us out already, so that means there's still a chance to frag the thing."

Harrow looked exasperated. "Do you honestly believe that?"

"No," she smiled, "but the longer I keep trying to work it out, the less time I've got to think about how scared I am."

There was a burst of static from the internal comms, followed by Godolkin's voice. "Mistress, the *Phaselis* is holding position."

"Great," Red called back. "Remember, nudge us away at the same time as the shuttle comes out. That should mask the manoeuvring thrusters."

"Your will."

Red flipped the shroud's helmet on over her head and sealed it, making sure her long hair was tucked down inside. The shroud was an awful thing to wear, a great bag of vacuum proof fabric-metal with gloved sleeves, legs with integral boots and a windowed bulge for a helmet. She had worn one before, when she had been trying to get aboard Xandos Dathan's planet killer, and had found it a trial then as well.

At least the shroud's generous proportions enabled her to carry a full complement of equipment over, and not have to stash it in a separate container.

The deck gave a sudden lurch, and Godolkin spoke again. "Blasphemy, we are clear. Be ready to leave."

"Notice how quickly he switches from 'Mistress' to 'Blasphemy'?" Red shifted about inside the shroud, feeling its weight drag at her. "Like he doesn't even regard calling me Blasphemy as an insult any more. I wonder what's going on inside that bloke's head, sometimes."

"Only darkness," said Harrow. His voice sounded flat and distorted through the shroud's sound system. "So hurry back."

"I'll bring you a piece of time engine," she grinned, and waddled over to the docking hatch.

Fury had three airlocks: a docking hatch on either side of the pressure cylinder and a larger lock chamber that only deployed when the landing spine was down. Red opened the hatch and clambered inside, making sure she was standing in the centre of the chamber. She didn't want to be pushed off balance when the pressure dropped.

The hatch swung closed behind her and locked. Red tried her comms. "Godolkin, do you hear me?"

"I do. Are you in the airlock?"

"Yeah. Harrow's equalising now..." She broke off as the lock chamber filled with a loud hissing. The pressure system was quickly drawing the air from it. In response, Red's vacuum shroud began to swell up.

In moments she was standing wrapped in a grey, metallic balloon. Moving her arms against its internal pressure wasn't hard, but the shroud's material had a tendency to spring them out to her sides again whenever she relaxed. The same went for her legs, and no matter how she moved her head the shroud's helmet stayed resolutely forwards.

"Sneck me," she growled. "This had better be a stealth mission. I'll die of embarrassment if anyone sees me like this..."

Godolkin's voice crackled through the comms again. "It's time, Blasphemy. I've tried to orientate *Fury* so that a jump from the lock will take you directly towards Ascension, but it will be up to you to locate the access hatch and get in."

"No problem. And remember, get *Fury* to a safe distance as soon as you can, and shut that bloody web down. You'll need it working if this all goes pear-shaped again." Although, Red thought as soon as she had spoken, the only thing really pear-shaped around here is this space suit.

She reached out and keyed the hatch open. It slid aside, and suddenly Red was looking into deep space.

There was an object right ahead of her, a dumbbell shaped cluster of cylinders made from flat, grey metal. It was hard to make out any details on it, because there were no stars close by, and so the only light that shone on it came from lumes on the object itself. It looked small, and close enough to reach out and grab.

An illusion of scale. Ascension was two kilometres from the blunt reactor housing to the cluster of towers and spines that formed the sensorium, and it was turning. Or rather, *Fury* was turning, its thruster burst taking it away from *Phaselis*, but giving it a slight spin at the same time. If Red waited much longer she could end up being rotated in completely the wrong direction.

"Now or never." She jumped.

Instantly, she was turning. She had given herself a good push away from the airlock, but the force her legs had applied could never be completely even. The stars began to arch slowly around her, taking Ascension with them. The shroud had a small thruster pack for corrective manoeuvres, but there was no way Red could risk using it. She didn't have a shadow web.

All she could do was wait, and spin, while the dark grey shape grew slowly larger.

It took a long time. The spin she had given herself took her, after about ten minutes, completely around until she was facing the wrong way. She tried to make out where *Fury* was, so perhaps she would feel a little less alone, but there was no way to see it. Every now and then her eyes would pick up a faint distortion in the stars, but they were probably just imperfections in the shroud's faceplate.

In another ten minutes she was facing Ascension again, and now it was like looking at a building. She could see panel lines and welds, the faint variations in colour where steel patches had been fixed over meteor holes. After another few minutes she began to make out external cabling.

She checked her course and realised that she was going to miss the station by a good hundred metres if she didn't do something. The thruster pack made little jumping movements against her back when she fired it, and although she couldn't hear it, her spin lessened.

According to *Fury*'s data files on this class of sensor station, there would be an engineering access hatch just under the big parabolic dish. Red fired the thrusters again, nudging her further along Ascension's spindle, and passed over the centre shield so close she could almost touch it.

The dish was very close now. If she hit that, someone would hear it. She made one last burn, dropped towards the shadows, and hit the spindle face first.

The access hatch wasn't where it was supposed to be, but it didn't take Red long to find it, which was a good thing, because by that time she was thoroughly sick of being inside the shroud.

She stripped it off and stashed it inside the access lock's chamber, behind some piping. If anyone tried to use the lock they would see it straight away, but Red was hoping to be long gone before anyone came this way again.

Along with the particle magnum, she had brought a trauma kit, a dataslate with a partial schematic of the station in its memory, a needle gun and the data-pick. The slate, however, only had a map of the station as it had been before the Archaeotechs had converted it, and as such turned out to be a lot less useful than Red had hoped. For example, it didn't show what the series of armoured modules at the base of the dish were, or what was in the spindle, or why the docking ring was so far away from the habitation decks. It made no sense.

Eventually she gave up looking at it, and ventured into the station with only instinct to trust.

The direction of gravity in Ascension was just as Red would have expected, with the reactor "down" and the sensorium "up". There were banks of elevators close by the access lock, and she was able to get into one without being spotted. Once there, she took a few seconds to examine the controls, and picked up some clues that way.

On the plus side, she could now see that the modules she had spotted earlier were laboratory blocks, which sounded hopeful. On the minus, even getting the elevator to stop on those decks would require an authorised crypt-disc.

Or a data-pick.

Red was able to find the time engine simply by following the chaos.

The device was obviously still being set up, which was hardly surprising. It had been here, along with whatever Archaeotechs had been in charge of it, for little more than eleven days. To install something as complex and danger-ous as a time machine was never going to be just a matter of unpacking it from the crate and plugging it in.

There were six modules around the spindle, each one wedge shaped and unconnected from the others past a circular, linking corridor. Red could see the value in that: if one of the experiments got out of hand and seemed likely to explode, its module could be jettisoned entirely. It would be hard luck on anyone inside it at the time, but could save the rest of the station.

For a time Red wondered if she should simply rig up the time engine's module to break free, and then blast it from

Fury when it was loose, but she quickly discarded the idea. She would never get back to the ship before the alarm was raised, and *Fury* would be shredded as soon as it tried to open fire. The Bastion was very close.

No, it would have to be destroyed from the inside.

Red moved around the circular corridor. It was of typical Iconoclast design, looking as if it would have been more at home in a cathedral than a space station. Arching braces were set every few metres, each one ornately carved, and the lumes between them shed a dull, bluish light onto the tiled floor below. The doors leading into the modules were wide double hatches cast from black iron, studded with rivets and warning plaques bearing brushed steel skulls, and their control panels were formed to look very much like church windows.

In terms of design it was hardly secure. Red was halfway around the corridor when one of the hatches began to slide open, but it was so ponderous and heavy that she had ample time to duck back and squeeze herself behind a brace. Her outfit – a fabric-metal bustier and skin-tight leather trousers – was black from head to foot, partly for stealth, but mainly because it looked good on her. Against the dark grey of the station's interior she blended in quite effectively, so much so that the man who exited the hatchway walked right past her without even knowing she was there.

It was the only time Red had to hide in the corridor. The next time she came across an open hatch, it was surrounded by empty packing material.

Red put her head around the doorframe and then drew back. There were at least four people in the room, and one of them was a Custodes trooper. He was talking to a slender, bald woman in black leather robes, while two drably clothed workers stood amidst a swarming nest of cables.

The woman was talking.

"He's up to something," she was saying. "Him and that modified helot of his. They've locked me out of so much data I can barely work."

"Are you sure it's not just station security? You are new here, and with the inspections tomorrow…"

"No, that fool Tullus wouldn't even know where to begin. This is technical data, Hirundo, station-wide power schematics. If he's so worried about security, why can I read full reports on the other experiments, but can't get hold of a simple power diagram?"

"Like what?" His voice was coming from a different direction now. He must have walked across the lab. "What *are* they doing here?"

"There's a discontinuity drive being built in the next module. The Manticore uses something like that to move around, tapping into the imbalances between realspace and jumpspace and just skating between them. There's a new communications array, although that's not working well. Oh, and some kind of temporal bomb, would you believe?"

"Weapons research? Here?" The Custodes was approaching the door. Red edged away, drawing the needle gun. "You're right, I don't like the sound of this either. I'll start making enquiries."

"Thank you, commander."

"Goodnight, doctor-captain. Don't work those helots too hard."

She laughed. "It's what they're for, but don't tell Caliban that."

The Custodes stepped out of the hatch. Red had moved behind a brace, but the Iconoclast whirled about immediately, reaching for the bolter slung at his side. Red was faster, bringing the needler up and sending a sheaf of splinters into his face and neck. The man opened his mouth, gave a wheezing gasp and folded forward.

Red was in through the hatch before his body had struck the floor, keying it closed and then scrambling the crypt-lock with the data-pick.

She had been fast, seconds at most. The woman in the black robes only noticed she was there when the pick chirruped its completion.

Red snapped the needler up and aimed it at her face. "Don't make a bloody sound," she snarled.

She glanced quickly around her. The two workers – helots, the Custodes had called them – were still toiling away as if nothing was wrong. The woman was over to the right of the lab, standing at a cluster of portable workstations, her face white with shock. The time engine, already fixed onto a new tower, was over against the far wall, surrounded by cables and power feeds. It wasn't moving.

Red drew the magnum with her free hand and waved it at the helots. "Okay you two, break time. Go and stand over there."

Neither made any indication that she had spoken. They remained bent over their work, the metal plates set into their skulls gleaming dully in the lab's dim light. "Hey! Tweedle-dumb and Tweedle-dumber."

"They're keyed to my voice-print, monster," the woman hissed. "They can't obey you."

"Well bloody tell them to get over there, then."

"Very well." She took a step backwards, edging away from the workstations, then shouted. "Helots! Kill the Blasphemy!"

Both helots snapped their heads up simultaneously. The lens arrays they had in place of eyes whirred, their bolted shut jaws worked soundlessly. They dropped the cables they had been working on and dived towards Red.

The workers were fast, and mechanically precise. Red got one shot off, a blast of charged particles that ripped the arm from one of the helots, but the wound didn't slow it. They struck her at the same time, bowling her over backwards.

She hit the wall hard, losing the needler. The helots pressed their attack, three hands reaching to tear her face. She batted them away, managing to duck sideways and get under their next attack, but they followed her all the way around.

It was like fighting machines. They had no instinct for their own preservation, just a programmed desire to rip her open.

Red dropped into a fighting crouch, then leapt sideways and kicked out as the first helot reached her. The toe of her boot caught it solidly in the head, flinging it over. It rolled to a halt among the cables, limbs flailing, sparks and fluid spitting from the side of its skull.

The second one, unbalanced by the loss of its arm, ran right into Red's fist. She punched it hard in the face, feeling a flare of pain as her knuckles met something a lot harder than bone under that white skin. Instead of the second punch she had been readying, she grabbed at the helot's throat, her fingers and thumb clawing into a lethal grip.

The helot reached for her wrist with its one remaining hand, but it wasn't strong enough. Red ripped back, coming away with a handful of flesh and metal hoses. The worker sank to its knees, spitting blood and breath from the wound, and twisted away onto the deck.

Red dropped the handful next to the convulsing worker, then turned to see the bald woman trying to get the hatch open. "Oh, for sneck's sake!"

She walked quickly over to the hatch, grabbed the woman's shaven head and bounced it off the metal. The Iconoclast sagged like a loose sack, crumpling among her robes.

The lab was suddenly quiet. One of the helots had stopped moving, the other was twitching fitfully. Red ignored them and trotted over to the time engine.

There was a circular area around the base of its tower that looked to Red as though it was due to be fitted with some kind of shield, and curved gantries curled up and around it like grasping talons coming up through the deck. The tower was lower here than in the lightning vault, and plainly rigged from a variety of materials. Whatever experiments the Archaeotechs planned here, they were still a long way from completion.

Red stood at the base of the tower for some time, then walked back into the lab. She raised the magnum, aimed carefully along the top of the barrel, and put a shot directly into the heart of the engine.

The bolt struck dead on, and caromed way with a deafening snarl. Behind Red, a workstation blew itself to fragments.

"Bloody hell!" Red ducked as chunks of metal and ceramic whipped past, streaking tracks of smoke through the air. The magnum bolt hadn't marked the time engine, hadn't even marred its liquid finish. It had reflected back with the same, if not more, power than it had left the barrel with.

Red looked back at the workstation, which was burning fitfully, sending a column of greasy smoke towards the ceiling. If there was one thing she wasn't going to do, she decided, it was fire at the engine again.

There had to be another way. She went back to the tower and began scanning the cables fixed into it. The power leads were obvious from their colouring and the warnings around their sockets on the tower base, but there were a host of others – data-feeds and pulse-monitors, links to sense-engines and crystal recorders. It was a maze.

It made sense.

Amazingly, Red found herself looking at the swarm of ducts and wires and knowing what they meant. Not from what she could see – the Iconoclast wiring protocols were fairly impenetrable – but from the way they connected to the time engine itself.

She reached up into the tower's guts and tugged one of the cables free. Something inside her, some distant part of her mind that she could access directly, knew what to do.

No. She *remembered* what to do.

One day, she would build this machine. In the timeline, the reality where she would become Brite Red, she would design the time engine from scratch, knowing it could be built, remembering, from this moment, how it should be wired. Which cables were the primary power feeds, which were the secondary voltage regulators, where the data inputs needed to be.

It was all clear to her, in a hazy, baffled way.

Red began to pull the cables free, twisting them hard to unlock them. She swapped three of the power feeds, rerouted the data into a feedback loop that would prevent the engine modifying its own energy supply, found a kilovolt socket and plugged a gigavolt feed into it. She worked fast, at times almost letting her eyes close. Trusting, as she so often did, to pure instinct.

By the time she'd finished, the woman on the floor was beginning to stir. Red thought idly about biting her, but decided against it. There really wasn't time.

She trotted over to the workstations. Apart from the one that was on fire, the rest were active. Red set up a command chain, looped it and hit the key to initiate the power feed. Then she put her fingers under the edge of the control board and pulled hard.

The board came up in pieces. Red pulled them free of their cable and hurled them away, then glanced back at the time engine.

It was starting to turn.

She grinned. The device would power itself up with a series of completely incorrect voltages, realise its mistake too late and then try to vent the power away, but the paths it would normally send the excess power to were rerouted back into its own sensors. The machine was doomed. It was going to blow itself to atoms and there wasn't a bloody thing anyone could do about it.

The bald woman was dragging herself into a corner. Red stopped on her way back to the hatch, picked up the needler and then went over to the woman, crouching next to her. "Hi," she said.

"Drink me if you have to, monster," she spat back, "but take it all. Don't enslave me like the heretic."

Red chuckled. "You really have got me all wrong, you know that?"

"Devil!"

"Oh, whatever. I just thought I'd let you know that your precious time machine's going to explode in about twenty minutes. So if I were you, I'd drag my sorry arse out of this lab and jettison it before it hurts anyone, okay?" She straightened up. "I'm going home."

There was more from the woman as Red left – threats, curses – but she didn't listen. There were more important things to think about now. She unscrambled the lock with the data-pick and opened the hatch, stepping out into the corridor.

The Custodes she had shot were gone.

Red paused. Either someone had found the man and dragged his body away, or Iconoclasts were more immune to the toxin in those needles than she had thought.

Both scenarios were equally bad. Red picked up the pace and began to run along the corridor. The sooner she was away from this place the better.

12. DISCONTINUITY

The Blasphemy was gone by the time Lydexia managed to get up. The blow the monster had given her had set Lydexia's head spinning, and her stomach threatened to rebel at any second. She was probably concussed.

It could, however, have been far worse. The first thing Lydexia had done upon waking, even before trying to get to her feet, had been to check her neck for puncture marks.

There were none. Then again, from what she had seen on the frozen corpse of Durham Red's duplicate, the vampire was not so careful when she fed. If Lydexia had lost blood to her, she would likely have lost half her throat in the process.

She looked around her, willing her eyes to start focusing properly. The two helots were dead, although not all their mechanical enhancements knew it yet. There was no sign of Hirundo. And the time engine...

The time engine was rotating on the top of the tower.

Lydexia ran to the workstations, batting away acrid smoke from the one that was on fire. The others told her a dire story – the engine was rigged, very effectively, to detonate when it reached emission point. Should anyone be in the lab with it when that happened, it would be even betting whether they would die by the unstable time wave which would hit them when the time engine reached critical, or by the explosion that would occur a microsecond later.

The real pity of it was that, by studying what changes the monster had made to the wiring, Lydexia could learn more about how to set up the time engine for correct operation than she otherwise could in a month of research.

That time, however, was gone. Lydexia stumbled over to the hatch, stepped over the threshold and keyed the locking pad.

Nothing happened.

She tried again, with the same results. Woozily, she crouched next to the pad, and by getting her swimming eyes close to the panel realised that the lights behind it were out. There was no power getting to the lock.

Suddenly, all the strength went out of Lydexia. She didn't have the energy to get up, to lie down, to speak. All she wanted to do at that moment was to stay there on her haunches, lean her head against the pad and let the universe go by without her. She was still there, a minute or two later, when a squad of Custodes troopers hammered along the corridor.

They stopped a few metres away. Lydexia looked around, squinting, and saw that they had bolters levelled at her. One of them looked a lot like Hirundo.

"Are you injured, doctor-captain?" he asked, his voice very level.

"She didn't bite me."

"Are you sure?"

"Hirundo, my throat's intact, even if my skull isn't. She hit me and rigged the time engine to explode while I was unconscious."

She heard him approach, carefully, and felt his gloved hands at her neck. She closed her eyes and let him tilt her head this way and that. "See?"

"She's clear." Hirundo stood up. "Fan out. Find that bitch and burn her."

The troopers scrambled away. Lydexia felt Hirundo's hand under her arm, drawing her upright again. "How long?" he asked.

"Less than twenty minutes, if she told me the truth."

"She spoke to you?" Hirundo sounded horrified.

Lydexia nodded, an action that set her brain bobbing in her skull. "She warned me about the explosion. Don't ask why, I don't know. Now something's happened to the door. I can't close it."

"What will happen?"

"If I can't stop it, either the chronoplast emissions or the explosion will kill everyone on this station."

Hirundo found Lydexia a trauma kit and injected her with a good dose of war-balm. Moments later, her vision cleared, and the pain in her head was replaced by a strange, airy coolness. Lydexia knew that the injuries weren't gone, just masked, but at least she could think straight again.

If the situation couldn't be resolved, it wouldn't matter anyway.

She returned to the workstation. Outside in the corridor people ran and shouted, Archaeotechs leaving their labs and bolting for the docking ring. She doubted if many would make it. The elevators could only take a small number at a time, and they weren't fast. Caliban had set their speed low to avoid jolting the sensorium.

"Fifteen minutes," she said, "or thereabouts. In God's name, where did she get the knowledge to do this?"

"That creature is capable of anything," Hirundo replied. "She's been trying to get to the time engine ever since Chorazin. The duplicate... There is a connection, I'm just not sure what it is."

"If we live past the next fourteen minutes, I'll buy you an ale and we can sit down and work it out together." Lydexia tapped out a command chain on an intact workstation. "Damn it. I can't access the program."

"Can we repair this machine?" He gestured at the station the Blasphemy had wrecked, but Lydexia shook her head.

"Not in time."

"Then we are lost."

"When the last minute passes," she snarled. "I'll not let that bitch thwart me. I worked too hard for this."

She moved away from the workstation and closed her eyes. It took three breaths for the calming effects to start, so great was her distress, and the cognitive catechisms didn't come easily. But the techniques slowly battered through her anxiety and anger, until she was finally able to still her mind, take control of her own thoughts, her own heartbeat.

Lydexia entered a computational trance.

The cabling of the time engine flowed out into her mind's eye, spreading until she could see more clearly what changes had been wrought. The time engine's momentum was already self-sustaining, she could see that now, well past the point where merely cutting it off from its power would have any effect other than a massive, catastrophic release of chronoplasts. If she severed any of the cables, even unplugged them to reverse what the monster had done, she would initiate the emission point and kill everyone on board Ascension.

But why wouldn't the door close?

She went deeper, trawling her own memories. It was a power fault, she realised, a function of the way the engine was wired. Electricity that should have been going to the hatch was being routed elsewhere, which made her wonder how the monster had got out of the lab in the first place.

Something here was very, very wrong.

Lydexia snapped awake and threw a glance over to the workstation. The trance had lasted for no more than thirty seconds.

She took her comm-linker from her belt and called Caliban. "My Lord Hierophant."

"Doctor-captain, I'm getting reports of a disaster down there. What's happening?"

"Sir, I have little time to explain. Durham Red is on this station, and she has sabotaged the time engine. Unless I can get the lab door closed and the module jettisoned in the next eleven minutes, Ascension will become a coffin."

"I'll get a tech-team down to you."

"My lord, there isn't time! I need the complete power-schematic of Ascension, uploaded to me here at the lab. There must be a reason why the power-routing has jammed the door, but I can't tell without that diagram."

"Very well," he replied. "I'll send that to you immediately. I leave this matter in your hands, doctor-captain."

Lydexia frowned. "What are you going to do?"

"Find that bloodsucking bitch and slaughter her where she stands."

"Best of luck," grated Lydexia, but she made sure the linker was off when she said it.

In terms of the power schematic, Caliban was as good as his word. The diagram came through to Lydexia's workstation less than a minute later. She began to scan it visually, at the same time running it through Ascension's data-engines, pulsing virtual packets of electricity through it to see where they went.

There was no answer.

Nothing in the schematics told her any reason why the door might have failed. Nothing the Blasphemy had done should have caused it. In fact, it appeared that the monster had been quite careful to leave any unconnected systems alone. Purely to further her own escape, obviously.

"There's nothing we can do," she told Hirundo after a minute or two. "There's no way to get the door closed. Even if we had enough time to lift the deck and get to the cabling there, the safety locks have engaged."

"Safety locks?"

"To avoid anyone being trapped in a compartment." She stepped back from the workstation, running her hand back over her scalp. "There's no way to halt the reaction, or to protect ourselves from it. Back in the lightning vault we had a forcewall, and we had..."

She trailed off. Hirundo tilted his head, aware that she must have been working something out, and unwilling to distract her.

"Dampers," she said finally. "I vented the power into a set of dreadnought class dampers."

"But there are no dampers installed here."

She shook her head. "I know, but there might be something else."

Her fingers flew over the workstation keys, making the machine's relays chatter wildly; it had probably never been worked so hard and so fast before. Lydexia didn't much care about that, as long as the machine could run at her pace for the next six minutes. "All right, I'm bringing up details of the other experiments here. As I said earlier, I've been able to access those from day one. Ah, here we are."

She scanned the list. Halfway down it she thumped the workstation in triumph. "That's it! The discontinuity drive!"

"Explain."

Lydexia stepped away from the workstation and headed for the hatch, beckoning for Hirundo to follow her. "The drive's still in its early stages. It can't power anything yet – all it can really do is route energy through its own systems and out into space. No one knows yet how to force the power into the discontinuity between jumpspace and realspace."

"You want to vent the time engine's power through the drive!"

"You'll make a fine scholar," she smiled. They were out in the corridor, running towards the drive laboratory. "Let's hope this door is jammed open too, or we might as well jump out of the nearest airlock."

Thankfully, it was. Lydexia ran in and began switching workstations on. "How long?"

"Five minutes." Hirundo ran to help her, then stopped in mid-stride. She saw him turn away, raising a comm-linker.

For this part, she didn't need him anyway. She began running the workstations through a bonding procedure, forcing a deep link between them and those in the next lab. Once that was done, she started to scan the activation protocols for the drive.

They seemed to be more complex than they should have been for something that didn't work yet, but nothing she couldn't handle. "Hirundo? What's happening?"

The Custodes paced back to her, clipping the linker back to his belt. "The Blasphemy has been cornered on the habitation deck. She ran into a crowd of panicking scholars, and a squad of Ascension's Custodes caught up with her. She's pinned down."

"Good. Hirundo, you should go. They'll need your expertise."

"But, doctor-captain–"

"I'll be fine. This is something only one person can do, commander. And I need you to keep the Blasphemy in place for me. If we die, so does she."

He nodded, and saluted her. "Thy will be done."

She listened to the sound of his boots beating the deck until she couldn't hear them anymore, then turned back to the workstations. The bonding procedure was complete, the protocols fused. When the time engine reached emission point, its energies would be directed though the discontinuity drive and out into the void. There might be some secondary effects, and Ascension would probably be off-line for a few weeks, but its occupants would survive, which would be more than could be said for the Blasphemy, if Hirundo caught up with her.

Lydexia walked away from the workstations, to the huge construction at the opposite end of the lab. That entire end of the module was a mass of gantry, heavy braces welded into place to hold the discontinuity drive in position. The drive itself seemed mainly pipework, a surreal conglomeration of tubes and helices cast from some pale, coppery metal. Several fat cables snaked out of it at various points to drape across the deck.

She checked the time and saw that there was a minute to go, maybe two at the most. She wondered if she should go in to be with the time engine, but then she remembered what the effects of the previous two emissions had been, and decided that she'd better stay where she was if she wanted to retain her sight.

The workstation began to bleat out an alarm. The time was down to less than a minute. Lydexia smiled to herself.

"This is where you fail, Blasphemy," she breathed.

The hatchway filled with searing white light.

Lydexia looked away, her eyes stinging, and was therefore facing the discontinuity drive when the machine at the heart of the gantry turned cherry red.

She cried out as the heat of it reached her, and dropped to the deck. The drive was shuddering in its metal cage, the vibration rattling the gantries, making the cables whip and writhe like decapitated serpents. The entire lab was shaking.

Impossibly, the light from the hatchway was getting brighter.

Something was going horribly wrong. The emission should have vented instantly, out through the drive and away, but instead the discontinuity drive was trying to store the power. It was building up a titanic charge within its own systems, a charge that it had never been designed to hold.

The vibration rose to a scream.

Lydexia had her hands over her eyes, but still the light from the hatchway was so bright that she could see her own finger bones through her closed lids, and it was getting brighter.

Behind her, the drive was still heating up. Had she been physically able to get her hands away from her face, Lydexia was sure that it would have been glowing white-hot.

And then, in the space of one heartbeat, the light died.

It didn't just fade. Lydexia still had her eyes covered, so she couldn't be sure if what she saw happen was real or a trick of her panicked mind, but it seemed to her that the light didn't just disappear, it *withdrew*, as though it was being sucked out of the hatchway and back into her lab.

In that tiny fraction of a second the light retreated and she was plunged into darkness.

The discontinuity drive detonated.

The searing hot core of it flashed apart in a great cloud of molten metal. Lydexia felt the air it displaced rush around her, scalding her, and she screamed, the sound of her voice drowned by the cacophony of the gantry exploding.

Great metal braces flew past her, crashing through the module's inner wall and into the corridor beyond, and as Lydexia saw them strike the module, the entire station was struck by a force so massive, so powerful, that her consciousness had no choice but to flee before it.

She awoke in a void, sightless and without feeling.

Panic gripped her and her heart hammered. Her eyes were open, blinking furiously, but she could see only blackness. She must have been lying down, but she couldn't feel the deck against her body. Even her hearing was affected – the hum of the air system was gone, leaving her in almost total silence. It was terrifying.

Then, out of the darkness, an orb of light drifted past her.

Lydexia stared at it incredulously, watching its light dim slightly as it slid along. It drew close, and she realised that she could smell it, the hot reek of burning metal, and feel its heat against the skin of her face.

Her perceptions switched with a jolt. She hadn't been blinded or left without feeling by the explosion. The power was out.

The orb was a blob of liquefied metal, probably from the discontinuity drive, which meant that she hadn't been unconscious for very long. She couldn't see because the module's lumes were dead, couldn't feel the deck because she was floating in mid-air. And the reason that there was no sound from the air system was that it had stopped working.

That sent another spike of panic through Lydexia's gut. Whatever had happened to the discontinuity drive had killed the power to this part of Ascension. If she didn't get out soon, she would suffocate, or freeze when the module's heat leached out into space. The air around her was already cooling.

Lydexia reached out, trying to find a surface, and eventually caught something with her fingertips and dragged herself close to it. Once she had a good grip on the object she began to run her hands over it, and by touch alone determined that she was holding onto the side of a workstation. That made it easy to orientate herself in the lab, and put her feet down on the floor. They wouldn't stay there if she tried to move, but she was pathetically grateful to find herself the right way up again.

She had trained in zero-g manoeuvres and combat, back in the archo-seminary, but had never expected to use them.

Now she knew where she was, she began to look around in more detail. There were small sources of light around her – more spots of glowing metal, an indicator from her comm-linker, but nothing from any device that drew power from the station itself. The module, perhaps even the entire lab deck, was totally without energy.

The indicator light on her comm-linker drew her attention again. She freed the device from her belt and switched it on. "Hirundo?"

There was no answer. She tried again and got the same result, so she switched channels to that of Caliban's crypt-key. "My lord? Elu?"

Silence from that, too. Lydexia began to wonder if she was the only living thing on the station.

She needed a source of light if she was going to go much further. There had been a container of tools next to the workstations when she had come in, left by some fleeing technician. Its contents were now drifting silently all around her.

Something tumbled past, and she grabbed it, brought it to her face and used the linker's indicator lume to study it. She'd been hoping it was a flashlight of some kind, but all she'd grabbed was a cabling burner, a precision blow-torch for welding and severing heavy power feeds.

It wasn't exactly what she had been after, but it was a start. Lydexia flicked the thing on, then spent a few minutes using its meagre, bluish glow to hunt down a flashlight.

Once she had that, it was time to leave the module. She pushed herself away from the workstation towards the open hatch, sailing quick and sure through the littered air, then grabbed at the frame to slow herself and peer outside.

The corridor was a tangled mess of wreckage and shattered gantry. To the right, the space was completely blocked from floor to ceiling. The left-hand way, back towards the time engine lab, looked just as bad, but when she examined it more closely she discovered a place near the deck where, if she squeezed, it would be possible to get through.

She touched the nearest gantry, lightly, and as she did the entire mass groaned a warning.

She backed off, breathing hard. The wreckage was unstable, and even without gravity any one of those mangled braces would be massive enough to flatten her. If she waited where she was, a rescue team might find her before she suffocated or died of cold.

There was every chance, however, that they would not.

Lydexia chose a quick death over a slow one, and shrugged out of her robes. The armour she wore beneath was figure hugging and quite smooth, apart from where the comm-linker clipped on, so she freed the device and slipped it into the top of her boot. Then, with a prayer on her lips and the flashlight clamped between her teeth, she put her head into the tangle and pushed herself through.

When she was halfway there, the lights came back on.

She saw the lumes above her blinking and flickering, and immediately the wreckage shuddered. The gravity was restarting.

A gantry above her, tonnes in weight, slipped down and hit her in the small of the back.

She screamed, spitting out the flashlight, and scrambled forward. The gantry had snagged on something, the gravity still not at full strength, and Lydexia was able to tear herself out from beneath it. She came up on the other side of the tangle just seconds before the entire mass shifted and collapsed down into the space below.

The gantry that had pinned her was now, she could see, buried half a metre into the tiled deck.

Lydexia got to her feet, slowly, her head spinning and stomach threatening to rebel. The return of gravity was making her internal organs settle back into their normal configuration, and after such a frantic struggle she was finding the transition highly uncomfortable.

It was brief, though. As her heartbeat slowed back to something approaching a sane rate, the nausea started to fade too.

She looked around, squinting in the dim emergency light.

Much of the damage seemed to be confined to the areas around the time engine lab and that containing the discontinuity drive. The rest of the corridor was reasonably clear, although the floor around her was littered with shattered tiles and broken panelling. Whatever had shaken Ascension had done so badly enough to cause structural damage everywhere she looked, which didn't make Lydexia feel very comfortable about the station's pressure integrity. She breathed quietly, listening for the sound of escaping atmosphere.

If there had been any, she would have heard it. Apart from the renewed, slightly wheezing hum of the air system, the deck was eerily silent.

She moved on, heading towards the elevators. As she neared them she noticed the corpses.

Two scholars were slumped on the deck, very still, sprawled and tangled in their own clothing as if they had been flung down by a petulant giant. Lydexia stopped to check for any vital signs, but there were none on the first body. There was no point checking the second, after she pulled the hood aside and saw what was left of its face. She couldn't even determine from that shattered mess whether the scholar had been male or female.

Blood and fluid surrounded the bodies in strange patterns. It had drifted in the lack of gravity for some minutes before dropping back to the deck.

Lydexia left them where they lay, stepping over the blood to reach the elevators. Along with the gravity and life-support, they should have been one of the systems fully restored under emergency power. Non-essential components might be reduced to half-strength or even left completely powerless until the reactor came back on line, but people would always need to get from one deck to another.

She pressed the call command. The elevator car must have been very close to the lab deck, because its doors parted almost immediately.

As they did, a gun barrel with a bore so wide she could have stuck her thumb down it poked from between them and stopped to rest against her forehead.

"Nice timing," snarled the Blasphemy. "Now how about telling me what the sneck you've done to this place?"

13. CENTRE PARKING

As soon as Red marched the Archaeotech woman back into the laboratory module, she saw that the time engine was still intact. She stopped at the threshold, covering the woman with the magnum, and glared at the silvery construction perched on its clawed tower.

"Bastard," she snarled at it. "What the sneck have I got to do to kill you?"

"You've already failed twice, monster," the Archaeotech hissed. "Here and on Chorazin. Why don't you give up and return to the pit you crawled out of?"

"Temper." Red lowered the gun and stepped closer to her. "What's your name?"

"You'll never know. I may lose my soul to you, like those others you've turned, but I'll not lose my name as well."

"I'll just call you doctor-captain then, shall I?"

The woman's eyes widened. "Where did you hear that?"

"Oh, sneck. You people, honestly." Red shook her head in exasperation. "One minute you're wandering around telling me I'm the ultimate evil, the arch-bastard who's going to bring all humankind to its knees, and the next you think I'm too dim to listen outside a door. I heard you earlier, just before I came in and you set those poor helots on me."

The Archaeotech looked slightly taken aback. "Sorry," she said reflexively.

"Forget it. I get that all the time." She holstered the magnum. "For the record, I'm not the ultimate anything, okay? Except possibly kisser."

"I'd rather not consider that."

"Don't worry, you're not my type." She leaned close. "I tell you what, though. You've got the worst case of sunburn I've ever seen."

The woman's hands went reflexively to her face, and Red saw her wince in sudden pain. Her face and scalp were a livid pink, with vague patches of paler skin on either side of her nose. Her lips were dry and cracked, the tattoos covering her head beginning to blur under flaking skin. She looked as though she had fallen asleep on a hot beach with her hands over her eyes.

"Cell damage," she whispered. "The heat from the discontinuity drive, maybe. Or the chronoplast emission..." Her face suddenly twisted in rage. "Curse you, monster! The time engine has poisoned me - this is your doing."

"I told you to shut the bloody door."

"It wouldn't shut," Her voice had risen to a scream. "Your infernal re-wiring robbed it of all power."

Red gaped. "What, me? Bollocks. I never went near the hatch cables."

"My wiring was correct."

"Sneck your wiring!" Red spun away and stalked across the lab. "It doesn't matter anyway. Whatever you did in here stopped the time engine blowing up, but took the main power out at the same time. By the time it comes back up I'm going to be long gone."

She flipped her comm-linker on. "Jude? You still with me?"

There was no reply. Red frowned at the linker, checked to make sure all its indicator icons were lit, and tried again. "Godolkin? Jude? Hey guys, don't make me start getting funny ideas about what you might be doing out there, okay?"

"I couldn't reach anyone either," said the Archaeotech dully. "I think the comms signals must be blocked."

"Why would anyone do that?" She glanced over at the woman, who was sagging against the workstation. "Hey, are you all right?"

"Blasphemy, I've been knocked senseless twice in twenty minutes, and now I'm being held prisoner by the creature that has terrified me since childhood." She looked up, her eyes glistening. "So no, I'm not all right."

"Childhood? I wasn't around then."

"The stories of you were. My father used to tell me the tales to frighten me, to make sure I spent enough time at prayer and my studies. God, the nightmares I had about you, Saint Scarlet of Durham, the mutant who ate babies and drank blood, and how one day she would wake up and tear the throats out of all the naughty children."

"And here I am," Red replied quietly.

"Here you are. Not the baby-eater I once feared, perhaps." The Archaeotech was studying her, looking her up and down. "Maybe just a mutant woman who drinks blood, as the heresies have been saying. But the fact remains that you are here to destroy my life's work. And in the process, you will probably kill us all."

"Not if I can help it." Red went back to join her. "You've got one thing right about me. I have come to destroy the time engine, because if I don't I know what you people will do with it. Surely you realise what a powerful weapon you've got there?"

The woman shrugged. "That's not my division. I'm an Archaeotech – we rediscover what was lost, learn all we can about it, and give that information to our superiors." She straightened slightly, pride giving her some strength. "We Archaeotechs rebuilt the Accord, monster, from the debris left behind after the Bloodshed. We gave humankind back the stars."

"And what will you give them with this? The future?" Red gestured at the time engine, waiting impassively on its tower. "Or a past where mutants never came to be? Doctor-captain, you're a smart girl. You know damn well they'd start a time war with this. Your High Command would rip the universe to shreds trying to re build history in their own image."

"You don't know that."

"Oh, I do. I'm a mutant; I know very well how things work around here. You gave them the Accord? How are you going to feel when they tear it apart again?"

The woman turned back to the engine. "I can't," she breathed. "I just can't."

"Don't you think," Red asked her, very gently, "that you've got more important things to think about right now?"

"Ascension..." The woman glanced back, startled.

"Yeah. I don't know about you, but something doesn't feel right about this place. The wiring, the jammed comms... Help me get in touch with my ship, so I can find out what's going on. And then we'll talk about the time engine."

It wasn't much of a deal, but perhaps the Iconoclast had as bad a feeling about the station as Red did. After a few seconds hesitation, she nodded.

"Good girl," Red grinned.

"My soul is forfeit," the woman replied, "and my name is Aura Lydexia."

Red had been in the middle of a particularly nasty fire-fight when the explosion had occurred. She had almost reached the access lock when she'd gotten tangled up in a group of panicking scholars, and then met a squad of Custodes coming the other way. They were obviously looking for her, which bore out her theory that the long-haired trooper had lived to tell the tale.

Iconoclast shocktroopers, she knew only too well, were tough. These Keepers of the Secret were tougher still.

The squad had driven her back into the habitation deck, and then set about trying to surround her. They had come close to succeeding, too – where many of the Iconoclasts she had met had simply waded into her in waves, certain that their righteousness would prevail, the Custodes had had more sense. They had kept formation, followed tactics and obeyed orders from people who were even smarter than they were. Red had found herself in something very much like a killing ground.

If there was one positive facet to her side of the battle, it was that she had managed to lead the Custodes away from her hidden vacuum-shroud. But the way things had been going on the hab deck, she had started to seriously wonder if she would ever get to use it.

Then the time engine had gone critical.

Red had thought that she still had time to go, but the heat of battle had stolen the minutes from her. When the moment came, it was fast: Red had just drawn a bead on one trooper who was trying to work his way behind her, and in the space between squeezing the trigger and the particle bolt hitting its target Ascension had turned on its head. Red had been bounced clear off the ceiling by the impact, and had hit it hard enough to lose consciousness for a few seconds. The only reason she had survived was that everyone trying to kill her at the time had suffered the same fate.

Some were worse off than others. The man Red had been aiming at was spared the particle bolt, but died anyway when his skull imploded against a ceiling brace.

The power had started to flutter then, but it didn't fail completely until about half a minute later, when Red was in an elevator and trying to get back to the access lock. There must have been some residual voltage in Ascension's systems, but it had run out just in time to trap her in the lift. When it came back on, the last place Red had wanted to be was in an elevator if the power was going to start playing silly buggers, so she decided to get out at the next floor and walk.

It was probably quite unlucky for Aura Lydexia, who had been waiting for that very lift to take her back up.

The communications weren't working because they were being routed through a suppression transceiver. "It's to stop transmissions interfering with the sensorium," Lydexia explained, peering at the diagram on her workstation. "Caliban's paranoid about it. That's why they put the shield halfway down the spindle."

"Caliban?"

"Ascension's operations manager." Lydexia grimaced. "I don't trust him."

"I don't trust anybody," Red replied. "What's your point?"

"My point is that he's hiding something, something big. There are things about Ascension that haven't made sense since I arrived, and I'm sure he's behind it." She left that screen and moved to another. "Here. This cabling trace should lead to the transceiver, but it doesn't, not directly. There's something in the way."

Red straightened up. Despite her success reconfiguring the time engine's cabling, this kind of engineering wasn't her strong suit. It all looked like lines to her.

"If the power was out when you first tried your linker, why didn't the call go straight through? Surely the transceiver wouldn't have picked it up."

"True." Lydexia began tapping at keys. "Um. That's strange."

Red peered over to the other station, looking at the diagram upside down. "Sneck, even I know what that is. It's a jammer."

"Linked to the power feed. So if the transceiver isn't getting power, the jammer activates under stored charge, then picks up from the emergency generators." She glanced up towards the dully glowing lumes. "Which are on now."

"Health & Safety would throw a fit." Red prodded the diagram with her finger. "If the power goes out the first thing you'd do is enable communications, not cut them off completely."

"I don't think safety has anything to do with this." Lydexia stood back, running her hand reflexively over her scalp. "This is Caliban's work."

Red could understand the idea behind the transceiver – if the sensorium was so finely tuned it could pick up sense-readings from a quarter of a light-year away, it would be sensible to try to protect it from stray crypt-signals. The comm-linker devices used in the Accord tended to be brute things, uncomplicated but powerful, forcing their signals into the quantum relay network for faster-than-light transmission. Caliban wouldn't want that kind of noise showing up on his scans.

To secretly install a comms jammer that would only activate in times of the direst emergency was the opposite of sensible. It was deranged. Either that, or an act of deliberate malice.

"Okay, so we know it's there. Can you shut it down?"

Lydexia shook her head. "Not from here, but I can read its pulse frequencies from this. I might be able to alter your linker to pulse in opposition."

She put a hand out for it, and Red passed it to her. "Push my signal out through the gaps?"

"That's right. Don't expect high quality, but it might be enough to transmit simple messages."

"I don't need complicated. All I need is 'What the bloody hell happened?'"

She watched as the Archaeotech began to open up her comm-linker. She had wondered, for a moment, whether handing it over like that had been such a good idea, but Lydexia was an intelligent woman. She must have known that if she'd tried anything Red would simply have knocked her out and taken hers.

The re-wiring took a few minutes. While Lydexia worked, Red wandered to the door. "I don't hear much in the way of activity out there, do you?"

"No. I'm hoping that's because people would have either stayed on the hab deck or gone to the observation platform for answers."

"Maybe they don't trust the lifts yet."

"Maybe." Lydexia snapped the casing of the linker closed, then tapped at some of its surface icons. "Try this."

Red came back and took it from her, then input *Fury*'s crypt-key. "Jude? Godolkin?"

Static blared out at her. She winced, holding the thing away from her ear, and tried again. "Durham Red to

Omega Fury, this is getting really bloody embarrassing, over?"

This time, the static came in jerks and jumps. Buzzing sounds were trying to force their way past it. And then, sounding as if it was coming through several layers of roofing felt, a voice. "*...Holy...*"

"Hey, Jude!" She grinned. "Good to, er, hear you."

"*One... Thought... Ascension was... Exploded...*"

Red shook her head. "I'm not getting enough."

"Tell him to alter their transmission frequency to match." Lydexia pointed at the screen. "Here, this value."

Trying not to shout, Red relayed the message several times. Eventually most of the static faded out, and Judas Harrow's voice became intelligible. "Holy one, where...you?"

"I'm on Ascension, in the laboratory modules."

"Impossible! Ascension is destroyed. Holy one, we saw... own eyes. There is nothing... of it."

Red looked around. "Well," she said to herself, "if this is heaven I'm bloody disappointed."

She lifted the linker again. "Jude, stay put. I'll get back to you. Lydexia, did you get that?"

"I did, but I'm not sure I understand it. Is your kinsman telling you that Ascension was destroyed?"

"Yeah, and Jude's got some of the sharpest eyes of anyone I know, Godolkin included. If he says there was an explosion, then something blew up. I think we need to have a look outside."

There were no external viewports in the lab modules, and in fact very few in Ascension as a whole. Lydexia wondered out loud if that, too, was a part of Caliban's paranoia, but Red thought it was more likely to be a matter of economics. Synthetic diamond ports, although quite easy to make, had a certain value. And Ascension had begun life as a military sensing post. Far better to save the money and give its occupants less to distract them from their holoscreens.

There were some sense-engine feeds on Lydexia's schematics, though. "The best images will come from the docking ring," she told Red, tapping at the workstation's keyboard again. "They have high resolution pickups there. Visiting starships can log onto them and see themselves approach."

"But you can log on from here."

"Of course, Blasphemy." Lydexia gave her a sideways look. "I believe I covered how to log onto a network feed in year one of the archo-seminary."

"I don't know exactly what you said just then, " Red told her warningly, "but it sounded sarcastic. Be careful."

"Oh, I always am." The woman tapped a final key and sat back. "There."

"Where?" The screen was blank, a slab of black with occasional lines of static tracking down it. "Did you pass year one?"

Lydexia chose not to reply to that, and instead tapped at her keys again. The black screen became the network diagram, then a series of options, then went dark once more. "Nothing," she spat finally. "How can that be?"

"Try another location. Are there pickups on the spindle?"

There were, but they were as lifeless as those on the docking ring. Lydexia threw her hands up. "Caliban. He's jammed the external feeds."

Red leaned in, over her shoulder, making her flinch away. "Don't panic, I'm just having a go. Let's see if there are any closer to home... Hey. Third time lucky."

As she spoke, the smile died on her face. Lydexia gasped out a curse, then a prayer.

The pickup Red had accessed was mounted just below the lab modules, and its view was aimed down the spindle. It should have been blocked by the shield halfway between the reactor and the observation deck.

The shield, however, was no longer fixed to Ascension.

Where it had once been mounted were now only a few twisted ribbons of metal. Some panels of it still survived over to the right of the pickup's view, but most of it was lost. There was nothing to protect the sensorium from the reactor, or the random emissions of starships as they berthed at the docking ring.

The ring was gone, too, and the reactor. "Holy Christ," Red said sickly. "No wonder the pickups were blank."

Ascension had been blown in half.

The spindle terminated just past the wreckage of the shield, in a sprawl of debris. Wisps of ruined gantry poked out past the ruptured plating, along with trailing cables and long metal tubes that would once have housed elevators. Some emergency system within Ascension must have closed off the lift shafts, along with every other open duct in the spindle, when the explosion occurred. If it hadn't, the station would have haemorrhaged its entire atmosphere in minutes.

The spindle looked like a severed limb, ragged and broken, its mechanics drooling out into the void.

"Harrow did see an explosion. He saw the reactor going up. When the time engine went critical it must have somehow overloaded the reactor, blown it to bits..."

She trailed off. Lydexia was shaking her head. "Blasphemy, you're wrong. Look at the stars."

Red put her face closer to the little screen, and with a jolt of panic saw what the Iconoclast meant. She'd not even noticed before, so stunned was she by the damage to Ascension. But around it, the stars were moving, arching down and away. Ascension was not only turning end over torn end, but it was racing through space at the same time.

It couldn't have been shoved that hard by the reactor exploding. Fist sized chunks of it, maybe, but nothing more intact than that.

"Here's the answer you seek, mutant," Lydexia said flatly. "Your Harrow saw the reactor and docking ring destroyed, and thought you had died with it, because the rest of Ascension was no longer there. We were already millions of kilometres away." She was bringing up a new screen on the workstation, one that Red recognised from *Fury*. It was a stellar cartography grid, its crosshairs homing in on a point in space.

"How?"

"The discontinuity drive." The Iconoclast nodded sideways, towards the next lab. "Caliban's records showed it to be almost useless, just a test bed for venting energy into space, but that was another lie. It's working, or rather it was when I used the time engine to power it up.

We moved almost a quarter of a light-year while the reactor was detonating, Durham Red. Directly towards the Manticore."

"I was right about you, doctor-captain."

This was a man's voice, from behind them. Red spun, drawing the magnum as fast as she ever had, bringing it up to firing position, and letting it drop before it was halfway there, as soon as she saw that the voice had come from one of the workstations.

She wandered over to it and peered at the flatscreen built into its control board.

The picture it showed was obviously a feed from inside some kind of starship. A man sat strapped into a luxurious command throne, facing the pickup, with a pale, grey robed young woman standing at his side. From the cut of his clothes, and the calm authority of his face, she knew instantly who had spoken.

"Let me guess," she growled. "Caliban."

"The Lord Heirophant General Malchus Caliban to you, monster." He spat the words. Beside him, the helot-woman flinched at the sound of his disgust.

He was older than Red might have expected, his eyebrows and beard silver grey against the deep tan of his face. His scalp was shaved, like every other Archaeotech scholar she had seen, and webbed with ritual tattoos, but that was where the similarity ended. This man, she could tell, was more warrior than scientist. He must have served his time in the regular forces before giving himself to the Archaeotech cause.

Caliban was clad in a long, high collared coat of black silk trimmed with gold, and the armour beneath it was ornate. "All dressed up and nowhere to go," sneered Red. "Oh, and that's *Miss* Monster to you, dipstick."

The man gave her a mirthless, twisted smile. "Such wit, for someone so nearly dead." He glanced back at someone cowering at the edge of the pickup's field of view – a small, florid official in black robes. "You see, Prefect? Hardly the nightmare we've been led to expect."

"Don't speak to it," hissed the official, quaking. "The filth will curse you with its witch tongue, Caliban. See – your doctor-captain already consorts with the beast."

Lydexia snorted. "Their opinion of you seems even worse than mine, Blasphemy."

"I'm used to it." She spread her hands. "So come on, Caliban. Fess up. How long have you been planning this?"

"I have no idea what you mean."

"Balls." She glanced at Lydexia. "What's he got here again? A drive that's finished when he says it isn't, and shoots half the station right at the Manticore. A comms array that's 'not working' either. What else was it?"

"A temporal bomb," replied Lydexia. "And I can guess that's far further along the developmental trail than your records might suggest."

Caliban sighed. "It is. Doctor-captain, I once told Elu that you were a risk to me, and here you are proving me right again. I should have brought you aboard far sooner – you were wasted on Chorazin."

"And what would I have done had you summoned me, my Lord? Helped you turn this station into a weapon?"

"Everything we do is a weapon, Aura." He leaned forward in the throne, his hands on either side of the pickup. On the screen, he loomed. "We both know it. We are Iconoclasts. Our duty is to the survival of the human race. That creature beside you is nothing compared to what's truly out there. Nothing!"

"Our duty is to knowledge."

"Our duty is to life! Aura, I know how dangerous the Manticore is. My father knew, and the knowledge killed him. But no one will listen, no one will let us do what must be done. So yes, I've turned Ascension into a weapon, in secret, because the Patriarch is in love with that nightmare." He jerked his thumb back over his shoulder. "He thinks it's going to give him access to time travel, if only we could study it hard enough."

"And what do you think?"

"I think you know I'm right. Even if you've been tainted by that creature at your side. Elu?"

"Yes, my Lord?" The grey cloaked helot turned her single remaining eye to him, and Red could see nothing in it but adoration.

"What time is it?"

"Twenty-three thirty-seven GST, my Lord."

Caliban nodded grimly. "Time we were away, then. Doctor-captain, I wish things were different. Fate and the Blasphemy have conspired against us. I always intended Ascension to be empty when it launched, but it was not to be. I'm sorry."

"You're sorry?" snapped Red incredulously. "Not as sorry as we'll be when the Manticore fries our arses!"

"That won't happen," he replied with little malice. "Your obsession with destroying the time engine has accelerated my plans, but not altered them. The Manticore has a tolerance range of just over one thousand kilometres. The temporal bomb is tuned to detonate at twice that distance." He leaned back in the throne and raised his head. "And when it does, everything within ten thousand kilometres will be projected roughly a million years into the past. I've heard that you are resilient, monster, and almost certainly quite resistant to aging, but I doubt that even you would last that long."

Not without turning into Brite Red, she thought sourly. "I don't know. Maybe I'll wait around for you and tell you all about it."

"In which case," he smiled, "have a good trip."

The screen went dead.

Red made a disgusted sound. "You know, back in my day we had people who acted like bastards because they were stupid and greedy and evil. Now everyone acts like that because they think it's the right thing to do..."

Lydexia rounded on her. "Is this really a time for philosophy, monster? Your actions have destroyed us all!"

"We're not dead yet." She lifted the comm-linker and showed Lydexia the 'transmit' icon. "Jude, did you get all that?"

"Much of it, holy one. And we're... our way."

"Tell Godolkin to put his foot down. He wouldn't want to miss this."

"Well...There, Red. Hang on."

The Iconoclast was glaring at her. "So what do you propose to do? Sit and wait while your friends rush to the rescue? Assuming that they can even get past the Bastion."

"Are you kidding? They'd never get here in time." Red crouched to pick up the magnum. "They'll get through the Bastion, but they haven't got time to calculate a superlight jump, let alone get here on thrusters."

"As I tried to tell you. We're lost."

"You might be. Caliban's an arrogant bastard, and that kind always makes mistakes. What we need to do is find the ones *he's* made and use them to our advantage. Get everyone off this station, into whatever shuttles or escape pods we can find, and get the sneck off this thing!"

Or, she thought worriedly, it's going to be a really long trip.

14. TIME TO DIE

The video feed from outside the station was still active on Lydexia's workstation. Red watched Caliban's ship peeling away from Ascension, its drives flaring. "Where did he get that?"

"It's the Prefect's shuttle," Lydexia replied. "Monster, you're not understanding me. It doesn't matter whether he has a ship or not. There's nothing he can do. Caliban was dead the moment the discontinuity drive activated. As I am, and you are."

Red pointed a finger at the woman's face. "You are starting to be a real killjoy, you know that?"

"We are inside the Gulf!" Lydexia yelled, slamming her hand down on the cartography screen. "There is nothing here; no surviving colonies, no life, no hospitable worlds. *Nothing*. The Manticore devastated it all – if Caliban was right about anything, it was about just how deadly it is."

"Lydexia, the Gulf's not that big. What, half a light-year?"

"It's not the distance, monster." The Archaeotech sighed, dropping into one of the workstation seats. "There's no way through. The Bastion isn't just a fleet – it's a total blockade. There are multiple layers of defence that have been built up over decades, purely for the purpose of making sure that nothing, not so much as a missile, ever leaves the Gulf. Atomic mines, jumpspace drones, vortex relays... It's possible, maybe, that your ship will get into the Gulf from outside, but it will never leave. None of us will. The Bastion is impregnable."

"Nothing's impregnable," Red replied. *Not when you've got an invisible spaceship, anyway.*

That last thought she kept very much to herself. *Fury's* existence wasn't something she wanted to broadcast, least of all to an Archaeotech. The shadow web was very much a lost technology, a relic of the Stealth Wars, resurrected by the Omega warriors. If Lydexia ever learned of it she would be stripping it off in seconds, just to see how it worked.

Red glanced back at the screen and saw that Caliban's ship had shrunk to a bright dot, only distinguishable from the stars by the way it moved. "Maybe you're ready to give up, but I'm not. You've got two choices, Lydexia. One is to sit here and wait for the bomb to go off, or for the Manticore to take a dislike to you and do what it did to that fleet back in six twenty-seven. Or you can try and get off this junk pile in time to watch the fireworks, and then think about what to do next."

The woman looked up at her. "What are you going to do?"

"What do you think?"

Lydexia sat for a few seconds, her hands clasped together, staring off into space. Red was just about to leave the woman to her misery when she spoke. "The bomb will destroy the Manticore."

"That's the plan."

"If the Manticore is gone, there'll be no reason for the Bastion to stay in formation."

Red shrugged. "That must have been what Caliban's betting on. He's a clever bloke, doctor-captain. He wouldn't have zoomed off without an exit worked out."

The Archaeotech seemed to straighten a little. "Don't count on it," she said. "Caliban must have been planning this for years, decades. His hatred of the Manticore must be overwhelming. A small matter like his own slow death by starvation wouldn't have stopped him, but no, you're right."

"I am? You're starting to convince me otherwise."

"Caliban must be found, and brought to justice. He's dishonoured the division, hoarded lost technologies for his own gains. That's not what we do, Durham Red."

"So you're up for getting out of here?"

She stood up. "I am."

"Good stuff. Now all we need to do is work out how."

Ascension was a bright disc on the stellar cartography screen, bracketed by indicator icons and vector markers. In its path lay the edges of several circles, concentric rings drawn from threads of coloured light.

Lydexia was bent over the screen, tracing the station path with a fingertip. "The discontinuity drive," she was saying, "threw us to this point. But once the drive was gone, so was the momentum. It didn't impart very much real speed to us at all."

"Hmm. According to that, about five kilometres per second." Red gnawed a thumbnail. "So how far away are we?"

"From the Manticore, no more than ten thousand kilometres."

She did a swift mental calculation. "Sneck. Half an hour. No, wait, that's until we hit the Manticore! The bomb will go off before that."

"Call it twenty-five minutes," said Lydexia. "How far away did you say your friends were?"

"Too far." Red sidestepped to the next workstation and sat down, quickly sorting through its menus until she found a plan of the station. She was vaguely aware of Lydexia glaring at her, as if disgusted that a mutant could operate Iconoclast systems so easily, but Red ignored her. She'd become very good at learning how to use other people's computers as a matter of survival.

The plan didn't look right until Red put her hand to the screen and covered half of it up. "Okay, this is us. How many people are left on the station, do you think?"

"About fifty Custodes, maybe seventy scholars."

"Helots?"

"Blasphemy, helots aren't people."

Red raised an eyebrow. "Caliban seemed to think differently."

"Yes, but he's insane. Most of the helots would have died when the power failed. They're permanently linked into device drivers, because there's so little left of their original brains they can't keep their organs functioning."

"Now that's just snecking sick." Red grimaced. "Can't you use robots or something?"

Lydexia looked at her as though she was mad. "Robots? Monster, even if such a thing were possible, who would want a mechanical person lumbering around? That would be horrible."

Red stared at her for a second or two, and then shook her head. There wasn't time. "So how many might be left ticking?"

"Another fifty."

"Right, that's two hundred and twenty people, plus you and me." She peered at the deck plan. "Tullus didn't berth his shuttle on the docking ring, that's obvious. So where did he put it? There's got to be a hangar deck somewhere."

Lydexia shrugged. "I never saw such a place. Then again, there was plenty Caliban didn't show me." She held out her hand. "Give me the comm-linker."

Red passed it to her. "Please would be nice."

"I'm sure." The Archaeotech tapped out a crypt-key and pressed the "connect" icon. "Hirundo?"

There was a few seconds of static, then: "Who's this? Identify yourself."

Red moved away. There was no video on the linker, not with the signal pulsed so brutally, but she felt better being out of range anyway. It was one thing for an uneasy truce to develop between her and Lydexia in these desperate hours, but quite another for anyone else on the station to see it that way.

Especially Hirundo, whom she had already shot once today.

Lydexia saw what she was doing, and nodded fraction-ally. She understood. "Surely you recognise my voice?"

"Doctor-captain?" Red could hear the sudden smile in his voice. "In God's name, I never thought to hear you again! The comms have been down since that impact, most of the hatches are jammed shut... Where are you?"

"Still in the lab module. Hirundo, I don't have time to explain everything, but there has been a catastrophe, and we are in mortal danger. Ascension has to be evac-uated."

"Very well." Ever the good soldier, Red noted. He hadn't questioned her words for a moment. "I'll start moving people down to the docking ring – the other Custodes will follow my lead. How long do we have?"

Lydexia made a face. "That's the problem. There is no docking ring."

"I'm not sure I understand."

"Hirundo, there has been an explosion. The docking ring is gone, as is the reactor. And everyone still on this station will die in roughly twenty minutes."

"Ah," he said. "In which case, we may have a prob-lem."

"Tell me about it," muttered Red, well out of audio range, but drawing an angry glare from Lydexia anyway.

"Hirundo, listen to me. General Caliban has already left the station. He used the Prefect's shuttle, and that must have been berthed somewhere above the spindle. Ask the local Custodes, if you can find any. I'll start making my way up. Where are you now?"

"Upper hab deck. Godspeed, doctor-captain."

Lydexia cut the connection and handed the linker back. "We need to leave, but if anyone sees you, monster, there will be even greater panic."

"Not to mention people trying to kill me, and I don't even want to go into what will happen to you if we're seen together."

"That's true."

"Go on ahead. I'll make my own way."

Lydexia shook her head. "No, wait…" She frowned for a moment, lost in thought, then beckoned Red to follow her out of the hatch. "You'll need a robe. Mine is on the other side of that debris, but there were those two corpses by the lift."

"Them? You're kidding." She followed the Archaeotech round to the elevator doors. The two bodies lay where they had been flung, blood drying on the cracked tiles beneath them.

One of the robes was in a better state than the other, but it still made Red look as though she had been hit by a truck. "It will give you an excuse not to talk," Lydexia told her, not without some satisfaction. "After all, you don't want anyone seeing those teeth of yours, do you?"

By the time they got up to the habitation deck, the Custodes had managed to force some of the hatches open, and Archaeotechs filled the corridors. Red followed Lydexia through the crowds, keeping her head low, trying not to listen to the sounds coming from the compartments no one could open.

For all Caliban's contrition about the fate of Ascension's occupants, the jamming of the hatches must have been part of his design, just like the blocking of the comms signal. The safety locks had been bypassed somehow. He had done quite a lot, Red realised, to make sure there would be no witnesses to his crimes.

It looked as though her estimate of two hundred plus escapees would have to be hugely reduced.

Lydexia took Red's linker again on the way, to make contact with Hirundo. The two met each other on the uppermost habitation deck.

Red hung back as Hirundo embraced the Archaeotech, noting that Lydexia, after an initial flinch, seemed to rather warm to the idea. "I swore I'd find you," he was telling her. "After we lost sight of the Blasphemy, and there was no answer to my calls, I feared the worst."

"I never doubted you would," she smiled.

He glanced over at Red. "And your companion?"

"I don't know her name." The woman's fingers were moving nervously, knotting and tapping. "She suffered injuries in one of the laboratory modules, and she can't speak. She helped me escape."

"Then I'm in your debt, my lady." He gave Red a bow, and she waved back.

Lydexia was looking around at the Archaeotechs and Custodes hurrying past them. There didn't seem to be all that many anymore as the crowd began to thin. "Did you discover Caliban's escape route?"

"Only just. There's a shuttle deck just below the sensorium, but it had been sealed for years." He started off down the corridor, and Red and Lydexia followed. "As far as anyone knew it had been filled with insulating foam long ago. The hierophant would never have allowed ships to berth so close to his precious sensors."

"I can only assume it wasn't as abandoned as everyone thought."

The trooper shook his head, the breathe-mask dangling at his throat. "I led a team in, and we discovered otherwise. There are also a number of life-shells stationed there, refurbished and set for launch. If this is all Caliban's doing, then he must have been planning his escape for some time."

"I've no doubt of that."

Red had noticed that Lydexia still hadn't told Hirundo what the true nature of their danger was, or even what had caused the explosion. Then again, there were some things probably best not explained in the middle of an exodus, if panic was to be avoided. If any of the fleeing Iconoclasts around them were to discover just how close they were to the feared Manticore, anything could happen.

By Red's calculations, they had less than ten minutes before it would be too late to care.

It took at least half that time to get to the shuttle deck. There were stairs that led from one habitation level to another, but to go further than that required the use of either elevators or the emergency access ladders alongside them. And Caliban had jammed the lifts, too.

Even Red was puffing by the time she had climbed up onto the shuttle deck.

Hirundo was by the hatch, helping the last few stragglers through. As he grabbed Red's hand and pulled her up the last few rungs their eyes met, and for an awful second she was sure that he had recognised her. But he said nothing, simply stepped aside and let her go through the hatchway.

The deck was long and curved, taking up at least a third of the station's circumference. The outer wall of it was studded with circular bulkheads, many of them sealed, and in front of a much larger set of double doors squatted the boxy, unlovely bulk of an Iconoclast shuttle, its drives glowing. Red saw Hirundo, who had now moved ahead of her, bend to say something to Lydexia, but with Archaeotechs still scrambling past her she couldn't hear what it was.

She began to trot forward. In front of her, one of the circular bulkheads blinked closed, and there was a hefty thump of explosive latches from beyond. The deck shook, and pieces of metal broke free from the bulkhead's frame and skittered across the deck.

On her far right, another life-shell exited in the same way. Red looked about to see if there were any others she could get into, but it looked as though she had just watched the last of them blast free from Ascension.

The shuttle it had to be, then. She started forward.

Hirundo snapped around to face her, his bolter centred unerringly on her sternum.

"I'm sorry." He reached down to his breathe-mask with his free hand, and pulled it up over his face. "You saved her, and for that I'm grateful, but I can't let you leave this place."

Red tensed slightly, preparing to leap. She wondered if she had left it too long, if he was too far away. Still, she'd have to risk it. "How long have you known?"

"She told me when I first saw her. Silently."

Battlesign, Red thought despairingly. The system of hand signals and finger movements Iconoclasts used as silent communications in combat. She'd seen Godolkin trying to teach Harrow the trick of it, but had never taken much notice. "Bugger."

Lydexia was on the shuttle's ramp. "Goodbye, Blasphemy," she said, and then smiled. "No more nightmares."

And with that, Hirundo pulled his trigger.

Her attention had been on the Archaeotech. Red saw the bolter flare and twisted away, the staking pin ripping a slice through her upper arm. She rolled, ducking into cover behind one of the shuttle's landing claws, hearing the bolter blast-firing more stakes in her direction. They hammered into the deck plating, shredding the metal and sending splinters up in a fountain.

Red sprinted around the shuttle's nose, just in time to see the ramp hingeing up.

"Snecking bastards," she screamed, picking up a stray staking pin and waving at the vessel. "I'll get you for this!"

The double doors were opening, the shuttle sliding forwards on a railed launch platform. Red thought for a second about running after it, somehow getting into the airlock with it and ripping her way in, but the only thing she would get out of that would be incinerated.

There was no one else on the deck. Hirundo had managed, without her even noticing, to manoeuvre her right to the back of the queue.

She stood where she was for a few seconds, then stripped off the bloodied robes and dropped them onto the floor. She'd not even had time to draw the magnum out. It had been hidden under the heavy fabric.

Had that been part of Lydexia's plan, too?

If her sense of time was anything close to right, Red had about three minutes before detonation, and that didn't

h time to stand around wondering. Instead she
and raced back to the hatch.

It was a lot faster going down the ladders than up
them, although running past compartments that were
still plainly occupied was harder than she liked to
admit. Adrenaline gave her speed and she had almost
reached the access lock by the time the temporal bomb
went off.

She felt it through the deck, a twisting shudder somewhere beneath her as she keyed the hatch open and
tugged the vacuum shroud from its hiding place. The
staking pin, she realised, was still in her hand, and the
particle magnum was on her belt. She swapped them
over, then pulled the shroud open and started shoving her
feet into the integral boots.

There was a breeze behind her, cold and strange.

It was hard not to panic, to rush and get herself tangled.
By the time she had gotten the shroud around her waist,
the temperature in the lock had dropped perceptibly, and
it was getting darker. More drain on the power system,
she thought, glancing back over her shoulder.

She was wrong about that. The end of the corridor was
wreathed in shadow.

Red swore explosively and dropped the magnum,
pulling the shroud up and around her. The helmet seal
jammed for an awful second, and she had to fight the
urge simply to pull it free. With her strength, she could
quite easily rip the shroud apart.

By the time she was in, the darkness was only fifty
metres behind her, and accelerating.

There was a sound, as well as the rising wind and failing light, a sinister rushing. Red grabbed the magnum
with fat, gloved fingers and stumbled a few paces away
from the lock. That took her closer to the onrushing darkness, and that awful, sibilant hissing. There were
whispers in it, she realised. Voices, high and quiet, like
mad children breathing threats in a language she couldn't
quite understand.

Red raised the magnum, set it to full yield and held the trigger down.

Energy snarled out of the gun and slammed into the inside of the airlock. The first bolts screamed and bounced inside, shattering cables and rupturing high-pressure pipes. Instantly the lock filled with vapour and sparks, and alarm gongs began chiming discordantly. They drowned out the whispering somewhat, which was a blessing.

She fired again, and this time the hatch gave way.

There was one instant between the first hole appearing in the metal, and the hatch failing entirely. Red saw the smoke suddenly cave in on itself, dragging the centre of the cloud back into the lock, and then the whole panel was off and tumbling away into space. A tornado of escaping air thundered after it.

It picked Red up and bowled her through the hatch, the shroud ballooning.

She was tumbling, whirling through space. Ascension was rolling around her, one second in her vision, the next at her back. She fumbled for the thruster pack's wrist controls, half wondering where her gun had flown off to. She'd lost her grip on it when the hatch had failed.

The "stabilise" control was large on the wrist pad. Red found it by touch alone and pressed it hard. Immediately the thruster pack began jumping and bouncing behind her, sending out timed bursts to slow her spin in each axis. Within seconds she was feeling heartily sick, but at least she was looking at a steady view through the shroud's faceplate.

Ascension was below her and to the right. She could see the ragged end of the spindle, and shattered fragments of the shield. And beyond it, a bright flare of thrusters, racing away as Hirundo and Lydexia escaped the coming storm.

Darkness was growing from the heart of the station.

The shadows she had seen in the corridor were spreading outwards, not increasing in size so much as building new layers of themselves, planes and spires of translucent shade – interweaving, linking and sliding over and through each other. It was like the way the time engine moved, seemingly passing through its own structure as it rotated, but that was a device, a construction of alien metals and electricity. This was something far greater, far more powerful. The time engine was a firecracker, this was the atom bomb.

Red tapped the controls, turning herself away from the sight, and hit the emergency burn. The pack slammed into her back as its main thruster fired, powering her away from the oncoming shadows, but she could already see them spreading past and around her. It was too late.

It had always been too late.

The pack ran out of fuel, its last stutters setting her spinning again, very slowly. She was moving fast now, Ascension dropping away from her, but the shadow-planes were racing up to meet her now. She had seconds, if that, before they took her.

She wondered if it would hurt.

As the thought crossed her mind, light crossed her vision. Searingly bright against the shadows, a thin, pure track of blinding light tearing out of the darkness and striking Ascension between the dish and the lab modules. Red saw it hit, saw the way it boiled through the temporal bomb's shadows.

She saw the star appear where it touched.

A sphere of pure white glare, utterly perfect and unmarred, had been born where the beam had touched the station's surface. It was expanding, much faster than the shadows had risen from their heart of darkness, swamping the planes and the spires. They were contracting in on themselves as the light grew, like the limbs of a burning insect.

The light rose up and out, world sized, its edges almost brushing at Red's booted feet. She looked down, leaning over in the shroud, and saw her own boots outlined against it, as though she was standing on a planet made of white light.

Without warning, the sphere vanished, leaving her vision full of stars, her eyes full of tears.

"Sneck me," she breathed, blinking furiously to try to stop the stinging. "What the bloody hell was that?"

Moments later, she had her answer.

It was a dot at the corner of her tear filled eye, and then it was a massive globe filling her vision. It had appeared so fast, stopped so quickly and so smoothly, that Red knew it could only have been driven by one force. The force that had torn Ascension in two and sent it hurtling clean through the Bastion's defences. A discontinuity drive.

Except that this one worked. This was the original.

The Manticore had arrived.

15. DEATH AND REBIRTH

In the Year of the Accord six hundred and twenty-seven, when Captain Verax and his fleet were destroyed in orbit around Kentyris Secundus, several of the ships involved had managed to send sense-engine data back to High Command before the Manticore's beams found them. The information had been classified upon arrival, but numerous security breakdowns in the decades that followed had brought the data closer to the surface. Red had managed to access some of it while she had been researching Ascension.

The images she had seen there had been difficult to interpret. At times the attacker seemed to be a great circle of orange light, at others a dark crescent against the stars. It was either polished smooth or insanely detailed. Eventually, after trying to make sense of the pictures for several minutes, Red had given up, coming to the conclusion that someone in the fleet had been taking photographs with their thumb over the lens.

Up close, though, the Manticore was a nightmare.

Red had seldom been so close to anything as big. She would have thought that the clarity of the vacuum and the lack of any background light source would have made it difficult to gauge the object's scale, but she would have been wrong. The insane mass of the thing was impossible to mistake. It had to be at least fifty kilometres across, and the glowing crater that it had turned towards her must have been twenty from side to side.

It knew she was there; she had no doubt about that. The Manticore's discontinuity jump had been executed perfectly, terminating within walking distance of where Red floated. It had matched her speed, her slow spin.

It was looking at her.

With the great, glassed in crater pointed at her like that, she couldn't help but see the Manticore as a giant metal eyeball.

The centre of the crater was almost featureless, marred only by faint gridlines that were probably the size of roads. Towards its edge it began to rise up into layers, growing more complex the further Red looked from the centre. Around the rim of the lens, and indeed over the rest of the object's surface, it swarmed with detail.

Red couldn't tell why, but it gave her the impression of something built slowly, over time, layer upon armoured layer. There was nothing in the Manticore's movement or form that spoke to her of anything but solidity. This thing was heavy metal, all the way down to the core.

There was a comm-linker built into the vacuum shroud, crypt-keyed back to *Omega Fury*. Red tried it, pressing the send key on the wrist controls. "Guys? Can you see this?"

Without Ascension to reroute and block the signal, Godolkin's voice came through very loud and sharp in her headset. "Blasphemy, we are still some distance from you. We were delayed breaching the Bastion's defences."

"Are you okay?"

"To a degree. Blasphemy, we have picked up an energy signature very close to your position." The shroud had a beacon built into the jump-pack. The things were mainly used for emergencies, anyway. "Has Ascension begun emitting power?"

"Ascension's gone," she said quietly. "And the Manticore's here."

Godolkin didn't say anything for a few moments, but she could hear Harrow shouting in the background. After a time the Iconoclast spoke again. "Hold your position, Mistress. We are accelerating."

"No!" She twisted in the shroud, reflexively turning to try to see *Fury*'s approach. It was a useless gesture, since the ship would be millions of kilometres away and still have the shadow web engaged, if they had any sense. "Keep away! If you get closer than a thousand clicks to this thing it'll cook you."

"Blasphemy–"

"I mean it, buster. It's come right up to me and not done anything yet, but I'll bet my saucy arse you won't get the same treatment. Stay a good distance away unless I tell you otherwise."

"Thy will be done."

"Maybe it won't do anything," she said hopefully, trying to work out how far the Manticore must have been from Ascension when it had fired. A lot further than a thousand kilometres, that was for sure. "It hasn't yet. It's just sitting there."

"Perhaps it finds you interesting."

"Right now, I'd rather it didn't." Her eyes scanned its seething surface, and once again the scale of it overwhelmed her. It gave her vertigo. "Christ, this thing is big. Godolkin–" She stopped in mid-sentence. "No, wait. Something's happening."

"What? Mistress, what is it doing?"

Red didn't answer. The Manticore was rolling.

It had started to move, very slowly, the eye crater tipping forwards as the entire structure turned on some invisible axis. It rolled through ninety degrees, and then slowed again. Red, despite the complete lack of gravity, got the distinct impression that she was now above it.

And it was rising towards her.

She could hear Godolkin's voice, but dimly, as if a gnat was in the shroud with her. His words became a buzz, thinning and attenuating until they were gone altogether, and she drifted in silence.

The surface of the Manticore was very close now.

Directly in front of her, part of the object grew a star. A point of light, pale and vaguely blue, appeared amidst the panelling, and swiftly began to spread out into several long, converging lines. The lines were thin at first, hair-fine to her eyes, but they expanded rapidly.

A circular door was opening up for her, dozens of metal segments hingeing up and out, each one dozens of metres long. The light expanded into a disc of cool, blue radiance, flooding out, enveloping her, and slowly drawing her down.

When the light faded, she was within the belly of the beast.

There was gravity here, she realised, sitting up, and, judging by the way the vacuum shroud now hung around her like a deflated balloon, air. Or at least pressure. Red had no intention of cracking the seal just yet.

She got up and looked around her, watching as the light receded into the walls, revealing the detail of her surroundings. High above her another set of segments was drawing closed, sealing her in. She must have travelled down a tube from the first opening.

An airlock of sorts, built to a massive scale. The chamber Red stood in now was a hollow sphere so big that *Fury* could have flown around the inside of it with ease.

The walls were as detailed as the outside surface of the Manticore, multilayered, panel upon irregular panel, with blue light flooding out from the gaps. Dark nodules, very glossy, studded the interior of the sphere as far as she could see, some the size of her torso, others as big as a shuttlecraft, and every size in between. They looked like some kind of bizarre metallic fungi, growing out of the wall in their thousands.

"Weird," Red breathed. "Totally snecking weird."

There was a noise in the chamber; not loud, but pervasive. It was a kind of immensely long, drawn out groan, a humming intake of air, rising slightly in pitch. As Red listened it rose higher, higher still, then stopped with a sudden, forceful impact. Something, far away, had slammed closed.

The sound began again, this time decreasing in pitch, moaning down the scale. After a minute or two it stopped as well, but this time it just faded away. And then returned, and started to rise.

Manticore was breathing.

The sound gave Red the shivers. It ground into her bones, her soul. As long as she was inside this monster, she would never escape the sound of its breath. That, alone, was reason enough to escape.

But in order to do that, she needed to know exactly what it was she was escaping *from*.

She moved closer to one of the nodules, one about the size of a small groundcar, and tapped it with her boot. It felt solid, heavy, fixed firmly onto the panels below. Quite dull. Red lost interest and began to move away.

Behind her something rattled and clicked, followed by a quick succession of thin mechanical noises. She turned around.

The nodule had grown legs.

Red shouted in horror and backed away, fingers scrabbling at her waist for a gun that wasn't there. The nodule had extended six long, slender limbs, each ten times the length of its own body, and hauled itself up off the ground. The body rotated backwards, bringing an asymmetrical cluster of eye-lenses up to glare at her, and a set of hinged arms unfolded from below it to snap at the air. There were instruments at the ends of those arms, and they glittered.

The machine took a step towards her, one long leg rising up, high above her head, the claw-tipped foot coming down onto the panelling at her side.

Red had never been all that fond of spiders, especially when they were bigger than she was.

She looked around, trying to find an escape route, a weapon, anything to put between her and this awful construction, but all she saw were more nodules coming to life. Everywhere she looked they were rising up from the inside of the sphere – from behind her, from above, to

every side. The inside of the chamber was suddenly a sea
of gleaming, chattering metallic motion, of glassy eye-
lenses and snipping claws.

Some of the machines were low and stubby, their legs
no longer than hers, making them look like bloated ticks
the size of gel-beds. Others were all leg, dancing their way
towards her with their tiny bodies bobbing. Smaller constructions were forcing their way up through the floor, the
walls, scuttling things no bigger than her hand.

The entire chamber was alive.

One of the machines darted at her, and its grasping
limbs snapped out faster than she could follow. It grabbed
the shoulder of the vacuum shroud, shook her violently
and then shoved her backwards. Another grabbed her
before she could fall; a third reached in with horrible,
snakelike tendrils flailing.

Red screamed in rage and kicked out, sending a gleaming limb flying from its moorings, but another ten
instantly took its place. Within moments they were pluck-
ing at the seals of her suit, finding the connectors and the
fastenings. Red felt a tugging, an insistent pressure, and
cold air suddenly rushed into the shroud as one of them
flipped the helmet back.

Red twisted away and dropped into a fighting crouch,
bringing her fists up despite the weight of the shroud-fabric.
"Come on then, you spidery bastards, I've had bigger than
you! All at once or one at a time, I'm not bothered- Hey!"

One of the machines, a fat tick with twenty or thirty
eye-lenses all whirring in unison, had grabbed her from
behind. Its limbs were solid and powerful, fed by thick
hydraulic hoses and coiled power lines, and once it had
her there was no breaking its grip. It took her by the
shoulders and hoisted her a metre off the ground.

Red writhed and snarled, but to no avail. The machine
was far, far too strong.

It began to walk.

Ahead of it, Red saw the others begin to move aside.
With their long limbs clicking, their pincers nipping in

razored lust, they parted in front of her like a biblical
ocean. As the tick holding her started to pick up its pace,
Red saw that she had a clear path through the army of
metal bugs and out the other side.

Long triangular panels were folding aside, spilling light
from between them. It was another door, opening in her
path.

The machines obviously had plans for her. Unable to
break free, and held aloft like a prize, Red could only hang
in the air and watch the door gaping to swallow her.

If Red had thought she had known nightmares before she
entered that circular opening, she was about to be proved
wrong.

The door led directly onto a tunnel, a wide tube five or
six metres across. Its sides were rippling with spider-
machines, shining black and smooth against the paler
panelling of the tunnel walls, while larger constructions
marched around her in every direction. Most ignored her,
the smaller ones not even moving out of the way before
the tick's heavy limbs crushed them, but the bigger bugs
seemed more interested. More than one got in her cap-
tor's way, eager to nip at her skin or pull her hair with
their grippers. To escape, the tick would often simply scut-
tle up a wall, or walk along the tunnel's ceiling for a time.
An effective enough tactic, but one that frequently left
Red dangling completely upside down.

All the time that she was being flung about like this, the
cold air rang with the moaning rise and fall of the Manticore's breath.

After several minutes of this treatment, the terrain
changed. Openings appeared in the tunnel walls, smaller
tubes leading away. Some of them were quite short, little
more than cylindrical antechambers leading to larger
spherical rooms. As the tick passed by one it slowed, and
Red was able to glimpse what lay inside.

It was a mistake, looking, and one that she would regret
for a long time.

The room's outer edges were covered in mechanical arms, larger and more complex cousins to that holding her shoulders now. The arms were still, some plainly broken or rusted into place, but the work they had once carried out was very much in evidence. For on a circle of tables in the centre of the room, held down with thick metal straps, lay dried, papery things that had once been men and women.

The floor was littered with rot and small bones that had tumbled from their desiccating owners as their skins had shrunk away. Many of the bodies had chest cavities that gaped like grasping hands, ribs teased apart to clutch at the air, and the brown, leathery bags that had once pumped and breathed within them had been extracted for view. These people, Red could see, had been dissected.

That would have been nightmare enough, had not the hand of one male corpse been outstretched and still clasping that of the woman next to him.

They had been alive when the arms had opened them up. Alive and conscious.

Red turned her head away, and was thankful when the tick moved again.

There was another chamber at the end of the tunnel, large and flattened, built from the same panelled metal as everything else here. The tick moved into the centre of it, then paused. At some invisible, inaudible signal it began to turn around on its clawed, stumpy legs, as if it was showing Red where it had taken her.

The arms holding her squeezed, painfully, and shook her. Red kicked and squirmed, but kept her silence, refusing to give the machine the satisfaction of a cry. Besides, she had other things on her mind.

She couldn't help but stare at what lay around her. Where the corpse chambers had been a nightmare, this was simply surreal. There was nothing here to make sense of.

In the centre of the room, on a wide disc of polished brass, was a squat cylinder the size of her torso. It was cast from what could only have been solid gold, and burnished to a high shine, while ranged around it was a wide ring of small, square boxes, each about the size of her head and raised on a pillar of grimy hoses and corroded steel cables.

In contrast to the cylinder, the boxes were roughly welded together from black metal.

There was something pale on the inside face of each box. Red couldn't see what it was at first, so she leaned closer. Obediently, the tick scuttled forwards, bringing her within a metre of the nearest. Easily close enough to see what had been stretched across its face.

Red recoiled. It was skin.

The front of each box was cut with a square hole, and the space inside the remaining frame filled with smooth, pale skin. And in the centre of the box was a mouth.

There was no chin, no other features at all, just a set of faintly-parted lips, the hint of teeth behind them. Red glanced across to the next box, and saw that it bore not a mouth, but a closed eye. Further along, an ear.

Eyes, ears, mouths, separated from the faces that once bore them and set into these awful containers, disembodied senses all facing that golden cylinder. Red squeezed her eyes shut. "Why are you showing me this?" she grated, struggling. "What are you doing to me?"

"Help me!"

The voice was high, startlingly loud. Red's eyes snapped open.

The mouth was screaming at her. "Help me!" it shrieked. "God, help me!"

Next to it, the eye had opened, and was rolling frantically.

More mouths were opening. Red heard laughter, pleading, threats. The mouths howled and shrieked at her, begged and pleaded, drooled and spat and gibbered. Instantly the room was filled with voices, their cacophony beating at her ears. She tried to draw away, but the tick seemed to sense her distress. Cruelly, it held her closer to the mouth, forcing her lips close to those working in that sheet of skin.

The eye was looking right at her. They all were. The mouth's spittle was on her cheek.

Suddenly, the tick jerked her back, spun on its claws and hurried away across the dais, so quickly that it knocked the golden cylinder askew. If that was somehow important to the machine, it made no sign, just continued on its path across the disc and out of the circular opening in the chamber's far side.

The voices went on screaming long after Red had left them. She could hear them behind her, their pleas a chorus of pain.

One last tunnel. One last chamber.

The tick scuttled into a spherical room at the end of the tube and dropped Red unceremoniously onto the floor. She hadn't been expecting that, and came down hard, rolling to a halt among cables and rough metal plates. By the time she had found her balance on the uneven surface and risen to her feet, the machine had already retreated. She caught one last glimpse of its glossy back as the chamber's door closed, spears of metal extending through the walls to form a disc in front of her, sealing her in.

She turned, slowly. There were no corpses here, no nightmare of disembodied eyes and mouths. Half the chamber was bare metal plate. The other half, or more than half, was made up of screens.

Red took a few steps forward and reached out to touch one. It was a flat glass panel, slightly warm, its surface matte and gridded. It looked very much like the displays on an Iconoclast workstation.

That was the last thing Red had expected to see. She stepped back, startled, and as she did so the screen lit up.

Something pale filled it, moving, its pixels swarming in grainy close-up.

Red moved further back as more screens came on. One near the top showed a pattern of black and crimson lines. In the centre, a shallow depression in the pale surround. In another something white and wet.

The rest of the screens flickered into life, and the picture they formed filled Red's view. She gasped.

It was a face.

Had it not been for one scarred, milky eye, and the maddened sneer on its lips, it would have been *her* face. And, given time, it might be again.

"Well," said Brite Red, glaring down from a thousand video displays. "Here you are. I've been waiting such a long time for this..."

16. FUTURE IMPERFECT

"You're dead," Red gasped, pointing up at the divided face looming over her. "I killed you, and the Iconoclasts froze you."

"Times change," said Brite.

"You haven't," snarled Red. "Still the same megalomaniacal bitch I chewed up at Salecah."

"Speak when you're spoken to," the face snapped, and pain blasted into Red's skull.

She cried out, dropping to the floor, her hands clasped over her head as though the pressure of them would somehow keep the agony away. She had felt something like this, weeks ago, when Brite had tortured Harrow and Godolkin and focused their pain into her mind, to draw her to the artefact and their final confrontation. That had been a scratch compared to what she was feeling now.

Just when Red thought that her brain was going to shatter in her head, the pain stopped. She slumped forwards, her hands twitching, her legs suddenly too weak to support her. She fell and rolled over onto her back.

"Oh, that felt so good." Brite's face was in something close to ecstasy, her good eye rolled back. "I've waited a long, long time to do that to you. All that pain I've been storing up, just for you." She looked down at Red and grinned horribly. "You know, it's true what they say. The longer you go without, the better it is when you finally get some!"

Blood was dripping from Red's nose. She wiped it away weakly and sat up. "So this is what it's all been about, eh? Getting me in here and snecking me over?"

"Yes. Absolutely." The face leered. "After four hundred years I've finally caught up with you, and now I've got you exactly where I want you. And oh, I'm going to make the most of it."

The pain slammed into Red again, but briefly this time. Just enough to make her cry out.

"A free sample," Brite smiled.

"Just enough to get you off again, huh?" Red forced herself upright. "I never realised I was into that."

"Oh, that wit will be the death of you, Durham Red. Eventually." The face seemed to flicker, a line of static crawling up if from chin to hairline, and something near Red's left boot sparked.

"Looks like this place isn't in such good repair, Brite. What did you do, fire the maintenance man?"

"Fired, dissected, I forget. I've been here so long it all sort of blurs into one. Don't you find that?"

"Not really."

"You will."

Red wandered over to one side of the chamber, flicking cables with her boot. She hoped the vacuum shroud was a good insulator. "Okay, Brite, spill the beans. Where did you find this thing?"

"I didn't find it, you pathetic idiot. I built it."

"Bullshit. Last time I saw you, I had half your blood in my belly and the rest was on the floor. How the sneck could you build a damn thing?"

Pain lashed at her, and she staggered. "You rancid little slut!" Brite screamed the words, her image on the screens jumping. "I'll burn your mind out! You don't know what pain is!"

"And you do?" Red had kept her feet this time. Either Brite's store of bottled agony was running dry, or she was getting used to it. "You wanted death, Brite! You begged me for it at Salecah – you built the artefact, the time engine, just so you could come back to kill me and wipe out your own past. All I did was give you what you wanted."

"And it didn't work, did it?" On the screen, Brite's eyes closed, her scarred face twisting. "God, Durham, you don't know what it's like. You can't know. The things they did to me..."

"Who?"

"The Archaeotechs. The ones who were on Ascension when Caliban's bomb went off."

Red blinked. "Wait a minute. You destroyed Ascension. How–"

"I didn't destroy it. That's not a weapon you saw me use, it's a time-grab." Brite sounded tired suddenly. Exhausted. Just from the sound of her voice, Red had a momentary feeling of just how long this woman had been alive, in one form or another. The thought chilled her.

"So Ascension went back a million years?"

"It did. I wasn't exactly alert at the time, you understand. I've had to fill in the gaps. But yes, the bomb went off. I hit it with the time-grab to stop it taking the Manticore back as well. That wouldn't have been good."

"You knew it was going to go off?"

Brite sighed. "I was waiting for it to go off. I'd been waiting for almost two hundred years!"

Red groaned and put her head in her hands. "Zap me again, will you? This is making my head hurt even worse than your bloody jolts."

"You know, all the time I've spent waiting for this moment, knowing it was going to happen, I never thought I'd end up explaining myself to you. I thought you'd have been screaming non-stop by now." The image flickered again, as if Brite's changing moods were affecting the screens. "But it's been so long since I talked to anyone."

"How long? Come on, Brite. You started this."

Abruptly, the image roared with laughter. "Did I? Oh, that's wonderful! You know, I really have no idea if I did or not."

"I didn't mean–"

"I know what you meant." Brite's face moved closer on the screens, filling them with her gaze. "Listen to me,

Durham Red, and I'll try to keep it simple. Caliban's bomb sent Ascension back a million years, with a hundred Archaeotechs still onboard. Do you know what the universe was like a million years ago?"

"No."

"Trust me, you don't want to. It was... occupied. I'll not speak of that again, and I didn't see much of it. But what I did see was enough." There was a coldness in her voice now, a horror. "They had to escape. They would have done anything to get back to their own time."

"Oh no..." Red gaped up at her. "They used the time engine, didn't they?"

"They tried. Oh, they tried, for years. But they always failed, until they realised the one component that was missing. The one part it could never work without."

"You?"

"I was clever in my youth, wasn't I?" She smiled, fangs showing. "Yes, me. They'd forgotten about my body, frozen in the hazardous waste store all that time. But that was the missing factor. I'd designed the time engine to operate specifically under my control. Without me, it's nothing."

Red closed her eyes. All her efforts in trying to destroy the thing had been in vain. She could have left it to the Iconoclasts, could have handed it to the Patriarch himself gift-wrapped, and without Brite Red it would have been no more use than just another bomb. "What did they do? Bring you back to life?"

"Oh no, they weren't that stupid. They just used a little of my brain tissue, accessed a few core functions. I was still dead. To start with, anyway."

"But we heal fast." Red thought about Brite's frozen brain, scraps of tissue being revived by the Archaeotechs to control the time engine, and all the time those scraps were growing, repairing themselves, reviving more and more of the surrounding neurons.

Eventually, consciousness would have returned. Thoughts and dreams. Pain. Madness. But Brite would have been clever, would have kept her newfound talents to herself, until it was too late. One day, the Archaeotechs would have woken up to find Ascension no longer under their control, but under hers.

And that would only have been the beginning. Red thought about the mummified bodies in the dissection chamber. Brite had taken them apart to see how they worked. "How long did it take? To kill them all?"

"Kill them? My dear, most of them are still alive. In a manner of speaking."

The mouths in their boxes, the eyes, weeping and screaming. "Sneck, Brite, you did that to them? Those cube-things?"

"What, the chapel? Oh, that was just an experiment. But I got tired of being worshipped very quickly. I'd been a goddess before, and it wasn't much fun then."

"I can imagine."

Fire sliced into her head, tore down her spine. "No you can't! You can't even *begin* to imagine!"

Red collapsed. She'd not been getting used to it at all. That burst had been short, but it was the worst yet.

"I'm the closest thing to a goddess these people have ever seen," Brite was snarling. "I remade them in my own image! I built the Manticore around myself, with the materials I gathered after it was finished. I looped time itself around me, to supply me with what I needed." She stopped abruptly, her eyes flicking to one side. "There's something…"

"What?"

"Never mind. It's none of your concern."

Red doubted that. And if she was right, she needed to keep Brite talking. "So those spiders out there are helots?"

"Some of them. The smaller ones are just machines, but the choicest Archaeotechs ended up as hired help. There weren't enough, so I designed the time-grab to get more. The ships that attacked me when I reappeared – I grabbed them and sent them back a million years, to when I was building the Manticore out of Ascension's ruins. Everything I grabbed, I sent back as raw material. Ships, cities, people... It took a lot to make this. There was..." She frowned. "Wastage. Not everything could be used."

Red's mind reeled. Even in that first battle, when Verax and his fleet had tried to defend Kentyris Secundus from the Manticore's beams, no ships had been destroyed. Those globes of white light she had seen in the classified images, and again consuming Ascension, were not death, but time. Brite had been building the Manticore out of men and machines that she sent back to the moment of its own birth.

The time paradoxes it threw up made Harrow's hypothesis look like a child's puzzle. There were loops everywhere, separate time lines linking and diverging.

"Oh my God. You built this whole thing, this entire bloody nightmare of a machine, just to come forward in time to the point where you could grab bits of spaceship and send them back in time to when you were building it in the first place?"

"More or less," chuckled Brite. "I was hoping to just come back to Ascension directly. I remembered what happened, and I knew that I, or you, would be here at a certain time and a certain place. But you'd damaged the time engine with that stupid overload plan. I couldn't get any closer than six-twenty-seven..."

Brite broke off, her eyes wide with shock.

The screens went blank for a full second. When they returned, Brite's face was fractured, in totally the wrong order, like a badly solved jigsaw. It took another few seconds for her to rearrange herself. "What have you done?" she hissed down at Red.

"Me? Why does everyone always blame me?"

"Because it's always your fault!" Brite's eyes were flicking madly. "I don't remember this. This shouldn't be happening. Something's outside, there's damage..."

"Really?" While Brite had been talking, she had pulled her right arm out of the shroud's sleeve, leaving it to dangle while she fished around on her belt. There, on the clip that had once held her magnum, was the only weapon she had left. Hirundo's staking pin. "What's the matter? Time-grab not working?"

"There's nothing out there to grab! Your accursed starship is attacking me!"

"And your time-weapons are line-of-sight, eh? That's useful."

Brite's face snapped back towards her, hair flying. "I'll deal with you later, bitch. You've distracted me long enough."

"Yeah? Actually, I'm just getting started!" Red flipped the pin out, caught it in her left hand, and slammed it down into the cabling.

Sparks erupted, sheets of light bursting against the shroud's glove. Above her, Brite howled.

Raw agony hit Red between the eyes, blinding her. She hauled the pin out again and stabbed back down into the cables, over and over, focussing all her rage and pain on that single action – stab, lift, stab again. It was like a mantra, an act of pointless violence that took her through the pain and out the other side.

The agony dropped away, and Red turned to see the tick rearing behind her.

Brite had told her too much. About the helots, the fate of the Archaeotechs, everything. Back at Salecah, Red had remarked that her future self had enjoyed the sound of her own voice. After all that Brite had been through – her revival at the hands of the Iconoclasts, her slow recovery to take over Ascension, the centuries she had spent building the Manticore to be both her weapon and the means of its own construction – she still did. All Red had needed to do was keep prompting, and Brite had spelled it all out.

There was something alive inside the helots, or something that had been alive once. Red leapt at the tick and drove the staking pin into its glossy body between its myriad eyes.

It shrieked.

The forward section of its carapace splintered, the needle sharp tip of the staking pin punching through the shell and into the systems behind. Red dragged the weapon free, and as she did so caught a glimpse of something pallid and fleshy through the hole she had left. The pin came out wet.

She drew back, ready for another blow, but the tick was scuttling madly on the spot, its limbs flailing.

Red darted past it, already knowing where to go. She ran back through the tunnel, avoiding another pair of helot-spiders that crashed through the wall plating to either side of her, and raced down into what Brite had called the chapel. The place where she was worshipped by the disembodied mouths and eyes of the Archaeotechs.

Machines, huge and clawed, were barrelling in from the opposite tunnel.

She jumped up onto the disc, rolling under a leg, feeling the knives at the end of it part the air millimetres from her face, and kicked hard at the golden cylinder. It had already been knocked askew by the tick on its hurried way into the screen chamber. Brite herself must have ordered the helot to hurry, and in its terror it had done half of Red's job for her.

The cylinder cracked free of its moorings. Ancient and ill-maintained, the metal sheered off at the base, bolts flying. Red grabbed it and shoved it back, off the disc and away.

Beneath her golden cover, the true remnants of Brite Red lay bare.

The Archaeotechs had put her in a small nutrient tank. Too small for all of her: only her head remained, her face against the glass, tongue grey and lolling. Her hair was gone, the scalp and skull beneath it gone too. The grey mass of her brain was a forest of implanted tubes.

"I should have done this a long time ago," Red breathed, raising the staking pin high. "I'm sorry."

She slammed the pin down, as hard as she could, through the glass and into the heart of Brite Red's tortured mind.

. . .

The Manticore took a long time to die, far longer than Brite did. Red could tell that her future self was finally at peace when the spider-helots around her stopped in their tracks and slowly began to fold themselves away.

Red went back into the screen room, and was rather surprised to see Brite's face still looming there.

It was a mere sketch of itself, and growing simpler as she watched. The eyes no longer moved; the hair was just a vague smear of scarlet and black.

"Dying," it said.

"I'm not surprised." She had discarded the staking pin, left it buried in the shattered pulp of Brite's brain. "Isn't that what you wanted?"

"It is, I think. I can feel parts of me shutting down, one by one. My mind is in the Manticore, but only traces. I'm fading, and it feels…"

"What?"

"It feels like peace."

Red sighed. She felt no triumph, here at the end. All she could bring herself to feel was a kind of belated satisfaction. Brite Red should have died for good at Salecah, but she had been forced to endure hundreds of years more at the hands of the stranded Archaeotechs. If it was finally over for her, the end had not come nearly soon enough.

"Red?"

"Yeah?"

"I have to tell you something. Something about your future."

Red violently shook her head. "Oh no! I don't want to know. Anyway, our time lines must have diverged sometime back then. You didn't remember me doing this, did you?"

"I don't know. But there are men who love you. Truly love you. Loved me."

Red blinked in surprise. "Godolkin? You're kidding!"

"Don't know. Too long ago. I miss him. I wonder… what happened… to… my… child…"

The screens went blank. Red couldn't move.

"My what?" she asked dully, staring up at the darkness. "My what?"

Without Brite's will to hold it together, the Manticore started to come apart soon after *Fury* had picked Red up.

The giant machine had been starting to shut itself down as she had returned to that first, massive chamber, its signal-blocking ability failing as she walked. Godolkin's voice had appeared in her helmet like the buzzing of bees, but it had been some time before she could bring herself to speak to him.

When she did, it was to tell him where to aim the antimat cannon in order to blow the segmented door off its hinges.

She was glad to be out of the shroud, although it had saved her life more than once that day, and it felt good to be back in the cramped little workstations that formed *Fury*'s bridge. Red couldn't help thinking about Brite, and how little joy she must have felt in all her thousands of years of life. No wonder she had gone insane.

Immortality, she decided there and then, was a curse. And not a route she would ever go down. "Short and happy," she muttered. "That's what I want."

"I'm sorry, holy one?" Harrow was standing behind her, watching the Manticore through her holos. "I'm not sure I heard you."

"Nothing, Jude." She paused. "Jude? Do you—"

"It's breaking up." He pointed. "Moon of blood, the whole structure's coming apart!"

He was correct, Red saw without much surprise. The machine was dissipating, its millions upon millions of components gently drifting away from each other. As they watched, it went from being a solid globe to a slowly expanding cloud.

Godolkin was in the pilot's throne. "Blasphemy, much of the structure is vaporising. Was it made of some short-lived compound?"

"No. I mean, I don't think so…" So much of the Manticore had been dragged through time, looped back in

self-sustaining paradoxes just to build the very machine
that had transported them back to its own inception. Perhaps, she thought dully, the loops were unravelling.
Things were going back to their proper order.

"I don't know. All I know is, I hope the Bastion's watching this."

"Do you think they will disband?"

"Maybe." Red kept her eyes on the holoscreen, watching tumbling fragments of the Manticore fading out in
front of her eyes. "We'll be in trouble if they don't."

"We found a way in," said Godolkin, folding his arms
defiantly. "We shall find a way out."

Red didn't answer. She was thinking about the corpses
in the dissection chamber, their hands linked for eter-
nity. In their last, terrifying moments, they must have a
found a small measure of comfort in that simple act of
contact.

She wondered if they were lovers. Whether, in some
time twisted parallel universe, they still were.

"There's no reason for us to be here," she sighed.
"Come on, Godolkin, let's find somewhere to sit things
out for a bit."

"What about Caliban?" Harrow asked. "Or Lydexia?
Their ion-wakes can't be too faded. If we act now–"

"Nah," she shook her head. "Let them go. I'm tired of
chasing things."

She sat back in the weapons throne, her eyes still fixed
on Manticore's slow dissolution. Caliban, she thought to
herself, had done what he set out to do. His great enemy
was gone. Not only that, but he had Elu to share it with.

And Lydexia had Hirundo, together with a long shuttle-
ride home. Even Brite had finally reached the peace she
so desperately desired. The only player in the game to
come out losing was Durham Red.

But had she? Brite had given her a prize, of sorts. A
glimpse of a possible future.

That was something to hold onto when the nights got
cold.

She grinned and hit the release control. The throne slid back, making Harrow step aside as it left the workstation. "Godolkin?"

"Yes, Blasphemy?"

"She's all yours. Find us somewhere quiet, but not too quiet. There's got to be somebody on one of these worlds." She stood up. "Get us somewhere that's got a bath."

The Iconoclast snorted. "After all your adventures, is that all you can look forward to?"

"Oh, no. Not by a long shot." She grinned and stretched, raising her fists to the ceiling and letting her spine click deliciously as it straightened. "There's loads I'm looking forward to, and more every minute."

"Like what?" asked Harrow, his eyebrows up in his hair-line.

"Oh, the usual. I mean, I don't know if you two are hungry, but I'm just dying for a bite!"

ABOUT THE AUTHOR

Peter J Evans has over four hundred pieces of published work to his name, ranging from the back covers of videos to big articles about Serious Stuff. He has produced regular columns for gaming magazines, short fiction, long fiction, reviews, interviews and a sticker book. His first novel, *Mnemosyne's Kiss*, was published in 1999 by Virgin Publishing, under their worryingly short-lived Virgin Worlds imprint. Evans previously contributed towards Black Flame with *Judge Dredd: Black Atlantic* (co-written with Simon Jowett) and *Durham Red: The Unquiet Grave*, *Durham Red: The Omega Solution* and *Durham Red: The The Encoded Heart*.